F
McGlothin, Victor.
What's a woman to do?

# What's a
# Woman
# to Do?

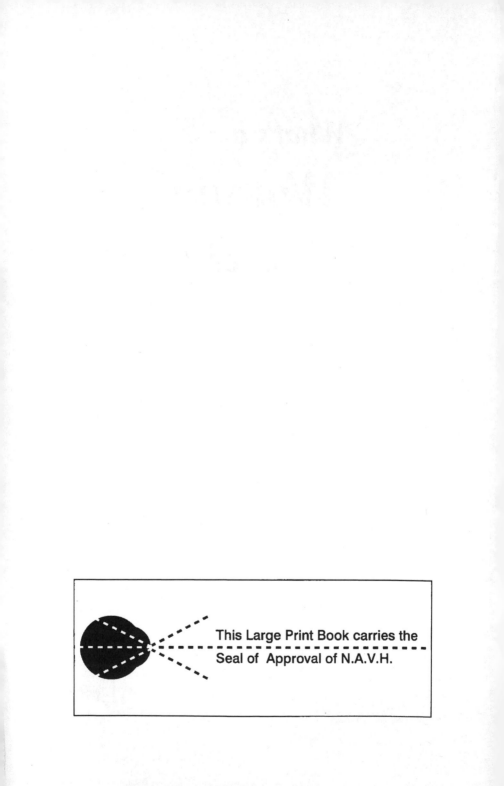

This Large Print Book carries the
Seal of Approval of N.A.V.H.

# What's a
# *Woman*
# *to Do?*

## Victor McGlothin

**Thorndike Press • Waterville, Maine**

Published in 2005 by arrangement with St. Martin's Press, LLC.

Thorndike Press® Large Print African-American.

The tree indicium is a trademark of Thorndike Press.

The text of this Large Print edition is unabridged.
Other aspects of the book may vary from the original edition.

Set in 16 pt. Plantin by Liana M. Walker.

Printed in the United States on permanent paper.

**Library of Congress Cataloging-in-Publication Data**

McGlothin, Victor.
    What's a woman to do? / by Victor McGlothin.
       p. cm. — (Thorndike Press large print African-American)
    ISBN 0-7862-7191-4 (lg. print : hc : alk. paper)
    1. African American families — Fiction.  2. African
American women — Fiction.  3. Dallas (Tex.) — Fiction.
4. Sisters — Fiction.  5. Large type books.  I. Title.
II. Thorndike Press large print African-American series.
PS3613.C484W48 2005
    813'.6—dc22                              2004028369

Oprah Winfrey —
Because you had the courage to share your pain with the hope that others may heal, undoubtedly many have.

This novel is dedicated to the women who've endured the weight of sins committed against them, for far too long.

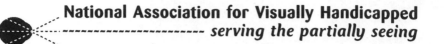

**National Association for Visually Handicapped**
*serving the partially seeing*

As the Founder/CEO of NAVH, the only national health agency solely devoted to those who, although not totally blind, have an eye disease which could lead to serious visual impairment, I am pleased to recognize Thorndike Press★ as one of the leading publishers in the large print field.

Founded in 1954 in San Francisco to prepare large print textbooks for partially seeing children, NAVH became the pioneer and standard setting agency in the preparation of large type.

Today, those publishers who meet our standards carry the prestigious "Seal of Approval" indicating high quality large print. We are delighted that Thorndike Press is one of the publishers whose titles meet these standards. We are also pleased to recognize the significant contribution Thorndike Press is making in this important and growing field.

Lorraine H. Marchi, L.H.D.
Founder/CEO
NAVH

★ Thorndike Press encompasses the following imprints: Thorndike, Wheeler, Walker and Large Print Press.

# Special Thanks

Thank you, Father, for keeping me focused throughout the entire two months and twenty-eight days while writing this story.

My family, for your support and for putting up with me when I'm in my "moods."

Book clubs, for supporting me and making a brotha feel like somebody, and for convincing me to write a story about a book club with some drama of its own.

Jennifer Enderlin and Kimberly Cardascia (a real gem) at St. Martin's Press, for all that they do.

Ginger Logan Canon, for breathing life into Janeen Hampton-Gilliam.

Pamela Walker Williams at Pageturner.net, for facilitating my home on the Web:

www.VictorMcGlothin.com

A "shout-out" to My Folks Out There Hustling Just Like Me: Vincent Alexandria, Kimberla Lawson Roby, Patrik Henry Bass, Eric Jerome Dickey, Lolita Files, Valerie Wilson Wesley, Pamela Guinn, Valorie Burton, Tajuana "TJ" Butler, Francis Ray, Donna Hill, Jewel Diamond Taylor, Dawn Knight, Tracy Grant, C. Kelly Robinson, Camika Spencer, Norma L. Jarrett, Eric Pete, E. Lynn Harris, Parry "Ebony Satin" Brown, Pat G'orge Walker, Carmen Benitez, Troy Martin, Jewell Parker Rhodes, Sara Freeman Smith, Maxine Thompson, Nina Foxx, Jacquese Council Silvas, Trisha Thomas, Travis Hunter, Evelyn Palfrey, Dionne "Diva" Character, and _____ (for those I forgot). your name here

# Chapter 1

# *If Walls Could Talk*

Janeen Hampton-Gilliam eased back slowly against her leather chair, crossing her shapely legs until her long frame was comfortably cradled in it. "I sat there staring at him for hours," she said just above a whisper. Softly clenching her bottom lip between her teeth, she allowed her mind to drift back to the most intimate moments of her life. It occurred several weeks ago in New York City while she attended a real-estate management conference.

Val, her good friend and longtime assistant, eagerly listened while taking in every word as Janeen continued sharing intimately provocative thoughts.

"His smooth chocolate-colored skin radiated beneath the bright lights of that lecture hall. Each day I tried to get a seat with a view. I would sit a row or two behind him, usually five or six seats over. You know, far enough away to stay hidden in the shadows of my world but close enough to hang on to the fringes of his."

"Shoot, let me close this door," Val said anxiously from the opposite side of the large mahogany desk. "Janeen, you sure can tell a story. It's like getting deep into a good book without having to turn the pages. You should be a writer, girl." Val wasted no time closing the office door and locking it. If she'd had a Do Not Disturb sign, it would have been hanging off the knob on the other side.

As Val returned to her perch and poised herself for an earful of someone else's business, Janeen drifted even deeper into the sensual thoughts that had her wishing for more of the catalyst, which caused them in the first place. "He was so beautifully black, like a rare onyx stone, tall, tailored, and smooth without trying to be. Everything about him was effortless. There were several other women who noticed that about him, too. Humph, some of 'em more than just noticed, but each time he'd give 'em the brush-off with a sultry 'No thanks' and keep right on stepping. It must have been hard for him to block the onslaught of women slingshotting their panties and room keys at him." Janeen smiled when that particular memory came back to her as crisp as a new dollar bill. "He was the kind of man that makes a woman wish she could trade hers in," she added with a slight head tilt for emphasis. "For four full days of that real-estate conference I watched him walk, talk, take notes on one boring speech after another without seeming bothered by them when mostly everyone else was trying their damnedest to merely stay awake. For those four glorious days I downloaded him into my memory, allowed him to captivate my mind, and welcomed him to become a part of me."

Val was so entranced by the idea of the gorgeous mystery man that she had to stop herself from drooling while catching her breath. She even had to clear her throat before she could speak. "Uh-uhh, all that heat. Whoo-weee. Is it getting hot in here or is it just me?" She began fanning her face with an open hand. "Why didn't you say something to him? You know, go on up to the man and introduce yourself. You got it going on. I see the way men look at you around here."

In fact, Janeen was a rather striking woman in her own right. Her smooth peanut-butter-colored complexion and short jet black curly hair accentuated the deepest brown bedroom eyes imaginable. She was an attractive package by anyone's standards.

"Oh, I wanted to, Val." Janeen blushed at the compliment, thinking back. "Almost did it once or twice, but I couldn't. . . . Out of practice, I guess. But more than that, I was terrified that we might have gotten to talking and enjoyed it too much."

"Would that have been so bad?" Val asked innocently. "*Just talking* sounds harmless enough."

Janeen smiled and wrinkled her nose. "No, no, no. You don't understand. With that kind of man, the conversation would have been superb; no doubt about that, but stimulating conversation is powerful. It can take on a life of its own. I've seen it happen. 'Just talking' can take you places you never intended to go and have you butt naked before you can even remember if you packed your diaphragm." Both women doubled over with laughter while momentarily forgetting where they were. "Can I get a witness?" Janeen added.

"Amen, sistah!" Val answered, with her

hand raised in the customary testifying position.

After coming back to their senses, Val glanced at an eight-by-ten photograph of Janeen and Raymond, her husband of fifteen years, sitting on the nearby credenza. "That brotha you can't seem to get off your mind sounds like the kind of man who tippin' out was invented for," Val suggested, with an I-won't-tell-if-you-won't wink.

Janeen's lips curled into a half smile. "Nah, I don't believe in that, but don't get me wrong, I ain't no saint. I've had some impure thoughts that a married woman shouldn't."

Val's mouth flew open. "Oooooh! Uhh-uh."

"Huh, on the last day of the lecture, he came in late and took the chair right next to mine."

"Nooooo, he didn't?"

"I almost lost it. I was so turned on when his cologne hit me that I felt a little tingle between my legs. I could feel my nipples pushing themselves against my blouse too, probably trying to get out and introduce themselves. Before I knew what hit me, I had jumped up out of that seat and bolted for the door."

Like a small child hearing her first bedtime story, Val leaned in closer with a twinkle in her eyes as the story climaxed. "Uh . . . where did you go?" she whispered, from the throes of deep suspense.

"Well, I couldn't make it to my hotel room fast enough so I ducked into the ladies' room in the hotel lobby, girl."

Val's eyes widened with disbelief as she placed her hand over her mouth to muffle the scream she held in. "Janeen, you didn't? Tell me you didn't."

"Huh, yes, I did. Told you that me and Ray haven't been too *cordial* lately, and I'm a very sensual creature, like all the women in my family."

The thought of getting that turned on over a man she'd never been with was too much for Val to fathom. She let out an unbridled shriek so loud that co-workers outside Janeen's spacious office took notice.

"Believe me when I say this, Val, *if walls could talk . . . they'd be too ashamed to tell.*"

Janeen sat there relishing her sinful fantasies, wearing a satisfying grin while Val tried unsuccessfully to hold herself together. Laughter and lust deferred were the orders of the day although they were both short-lived as Janeen peeked at Ray's photo and immediately allowed her joyous mood to slip away.

Suddenly the office telephone rang with the urgency of a runaway fire engine. Janeen leaned in closer to it, noting the caller ID readout. She instantly dismissed the pleasantries she'd cherished only seconds before and replaced them with her patented nine-to-five take-no-prisoners corporate-game face.

As Janeen pressed the speaker button to answer the call, Val took a deep breath and exhaled slowly to compose herself. "Yes, Mr. Bragg," Janeen said flatly in the telephone's general direction.

"I hope I'm not on speaker, Janeen. You know how much I despise that," a distinguished voice remarked.

Val grimaced sharply and headed for the door when she recognized who that distinguished voice belonged to. It was that of Mr. Jacobson Bragg, the company's president. He had a lot of hang-ups, and discussing company business while others could listen in was one of them. Janeen acknowledged her assistant's departure with a silent nod as Val discreetly crept out, pulling the door closed behind her.

Mounting a terrible facsimile of a smile, Janeen reached over to pick up the telephone receiver. "No, of course not. I am well aware of your disdain regarding modern telephony hand-free features."

During the dead quiet, she could almost hear him thinking of how easily she always seemed to put him at odds. She listened as he tapped the end of a pen against a notepad on his desk.

"What?" he managed to utter, amid his confused frustration.

Over the past forty years, Jacobson Bragg had made millions of dollars but despised modern technology as if he held a personal grudge against it. The elderly Mr. Bragg was used to getting his way and he couldn't understand for the life of him why anyone would irritate him for no apparent reason. Actually, Janeen's refusal to bow and shuffle like all the other executives employed by First World Mortgage endeared her to the old man, which is what they called him behind his back.

Determined to get back to the reason she'd received a call from the owner of the company, Janeen jumped in with both feet. "Never mind, Mr. Bragg, I'll explain it later. What can I do for you this morning?"

"I need to see you right away," he answered, before hesitating. "Uh, if you don't mind."

Janeen giggled deep down inside when she acknowledged that he had to check himself when addressing her despite having free reign to bark marching orders to everyone else in the company. Everyone else stood for it. Janeen didn't.

"No problem, sir, I'll be right up. Would you like to meet on sixteen? All right then, I'm on my way."

Eventually, Janeen opened the door to her office. Before she could step one foot out of it, Val turned to face her manager from her own desk, where she had listened in on the entire conversation. "Uh-uh-uh. You ought to be 'shamed of yourself. You're the only person that old man allows to treat him common like that."

Janeen strolled past her, whispering, "That's why I do it."

"Go on, girl! I know that's right," Val signified, adding a gratuitous finger snap in honor of the way her boss continued to pull off the unimaginable with matchless grace.

Remnants of Janeen's prideful expression were still apparent by the time she had disappeared among hundreds of workstations covering the better part of the eighth floor. Frequently, when she passed through the countless rows of cubicles aligned like a field of planted crops, Janeen felt a sense of comfort. Each time she passed them by, she slowed her distinguished stride enough to reminisce on her early childhood in the farming community of Newberry, Louisiana, where acres of corn, wheat, cotton, and sugarcane seemed to just go on for days. Sometimes she'd gleem a bright smile and other times the memories of that small town forced her to cower behind the walls of her soul. But this time she had to hold in the laughter. It had been a good day up to then and she vowed not to let anything or anyone steal her joy.

Janeen folded her arms over the black leather business portfolio that often accompanied her to Mr. Bragg's office, not so much as a management tool but because she liked feeling as important as she knew the company's owner was to thousands of employees. Besides, she typically used the meeting time to remind herself of various important appointments she'd scheduled or update her to-do list between his long lectures about this and that. However, despite the trouble she'd given him on occasion, Janeen respected Mr. Bragg, but even more than that, she liked him. She liked him a lot.

Mr. Bragg was an educated man who, over the past four decades, had helped more than two thousand employees complete college via his tuition-assistance program. He was undoubtedly a good man, a good man at the end of his career and tired of running a company that had grown too large for him to handle all of its concerns.

The magnificent brass light fixtures enchanted Janeen when she stepped off the elevator on the sixteenth floor, just as they always did. The old man's propensity for nice things and neatness was evident by the spotless rosewood office furniture that elegantly landscaped the waiting area.

Mrs. Aderly, an antique little lady who resembled the granny character from the *Beverly Hillbillies* television show, sat at the reception desk knitting. She was the company's oldest employee next to Mr. Bragg and Thomas Salley, the head janitor.

Mrs. Aderly showcased a new blond wig and the same pleasant grin she was well known for when Janeen approached the president's office.

"Well, hello there, sweetie," Mrs. Aderly greeted cheerfully. "Go right on in. He's waitin' on you."

"Thank you very much, ma'am, and I just love your new hair . . . do." That was a nice save considering Janeen noticed that the charming little woman's wig was sitting on her head crooked, though she didn't have the heart to tell her.

Trying to shake the bad-hair-day image from her mind, Janeen found herself thinking more pleasant thoughts, like those she had earlier. She pressed for naughty images of a tall, dark, and handsome stranger but the reality of what probably awaited her on the other side of the door upstaged every scandalous vision she managed to conjure up.

Never before had the company president called and asked to see her right away. Normally, he would have Mrs. Aderly call to schedule a meeting time, so Janeen figured this had to be something tragic. *I hope nobody died or got caught with their pants down again,* she thought.

After giving her crimson designer suit a once-over, she took a deep breath and prepared herself to accept a direct order to clean up someone else's mess.

Sitting behind a massive hand-carved mountain of a desk on the other side of his ridiculously oversized office, Mr. Bragg was decked out in a banker blue pinstripe suit. His white hair and thin frame made him appear tired or sickly at times but actually he rarely missed a day of work due to illness. When he noticed that his vice president of corporate leasing had arrived, he quickly put the papers in his top drawer, then immediately closed it before springing to his feet. "Uh-huh, Janeen. Thank you for meeting with me on such short notice. Have a seat over here, please."

He extended his hand toward the lounging section of his office. Janeen often wondered how it would feel to be invited to hang out over there. Now that her time had come, she was concerned. She had a distinct feeling that the discussion was either going to be extremely favorable or piss her off to no end. Nonetheless, she accepted his offer and made herself comfortable on the extravagant creme-hued moleskin sofa. Mr. Bragg took a seat on the matching high-back chair next to it.

"Thank you, Mr. Bragg," she stated plainly, with a faint hint of suspicion.

He removed his bifocals, then placed them on the brass coffee table covered with a thick beveled smoked-glass top. "Now, let's get down to business," he announced, staring directly at her.

Janeen smirked politely while she opened her leather portfolio binder. She considered how much that sounded like the beginning of something unfavorable. It was quite difficult to maintain her usual upper hand while being caught off guard, lounging on the casual side of life. But no matter what he had to say, she promised herself to take it in stride with unrelenting dignity.

"Yes, sir. What is it that's so pressing? Another board member get caught in a compromising position with a young boy?"

"No, no," he replied, frowning. "Nothing like that. And you were never to mention that again. Mr. Smaltz is seeing a well-respected psychologist about his condition. He'll be away for a few more months."

She knew all the dirt on the higher-ups in the company, including whose little habits got them arrested, committed, or tucked away in the finest treatment centers this country has to offer, covered by the golden-parachute protection plan, of course. Mr. Bragg took great care of his own, whether they deserved it or not. Many of his senior-level corporate leeches didn't.

By the constipated expression on Mr. Bragg's face, this meeting was about someone close to him. Poising herself for some damaging news, she placed her pen on the table and put the binder aside. She'd learned a valuable lesson over the years concerning when to commit things to memory due to the threatening possibility of personal notes falling into the wrong hands.

"All right, then. Who is it this time, your brother Bill?"

"I'm afraid not." He lowered his head before answering her. "This time, it concerns you, Janeen."

"Me?" she responded. Her surprise couldn't have been concealed if she'd tried.

Janeen was totally unprepared for whatever came next. She felt her heart beating faster. Her mouth suddenly became uncomfortably dry. After swallowing hard, she fought desperately to regain her composure, thinking maybe she had pushed the envelope one too many times with him or perhaps something that one of her staff members had gotten themselves into had come back to haunt her.

"I'm sorry, but I don't understand," she replied, when nothing else came to mind.

"Don't be alarmed. It's not that serious, but I do owe you an explanation before the news is leaked and you hear it from someone else."

Janeen leaned in with her eyes narrowed.

What she heard him say was "I do owe you an apology before the news becomes common knowledge." It was obvious by then that he had done something to piss her off all right, something magnanimous.

He still hadn't looked at her. He purposely avoided making eye contact as jurors do with the accused after they have returned from deliberation with a guilty verdict.

She listened intently as Mr. Bragg began his explanation. "Now, you know that our board has veto powers over my candidates for senior executive positions. Of course that's why your first bid for a promotion was denied, and believe me, what I'm about to tell you isn't going to make you feel any better." Mr. Bragg started to stammer a bit. He knew that she would be very upset when she heard the board's latest decision so he figured she might as well get it from him firsthand.

Saddled with a placid expression, Janeen braced herself. "Hmm. Well, I guess we had better get on with it then," she echoed.

Her jaws were clenched tightly now. She knew that whatever came out of his mouth next, countless others in the company already knew about it. She couldn't stand the thought of that.

"You're right. I should have just come right out with it," he agreed wholeheartedly while deliberately choosing his words. "The thing is this; we've created a new position, executive vice president of property recovery. And I know you are next up for a senior-level spot, but the board thought it best to give it to an outside candidate that —"

She popped up off the couch so quickly that Mr. Bragg recoiled with surprise. "An outsider!" she yelled, before her back was even straight. "Someone off the street?" Mr. Bragg winced as if she had punched him in the stomach while she continued her tirade. "You mean to tell me that I've slaved and made this company a lot of money, played by a long list of rules that didn't until recently include people who look like me, and now you've . . . let me get this straight . . . created a position for someone who has *never* contributed a damned thing or made this company one thin dime?"

The old man began to massage his temples with the tips of his fingers as he stood and backed away from the lounging area. "I knew you'd be upset, Janeen, and I'm sorry, but believe me, I had no other choice in the matter or in the decision to have you show him the ropes."

That last bit of news floored her. Janeen's knees weakened. She felt herself sinking down until the couch stopped her descent. The idea that a coveted position, which rightfully belonged to her, was being awarded to someone who had not given blood, not given sweat or tears for it, was too much. *The nerve,* she thought, *these white folk are going to be the death of me.* She sat subdued by the shock of it all until Mr. Bragg came nearer.

"Janeen, please listen to me. I know that you're due, past due, but believe me, you've got to give this thing a chance. One month. Promise me that you'll continue to stay aboard for one month. After that, I'll accept your resignation if at that time you still don't want to be here any longer. One month, and if this thing works out like I think it will, you'll be very happy you toughed it out. Can I count on you?"

Janeen felt empty inside. She honestly believed that corporate soldiers were supposed to follow orders with no questions asked, but she'd just been hit with a bullet from a firing squad herself. She spent several moments shaking her head in disbelief. "I've never let you down before, have

I?" she muttered solemnly. "One month, huh?"

"That's all. One month. If it doesn't work out for you, I'll put together a substantial compensation package for you myself." His expression conveyed that he wanted her to stay on even more than his words could have.

After lamenting briefly, she responded with her answer. "I'll do it. I can't say why, exactly, but I will."

As she dragged herself out of his office with her tail tucked between her legs, she lifted her head high and turned to face him. "You know what it is? For all you've taught me about this business and for all you've done for others in this company, I owe you at least that much. No hard feelings. I understand, it's just business, right?"

Her feelings weren't hardened. On the contrary, they were severely bruised. Oddly enough, when Janeen left Mr. Bragg, he felt worse than she did, and she knew it, too, although she didn't know why yet.

While waiting for the elevator to arrive and take her back to her office on the eighth floor, Janeen heard someone's familiar voice behind her. "Sorry, sweetie. The old man couldn't do anything about this one." The soothing voice belonged to Mrs. Aderly.

As the elevator doors opened up, Janeen turned toward the executive assistant with the well-known grin and nodded a thank-you before backing into it. Janeen caught a quick glimpse of Mr. Bragg watching her with repentant eyes from the door of his office as the elevator doors closed.

Janeen was too caught up in the disaster that just happened to her career to notice that she wasn't alone. Val stood next to her wiping her eyes with tissue. Eventually, Janeen came out of the spell to see her good friend welling up.

Janeen became immediately concerned. "Val, you all right? What's the matter? Someone bothering you?"

Val continued to press her eyes with a handful of tissue. "Nobody's been messing with me. I just had a smoke break and Mr. Salley told me the news."

"Mr. Salley, the old janitor?" Janeen replied defensively. "And what news is that?"

"The news that you just received about being passed over again for a promotion that somebody from outside the company landed."

Janeen was livid. She painstakingly exhaled through her frustration. "That's just great. My business is definitely in the streets now, but you need to put those tissues away. If they think I'm taking this lying down, they've underestimated me. There's nothing more dangerous than a black woman with nothing to lose. And by the way, next time you can tell Mr. Salley for me to keep his goddamned nose out of my business!"

Janeen was amazed at how fast the company grapevine transmitted bad news. Even though it just happened, Mr. Salley knew all about it and passed it on to Val and God knows who else, adding insult to injury. Calm days that started out as well as hers did should have never ended up like this. All of this drama before lunchtime just didn't seem plausible to Janeen.

To make matters worse, she had a message from her younger sister by thirteen years, Janeese, when she returned to the solitude of her office. Janeese was also known by her childhood name of Sissy by those who knew the family back in the old days. Although Sissy was a grown woman paying her own bills, she developed a knack for getting herself in the worse kind of trouble, someone else's.

# Chapter 2

# Scenes from a Sistah

Five blocks away at the Blue Water Café, a trendy upscale seafood eatery near downtown, lunch-hour crowds were willingly put on the usual waiting list. The cuisine was that satisfying and the ambiance even better. Beautiful people frequented the restaurant, which offered overpriced entrées and occasional celebrity sightings, which meant lines out the door. Lines were always great for business.

Several of the businessmen seated near the magnificently ostentatious wall-to-wall fresh-water fish aquarium enjoyed their lunches more than they usually did. They had Sissy and Morgan to thank for their midday entertainment.

Sissy twisted a lock of her naturally curly

coif, what some people might call good hair, around her index finger. Her fair complexion caused white men, especially, to take a second or third look, but not one of them with decent eyesight found it in themselves to ignore her rather revealing tight white hot pants, red polka-dot halter top and flashy high-heel pumps ensemble. She also had long sculptured legs, a tiny waist, and full C cups to work with. Sissy felt that hours a week in the gym and a private visit to a breast augmentation specialist gave her the right to flaunt both what her mama gave her and what she'd bought for herself — all the trappings of a woman who was quite accustomed to getting what she wanted from men.

Morgan, Sissy's protégé, was a petite Asian college coed with a lot on the ball, too. She had a model's face, breast implants, and four-inch heels to accompany her scandalous appetite for making fast money as well. She was just one of Sissy's business associates. There were twelve of them in all, young ladies working their way through college, medical internships, and law school. Morgan's code name was September because she was the ninth girl added to Sissy's lucrative dating service, which had started out as "just doing favors" for powerful people.

Sissy wrapped her red-painted lips around her soda straw with the provocativeness of an adult film star when she noticed she'd gained the full attention of four men who sat at the next table. One of them didn't try hiding the fact that he was imagining himself between her legs. Mentally he had been down there so long he could scarcely find his way out. By the looks of his potbelly, his heart couldn't have withstood the strain if he had gotten lucky. The sweat pouring down his face should have been the second clue.

Morgan looked on and giggled like a schoolgirl hearing a dirty joke. "Oooh, Janeese," she whispered across the table, "you're gonna give the fat one a heart attack."

Sissy shook her head slowly while adding a little tongue action to the sensual game she initiated. "Uh-uhhhh," she moaned seductively as she began to slide her fingertips up and down the straw. "I just want him . . . to . . . remember . . . that he's still alive . . . and too damned fat to think that any part of his anatomy is going anyplace . . . his mind's been for the past . . . half . . . hour."

Her seductive stunt drew the gaze of

other men too. Some of them had female lunch dates but that didn't stop their jaws from hitting the table, much like the sweaty man who took his napkin and began wiping the streams of perspiration from his face. He swallowed hard to force the tension past his arid mouth. "What I wouldn't give to be that straw right now," he said to himself.

One of the other men overheard him thinking aloud and agreed wholeheartedly. "You're telling me. I don't know if I could make it out alive but you wouldn't be able to sandblast the smile off my face if I didn't."

When the waiter arrived with lunch for the ladies, the burlesque show abruptly ended. Sissy didn't play when it came to good food, although hours of dedication in the gym erased any evidence of that.

After the waiter disappeared, Sissy looked at the guys who anxiously awaited more. "Sorry, gentlemen," she apologized with a sexy frown. "That'll be all for today. A girl's gotta eat."

Although she was speaking to the men at her nearest table, there was a resounding "Awwwwwww," followed by applause from men seated in her section. That ovation put a bright smile on her face.

"Why do you do that, Janeese?" Morgan managed to ask between giggles. "You're such a tease. You haven't made time for a man in the two years I've known you."

"I don't know why I trip sometimes, girl. Funny thing is, I call myself saving it for someone special, someone I used to know. But today, Mo, I'm just getting my kicks."

During lunch, Sissy reached in her red leather purse and came out with an envelope. She casually placed it on the table. "Mo, you sure you're up to the engagement tonight? Cool. Now, it needs to be wrapped up by nine o'clock, I guess so he can get home to wifey, but that ain't my concern."

"No problem," Morgan answered without taking an eye off the envelope. "He never lasts more than five minutes anyway."

Sissy handed over the envelope. "Well then, that's two hundred dollars a minute. There're ten bills."

Morgan quickly placed the envelope into her purse. She had seen her share of payment envelopes but the amount was out of order. "A thousand?" Mo asked. "Why is it double the normal rate?"

"You've got skills and they are in demand. The man wants to pay twice as much for the same show and you've got a problem with that?"

Morgan shrugged. "No, I'm not complaining. It's just that he isn't as bad as most of them. He's funny, makes me laugh. I'd do it for half that. Next time tell him the standard five hundred is enough."

Sissy was applying lipstick when Morgan's words caught her with her guard down. "Mo, don't ever say that again. Don't ever think that again. They all gotta pay to play. Another year and you'll have your master's degree. You've got bills and skills and they've got the money to pay for that honey," she lectured, leaning in closer to make her point. "Listen to me and don't you forget this, ain't nothing meant to be free that's worth paying for." Sissy sat back against her chair. "We understand each other, Mo?"

Morgan's expression, riddled with the embarrassment of being scolded like some back-alley streetwalker, quickly faded. "Yeah," she proudly answered. "I will have my master's this time next year, won't I?"

While taking a visual inventory of her expensive platinum timepiece and nice clothes, Morgan nodded her head. "Yeah, Janeese, we understand each other real well."

Both ladies raised their glasses and toasted, "The finer things."

After lunch, Sissy whizzed down Interstate 75 in 102-degree heat to transact her next order of business. Texas summer days are notorious for being hotter than a crack house raid and sometimes just as dangerous, so when Sissy's air-conditioning unit in her Mercedes coupé had decided to surrender to the forty-ninth consecutive day above 100 degrees the night before, she vowed that it had to be fixed immediately.

Turning left on Forest Lane to Greenville Avenue, she decided to whip her maroon two-seater around an old rusted-out station wagon that moved too slowly for her taste.

Kelvin heard the screeching tires of Sissy's latest driving maneuver and raised his head from underneath a BMW thinking an accident was about to happen; maybe an accident he could get some business from. Kelvin Clark managed the European Sports Car Repair Center at the corner. He was a stump of a man in his early thirties and related to Sissy by marriage. He'd pledged holy matrimony to her oldest sister's daughter, Kyla.

He watched Sissy's car pulling into his service bay. Before he could duck back under the hood of his immediate concern, her car door seemed to glide open. Two other auto mechanics literally dropped what they were involved in when they watched her sultry body as she climbed out of the car, all high-heeled and polka-dotted up like a woman on a mission.

Mechanics, like policemen, meet tons of attractive women who are always on the wrong end of a bad set of circumstances. The women are either in desperate need of something while offering nothing in return or eventually cost a lot more than they are worth. Sissy was indicative of the latter. Surprisingly, she did have a big heart as well as a fat bank account.

As cars passed by behind her, she shielded her face from the blinding midday sun. The greasy neighborhood automotive shop sat in front of her like a broken-down old man. Sissy concentrated on the nearly motionless warehouse of an oil pit. The only movement inside the dimly lit garage was Kelvin slowly shaking his head in disapproval of the effect she had on his employees. Kelvin's two assistants were identical twins, Orang'jello and Le'monjello. They stood quietly side by side, afraid to blink because they didn't want to miss anything. They were barely twenty-one, on probation, and hadn't ever laid eyes on anything like her, an alluring woman with loads of book sense, common sense, and street sense to match. She was something to see, and she liked it that way.

"We're closed, Sissy!" shouted Kelvin just before she entered the service bay. "Besides, customers aren't allowed in the work area."

As the befuddled twins looked on, Sissy said something into her cell phone, then flipped it off. "Come on, nah, nephew," she teased.

Kelvin was actually her nephew by marriage although he was five years older than she was, but that didn't stop her from poking fun at him. She knew how much he hated being called that by her in public, which always meant he'd be explaining it to somebody later.

"Ah-ah-ah! Don't you be starting with that nephew stuff and bringing confusion up in my establishment. Look at 'em." Kelvin pointed toward the twins, neither of whom had moved an inch since she arrived. "They're good workers and now you've got 'em in my pocket and standing around on my clock." He was fuming to the point of getting hostile, but both of the young men stood their ground. "Dammit!" he barked loudly, "do either of y'all understand English? Damn crack babies. I ought to call y'all's probation officer."

The thought of that phone call broke the spell she had on them. Kelvin often gave young men with troubled pasts a shot at honest work. He would never have reported their poor conduct but they almost broke their necks getting back to work just in case he did.

Seeing that she might have to add some extra jelly, figuratively speaking, to the jam she was caught in, Sissy put her hands on her hips and let her backbone slip to the side. Before he knew it, even Kelvin had raised his brow to acknowledge the heated intensity she caused, and that wasn't the only thing on the rise.

Feeling more than a bit nervous himself, the reluctant nephew began having problems getting on with his previous business. "Whu-whut-whut-whut's wrong with your car anyway," he stuttered, trying to avoid noticing her sensual pose. "It's under whoo-whoo-warranty anyhow."

Kelvin was kicking himself for losing his composure. Each time she came to the shop to ask for a favor, he promised it would be the last time he'd oblige. Even though he loved and was married to her niece, Kyla, who was only three years younger than Sissy, Kelvin was still a man, not a dog. He just suffered from that most common of all male dysfunctions: when the little head wakes up, the big head takes a nap. Sometimes it can barely find its own way home before the sun comes up.

After watching the whole incident from the mechanics' break area inside the garage, J. R. Cooper applauded as he stood with the sports section of the newspaper tucked underneath his arm. "Bravo!" he announced. "Bravo. That's the same routine you used in senior trig. Those hips got old man Hester to change the test dates around so you could rehearse for the spring pageant."

"I won it too, didn't I?" she replied with unadulterated certainty, although her usual seductive demeanor was blindsided by a struggle to shield her surprise at his unexpected presence. Actually, she almost choked on her words.

As Kelvin leaned back to get a look at Cooper, who was taking in an eyeful of Sissy, she pretended not to be impressed by Cooper's strong hands, muscular arms, and fantastic looks.

"Yeah, yeah, you did," he answered, without blinking.

Kelvin decided to get out of the way while they caught up on the good old times. Unfortunately, not all the old times were that good. Sissy had tried extremely hard to forget theirs. Cooper hoped that she couldn't, not after what they experienced together.

As Cooper approached the wide doorway of the garage, Sissy made a poor attempt at keeping her tough-girl persona intact. It's interesting how an ex-lover's presence can get a woman hot and bothered, even if she doesn't want to.

"So, Janeese, how've you been?" asked Cooper, unleashing a dazzling smile and showing his sparkling white teeth. "Looks like somebody's taking care of business these days."

Instantaneously Sissy cocked her head back in objection to her personal business being brought up in a greasy auto repair shop. She pulled the sunshades down over her eyes from resting atop her head, metaphorically blocking him out of her world. Before strutting away toward the customer waiting area, she twisted her lips as if she smelled something rank. "Uh-uh. Don't go there, because you have not been invited, *Cooper*. Tell you what, though . . . you want to know how I've been? I've been without my air-conditioner. Tell Kelvin to get right on it," she demanded matter-of-factly, then disappeared into the cool part of the building to wait.

Cooper responded to her blatant rejection with a sly chuckle, like a man in the middle of something he could see the ending to and liked what he saw.

Kelvin approached his new employee while thoroughly looking him up and down. "You don't know what you're getting yourself into. Believe me, you don't want any part of that."

As Cooper peered at Sissy standing inside and fanning herself with an outdated magazine she'd found at the reception desk, he grinned knowingly. "Too late, Mr. Clark," he replied without regret, "I can't help remembering how good it was when I had better . . . things . . . to do with my time."

Kelvin's eyes bugged, displaying his disbelief. "And you lived to tell about it? Humph, you must be one hell of a man, Coop. One hell of a man."

Sissy immediately began checking the messages on her cell phone as she surveyed the large dusty waiting area with grungy floors and faded walls. There was no way she would allow anything in that filthy room to come in contact with her behind. No way.

Cooper spoke briefly with Kelvin regarding Sissy's request to have him service her car. Kelvin made some unflattering remarks among his general refusal to go anywhere near her *whip,* as he put it, but told Cooper he could take care of it if he wanted to — off the clock, of course.

In the waiting area, Sissy grimaced with disgust. It was extremely difficult to detect what the thick film consisted of, covering the large plate-glass windows encasing the room where she took refuge from the even more repulsive service area.

"Why don't they ever think of cleaning this place?" she said aloud as her cell phone rang for the second time. "Hello, this is Janeese."

Sissy watched tentatively as Cooper leaned over the driver's-side door and felt around underneath the dashboard panel until his fingers found the hood release lever. She stepped closer to the window to get a better look at his tight butt pressing against his soiled navy blue work pants. "Dayyy-um . . . he's still fine as cat hair," slid right out of her mouth. "Oh, nothing, girl," she answered, into the small handheld telephone. "I just slipped, is all. Don't mind me, I just slipped."

When it seemed as if Cooper were turning around to face her, she quickly did an about-face to avoid being busted for peeping. "How'd you know it had anything to do with a man?" she said defensively to the person on the phone. "Oh, your telephone just got hot. That's real cute. Very funny."

Sissy tried to disregard the fine brother maneuvering his way around under her hood but there was something magnetically pulling her attention his way. Before she could blink, the thought of his strong arms lifting up more than just the hood of her car crossed her mind. Tempted more than she could stand, she turned slowly to see if she could get another quick look at him without being noticed.

"Uh-huh. Uh-huh. Uh-huh," Sissy uttered, while stretching her neck. When it seemed that someone might discover her attempt at surveillance, she resorted to hiding beside a relic of a cardboard tire advertisement in order to secretly keep him in her sights.

"What? Oh, I'm sorry, Gigi, but you're

gonna have to forgive me. A heat wave just ran over me and woke up ma' girl. It's a shame, too, because I have bathed her, perfumed her, kept her 'do perfectly coiffed, dressed her in the rarest silks, paraded her tail to the best hot spots in the city and around the wealthiest men and she's always been a lady, but you let the one fine-ass-*broke*-rusty-butt roughneck that I've been dreaming about since high school cross my path one time and she starts embarrassing the hell out of me. Girl, I got to get out of here before she starts singing to the man. I'll catch you later." She sighed deeply, then flipped the tiny cell phone closed. "Where has he been for the past few years?" she heard herself say. "And why in the hell didn't he have the decency to call me when he came back to town?" She shook her head to shrug off all of the leftover feelings she still held for him when they came rushing back. "Uh-uh, girl, don't even stress, and never let 'em see you sweat."

Cooper thumbed through a thick directory at the far end of the shop when Sissy made her way back into the garage. She hoped that no opportunity to speak with him again would present itself. Tragedy may have been eagerly waiting on the other side of a drawn-out conversation and she already had too much drama going on in her business life to return to something that was once so personally damaging.

"Hey, Kelvin!" she called out into the opened garage, as if it were too much trouble to look for him.

"What!" he answered back, as rudely as she'd called for him. He was up to his armpits in someone's ultimate driving machine.

"When is my car going to be ready? I've got things to do and places to be."

He peeked his head out just enough to display his frustration, then ducked back under the hood. "I'ont know. Ask Coop. Said something about needing a special hose you can only get from the dealership, *which is where you should have taken it in the first place!* I'm one man short as it is."

Sissy was too out of sorts to argue the point but she could not see herself sweating another day in the Texas heat without cool air blowing in her face. When Cooper hung up the phone and headed toward her, she swallowed hard. All of a sudden she felt sixteen again, young and liking the idea that boys seemed to be evolving into strapping young men overnight. Dreading the inevitable, she called out to Kelvin again. Her voice was uneasy and overrun with panic.

"Heyyy . . . Kelvin?"

"What you want now? Can't you see that you're not the only person on this earth who's got business to tend to?"

"Whutehvah, anyway . . . how long does it take to get a hose thingy?" She was hoping to receive the answers she needed from the shop owner before Cooper was staring her in the face again.

Tired of yelling, Kelvin walked around to the side of the car. "Coop, come on over here for a second," he commanded. "You get an estimate on how long it'll take to get that part sent over?"

Cooper wiped oil from his hands with a red cloth as he approached them. "The man said he couldn't get it here until tomorrow, something about the delivery truck breaking down."

Kelvin's thick lips relaxed into a sheepish grin. He winked at Cooper before gleefully addressing Sissy's concern. "Well, well. Seems like you gonna have to leave that car here overnight, mahdam. Mr. Cooper here can run you to wherever you need to go. Right, Coop?"

Cooper's expression turned sour as he looked down at the ground with false apprehensions. "I'ont know, Mr. Kelvin, suh," he teased, with a rather impressive Amos-and-Andy dialect. "A fine woman like this'n here might not like the confines of my modest open-air Jeep when she been spoiled by that grand chariot over yundah." Like an imbecilic half-wit, he raised his arm slowly and pointed to her Benz.

Kelvin and Cooper both found the co-medic stand-up routine to be hilarious. They laughed aloud and slapped high fives at Sissy's expense.

She was not amused. "That's just great. I'm stranded and I've got Heckle and Jeckle making jokes. That's just great!" She was outdone by a tag-team purposely working to water down her attitude, which proved impenetrable. On the contrary, she put on her best smile and changed her strategy. "Tomorrow, huh? Then how am I supposed to get home from this paradise of yours? A true black man wouldn't just leave a girl standing on the corner," she ex-claimed, going out on a limb to appeal to their sense of chivalry. Unfortunately for her, they saw her pitiful helpless-girl act coming a mile away.

Kelvin stroked his scraggly goatee with malicious intent. His mischievous grin returned as he came up with what he thought to be a great idea, as well as a challenge. "Nah, not us. Fine upstanding Negroes like ourselves would never think of such a thing." Sissy should have seen the "but" coming. "But what I will do is give you this-here dollar to catch the bus that stops right over there every fifteen minutes."

Sissy was boiling mad by then. She had to press her lips together tightly in order to suppress the high degree of piss-tivity she felt. "No thank you, gentlemen. I'll work it out myself."

She slung her long purse strap over her shoulder and headed for the intersection. A city bus was about to pull away from the curb as she sauntered toward it.

"You'd better hurry up, Cinderella, your pumpkin is leaving without you," Kelvin shouted, to get in one last ribbing.

Instinctively, Sissy flipped him a nasty little screw-you finger over her shoulder for good measure. "Whatehvah, fat boy, right back at ya."

She proceeded toward the bus, which had actually passed her by then. As Kelvin yelled, "Run, Cinderella . . . run!" and Cooper busted a gut, Sissy put a little extra wiggle in her git-along with hopes of capturing the bus driver's attention. When he did notice her out of his oversized rearview mirror, the three-hundred-pound brother bugged his eyes and mashed his size thirteens against the brake pedal as if his life depended on it.

Dust kicked up behind the skidding bus. Several automobile drivers leaned on their horns to protest the blocked intersection, which the bus made impossible to get through. Amidst all the noise and near pandemonium, the mountain of a bus driver with a shaved head and a predilection for sexy women, graciously welcomed Sissy up the bus steps. When she asked him where exactly the bus stopped, he was more than happy to tell her it would stop anywhere she wanted it to.

Sitting a few rows down the aisle, a rusty brown-skinned dread-headed brother looked on casually. He appeared undisturbed from the other side of a shoe box full of marijuana as he methodically rolled joints using the box lid to separate the seeds from the weed.

Before Sissy was comfortably seated, she stole a glimpse of Cooper still standing near the opened hood of her car. A man who was talented with his hands was a good thing to keep around, she reasoned.

And, as the bus made its way into traffic, Sissy thought back on how Cooper used to make her feel, his sweet slow lovemaking style, and why she began making love in the first place. She also remembered for the first time in years why it was possible for anyone to fall in love, even if it happened to be with the wrong man.

# Chapter 3

# Something's in the Water

Having tried desperately to get the trouble-some memory of Friday's meeting off her mind, Janeen dreaded being forced to deal with it on the following Monday morning, but in the meanwhile Saturday night couldn't come fast enough for her. The third Saturday evening of each month provided an opportunity for the Good Book Club to visit, share in each other's lives, and peel back some layers of the latest best-selling novel.

The group was formed by Janeen and her older sister, Joyce, before reading clubs were all the rage, and it didn't take long before other family members and close friends soon joined in. Ten years and lots of good books later, each member looked forward to sitting down to wine and finger food and getting intimate with the chosen selection of the month.

When the sun began its descent on Saturday evening, cars were lined up outside of Janeen's palatial two-story home on Mimosa Drive in an exclusive gated community. Six large white pillars graced the entrance way to the beautiful white house with eggshell trim. The house featured an antebellum style that reminded Janeen of the grandiose plantation houses she'd trod past as a child on her way to pick cotton and chop sugarcane. In her formative years, she often dreamed of living in a house like those herself but often wondered if she had to be white in order to do so. After she was promoted to vice president at First World Mortgage four years ago, she finally stopped wondering.

"Come on in, y'all," Janeen welcomed, after she pulled open the oversized front doors decorated with marvelous stained glass in a montage of primary colors. "Kyla, let me help you with that."

Janeen received a large platter of southwestern egg rolls from her niece. "Where's Joyce?" she asked, stepping out onto the vast front porch. "I thought your mother was coming with you?"

"Hey, auntie. She's in the car praying," Kyla huffed with disdain.

Janeen wrinkled her nose and thought aloud, "Praying for who this time?"

The ivory-and-gold-colored telephone rang from the redwood table near the front door. Janeen stepped back into the house to answer it. "Hello. Hey, Sissy. I know you wanted to stop by and talk but the book club is meeting here tonight. Yeah, we'll probably get started in about thirty minutes or so. Did you read the book? Don't come unless you've read it. You know you will get clowned if you don't have anything to contribute to the discussion. Kyla's the club president now and she's serious about her post. Save yourself some humiliation. Huh? Ten o'clock is fine. We'll be all done by then. I'll see you later."

Just after she set the phone down, Janeen returned to the door to greet other members coming in with hospitable "Hey, girl" and "I'm glad you could make it" salutations. The warmth with which she welcomed her guests into her home made everyone feel at ease, considering the house was valued at over $1 million. All the homes on Mimosa Drive were worth at least that much. Janeen snagged hers at a foreclosure sale for half the price. She

54

bought everything else on sale when she could, just as her mother trained her, so why not her house too?

Eventually Joyce got out of her daughter's Astro van and slowly made her way up to her sister's castle of a home. Kyla was setting up the seating arrangements and placing huge pillows on the recently buffed hardwood floor as some of the new members toured all eight fully furnished bedrooms. Janeen suggested they make themselves at home while she checked on the refreshments.

In the spacious kitchen, Joyce hummed a pleasant tune that reminded Janeen of their mother, who'd spent most of her days in the kitchen humming while preparing meals for the family. She couldn't help but think that the two seem to go hand in hand, cooking and humming.

Joyce paused when she looked up and noticed an impressive copper cookware set suspended from the ceiling on a six-by-three-foot black wrought-iron rack. She shook her head at its grandeur, then began humming the same delightful tune.

Watching her older sister fussing around the spice canisters, hunting for sugar, Janeen smiled and folded her arms. "You know, you're getting more like Muh'dear every day," she mentioned in a complimentary way.

"Oh, it's you. I knew somebody was looking me over." Joyce turned her head just enough to catch a glimpse of Janeen's face. "Thought maybe it was one of those funny crows. You know, it's not beneath them to take a good look at another woman's wiggle box."

"Ooh, stop, Joyce. The wrong somebody's going to hear you and get their feelings hurt."

Joyce could be cruel when she felt the need to be. Lila and Bertha Crowe had a well-earned reputation as nosy cousins. Rumor had it that they were also kissing cousins, in a twisted, incestual kind of way. Admittedly, they were lesbians and eternal roommates, but Joyce's play on words did not go unnoticed.

Only a few years older than her sister, Joyce had felt responsible for Janeen's well-being since their teen years. It's funny how a terrible childhood tragedy can bring rival siblings closer together when all the parental lectures under the sun couldn't. Sometimes sisters have to go through trying ordeals together in order to get where they need to be.

Barely forty-two herself, Joyce seemed as

if she were at least ten years older by the way she carried herself. She was never in a hurry for anyone or anything; that was just her way. She usually had an easy spirit. That part of her was passed on to Kyla, her only child. But, that evening, something was weighing on her, something heavy.

Janeen could always sense when her sister was shouldering something because she would spend a lot of time praying. The fact that Joyce never once prayed for herself or set foot in any church in over twenty-five years didn't seem in the least bit strange to Janeen. She knew why and fully understood Joyce's rationale, although she didn't necessarily agree with it. On the other hand, considering Janeen's past experiences, she couldn't blame her sister for it either.

Kyla dashed in to get something to drink. "Auntie, I like the new floors," she said, while reaching into the cabinet for a water glass. "They remind me of Muh'dear's old house."

"That's why I had the carpet pulled up," Janeen reminisced. "Muh'dear would say, 'Nowadays people try to put covers on things that don't have no business being covered up.' So one day I lifted a piece in the corner of the living room just to see what was underneath and there it was, dusty but beautiful hardwood just waiting to be looked at."

"Now look who's getting like Muh'dear," Joyce quipped, having a laugh after making a well-timed comeback.

After a brief laugh among family, Kyla barked instructions before darting out as quickly as she came in. "Uh-oh. I think I hear Bertha and Lila out there, so I'd better go and get things started before they get going themselves and somebody gets offended. Now, I know y'all like to talk as if y'all don't see each other every week but we came to get into the book, so hurr'up! Pleeeease. I just might need some backup. This book was hot."

Janeen walked over to the counter lined with spice canisters, poured two cups of coffee, then dropped two cubes of sugar in each of them before topping them off with a healthy swig of Bailey's Irish Cream. Joyce dipped her spoon in one of the cups, then laid it on her tongue. "Mmmm . . ." she moaned. "That's nice. I can remember when a li'l spoon taste was all I got. A few times Daddy caught me trying to dip my spoon twice and I got more than I bargained for."

"I remember, but that didn't stop you

from trying, though," Janeen offered without a word of response from her sister. "Uh . . . Joyce, your daughter told me you were in the car praying earlier . . . and I know you well enough to know *that* prayer was for somebody who lives in this house, and since your prayers never include Ray, I know it wasn't for my husband."

Joyce took a long sip of coffee, then stared in it for a while before answering. "It might not be anything but I saw Sissy and Ray arguing up a storm in his car outside the Rib Shack. I didn't say anything about it before now because I wasn't sure, but the more I thought about it, I just didn't like the way it looked."

Nothing appeared to be out of the ordinary about that as far as Janeen was concerned. "It was probably nothing," she reasoned. "Sissy has been working with Ray on a part-time basis as a client development agent. Anyway, he has been more like a big brother to her than a brother-in-law. I'm sure it was just business and —"

"It was a lovers' quarrel, Janeen!" Joyce interjected harshly. "Fussing like a man and woman who's got more than public business between 'em."

Kyla apprehensively stuck her head in the kitchen. "Is . . . everything all right?"

she asked cautiously, surveying their faces. "Sounds like more drama is going on in here than out there."

When a woman is informed that her husband and her sister were seen dangerously close to one another, it could mean there might be some explanation worth hearing. On the other hand, a report from someone she trusts, that some kind of intimacy between the two has taken place could also suggest that somebody is going to get hurt.

Moments later, in the large family room, lively conversation captivated each of the eighteen book club members who attended the meeting. They raved about how good the novel, Skin Deep, was, and agreed that everyone had their own inner demons to contend with no matter how their lives appeared to be on the outside.

Throughout the discussion, Janeen's blank expression concealed the war going on inside of her. The idea of her baby sister and her man being involved in an affair caused a burning rage within her. She didn't know whether to be more upset with the thoughts of her husband sneaking around on her or the fact that she'd stayed around long enough for him to make a fool of her twice. Sissy's potential part in the alleged act of betrayal never entered her mind. She wouldn't allow it. Janeen simply refused to believe that it could have happened with Sissy. She simply refused to. Denial always has been heartache's favorite bedfellow, and once they get together, it generally takes an epiphany of earthquake proportions to separate them. Sometimes, a real good knockdown sucker punch will do just as well.

"Janeen! Janeen!" someone shouted.

"Janeen!" bellowed Kyla once more, from across the room.

Blinking her eyes rapidly to regain focus, Janeen felt as if she were awakening from a bad dream. Every eye in the room looked on with concern.

"What did you think about the book?" Kyla asked again, to help her obviously troubled aunt along. "The book? How many stars did you give it?"

"Umm, five stars. Yeah, I gave it five stars," was all she could manage to say while languishing in a fog of uncertainty.

Strange looks from nearly everyone followed. Joyce nodded to Kyla, suggesting they'd better adjourn the meeting to grant her sister some time to herself.

Kyla called the meeting to a close, then

remembered something important. "Oh, oh, oh! Y'all, I almost forgot. As y'all know, next month is special because it's our tenth anniversary meeting and . . . and I'll have a special treat for you. So make sure you run out and get *The Women of Newberry* by Eric Bynote. It's a Black-Board best-seller and he's one of the few brothas ever to get on Oprah's list, so you know it's hot. Besides, he's from Newberry, Louisiana, that's my family's hometown."

The crowd began picking up plastic cups, paper napkins, and personal belongings as they made their way out into the uncomfortably warm night. Janeen stood near the door thanking everyone for coming when she remembered Sissy was supposed to be stopping by. She overlooked the comment she heard her cousin Bertha make regarding "Don't nobody need eight damn bedrooms when you can't screw but in one at a time nohow."

Lila co-signed the statement with her own worthless two cents. "Uh-huh. Word on the street is she ain't the only one getting screwed."

Suddenly, Janeen became particularly interested in knowing why she had received two calls in two days from Sissy, asking for an audience, who could have easily stopped by any time without a formal invitation.

It must have seemed like yesterday to Janeen when she carried Sissy around on her hip like a doll, considering she was already thirteen when her younger sister was born. There had to be some other reason Sissy was so pressed to meet, and there had to be some other explanation for the heated exchange Joyce had witnessed and informed her about.

As the last good-bye rolled out of the front door, Janeen sighed and headed for the kitchen. She pulled two wineglasses down from the bottom shelf and smiled what could barely be considered a smile in the reflection of the second glass.

*A generous glass of merlot for one,* she thought as she poured slowly. The other glass sat there empty, just as it always did when any of the sisters drank alone. Thanks to their father's old superstition, it became a family custom to leave the second glass empty so that any spirits in attendance could feel welcome to join company if they felt so inclined. Janeen had thought it was silly as a child witnessing the quirky undertaking, but as a grown woman she learned in due time that being alone and feeling alone weren't necessarily the same thing.

While adjusting the top of her tightly fitting fuchsia-colored sleeveless designer pantsuit, Sissy composed herself enough to ring the bell. After minutes of pacing back and forth on the porch with both hands clasped behind her, she knew it was time to face Janeen and show the woman she respected most on this earth that she was a stand-up person, one who could own up to the decisions she'd made whether they were right or wrong. However, she didn't know if Ray was home. What she went to Janeen's to say would have caused a train wreck of accusations if he did happen to be there.

She took another moment and drew a deep breath, then pressed the bell. It was too late to turn back now, she kept telling herself. Anyway, it was the right thing to do.

Janeen made her way into the living area. She assumed that one of the book club members had forgotten something after the meeting concluded. Without checking to see who'd rung the bell, she opened the door with a pleasant smile gracing her attractive, angular face.

Sissy stood there beneath the lazy

flickers of the nineteenth-century-style gas-powered porch light, rocking on the balls of her feet like a woman who was moments away from an anxiety attack. "Hey, big sistah," she said, nervously. "Aren't you going to invite me in, or am I intruding on somebody's quality time?" Sissy was almost sure that no one else was inside because she'd staked out the house from the corner until all the cars were gone. Ray usually hung out late with the boys on Saturday night, playing dominoes or poker, that's one thing she hoped she could count on.

"No, Ray's out," Janeen answered, as calmly as possible. "Come on in out of that heat. It's a shame that it's still in the nineties this late into the evening."

Sissy was family so Janeen had never looked at her from the standpoint of being "another woman" before despite the obvious fact that she had grown into the kind of woman that men were interested in getting to know better, with a tight body and a healthy sexual appetite. In addition to her physical attributes, she was also very smart and just a term away from completing law school. Although Sissy wasn't perfect by any means, Janeen knew what most men fantasized about and her younger sister was well equipped with most of it.

In an attempt to remain positive, Janeen shook her head briskly to ward off any negative energy that worked hard at sticking around. Lost somewhere in those suspicions was her accommodating disposition, which Sissy loved so much about her.

"Is something wrong, Janeen?" Sissy asked peculiarly, while gazing at her the same way the book club members had only moments before. "You don't look like yourself."

"Oh no? Then who do I look like?" she snapped back.

Wonderment cast a shroud over Sissy's face. Before she could react to the comment, Janeen caught herself. "Dammit. I'm sorry, Sissy. Just had a lousy day at work on Friday and I can't seem to let it pass. Let's go in there and sit down. I know you've been wanting to talk to me about something."

Both ladies crossed through the formal dining area into the family room. Sissy was still quite reserved. There was something altogether wrong with her sister, more than what an unfavorable job situation could explain, but Sissy had her own peace to make.

After they were comfortably seated on the couch, Sissy reached into her purse. Uncharacteristically, Janeen jumped back. Her sudden movement startled Sissy.

"What in the hell is going on with you?" Sissy asked, two octaves higher than normal. "You act like someone is hiding under your bed or something. I've never seen you like this."

Pressing both outstretched hands against her sister's face, then moving them downward slowly, Janeen stared into her concerned eyes. "Sissy, I'm just going to ask you this woman to woman," she said flatly, "and please don't lie to me."

Sissy was scared now. Janeen always had a strong hold on her emotions but she appeared to be a woman hanging on by a very thin thread. "I would never lie to you, Janeen. You of all people should know that. What is all of this about, anyway?"

Taken by surprise as her younger sister reached for both of her hands, Janeen pulled hers away instinctively. "Be straight with me. Is there something between you and Raymond that you want to tell me about?"

Sissy's face turned white as a sheet. "What about me and Ray?" she muttered rather suspiciously. She didn't want to confess to any more than necessary and it was obvious she had something to hide.

Clenching her jaws together tightly enough to make diamonds, Janeen asked again. "What about you and Ray?" she repeated. "Janeese, don't you play with me."

There was little room now for the affectionate childhood name she readily used before. This was grown-folks' business. As Janeen battled with the idea of it being remotely possible, asking became twice as difficult. "Are you and Raymond having an affair?"

When the accusation hit Sissy like a misguided backhand, she leaped off the couch screaming, "Hell, no, I'm not messing with Ray! Are you serious? I can't even believe you'd ask me something like that. You're my sistah!" Sissy fought back her tears. "Is that what you think of me? Huh! After all you've done for me. You've raised me like you were responsible for me, put me through college and now you're footing the bill on law school. I don't believe this." Sissy's eyes began to well up from the hurt. "I might be a lot of things but I would never, under any circumstances, think of doing anything to hurt you. Sometimes I think I love you more than I love myself."

Janeen was in shock too. Having her

words and torrid accusations thrown back in her face rocked her as much as they did Sissy, who was trembling.

"I just came by here to give you this." She reached into her purse again and came out with a greeting card and a cashier's check for $37,000. She began reading the card between attempts at wiping the tears from her eyes. "Because you've shown me the kind of love I need, I've learned to appreciate what plans you've made for me and in spite of myself, your love . . . is helping me to become the woman I was meant to be."

Choked up on the sentiment when Sissy handed the card to her, Janeen was frozen, filled with pride and confusion. It didn't help the situation any when her younger sister held the cashier's check up for her to see.

"And this . . . and this is just a little something to pay you back for helping Muh'dear to raise me after Joyce moved out and for buying me things when I needed them. I know I can never repay you but . . ." She couldn't go on due to the flood of emotion rolling down her cheeks.

The gratitude Sissy displayed caused a prideful knot in Janeen's throat and at the same time plastered a heavy coat of shameful remorse on her face. "I'm sorry," she apologized. "Sissy, I'm so sorry. Please forgive me. I should have known better. I never should have even considered such a thing. Please forgive me."

They spent the next hour holding each other and reminiscing about the tough times bringing Sissy up after their father died in a terrible car accident. Janeen did have issues with the hefty personal check, though. She'd never intended to be repaid for her kindness and generosity. Taking care of family business was like breathing. It was second nature to share what she had and it was the first time in a long time that they actually sat down and discussed some things that mattered. However, their conversation did hit a snag when Sissy informed her that she'd saved the money by dropping out of law school to make a good income by developing business for Ray. That was something Janeen promised herself to take up with her husband later.

Whatever Joyce saw transpiring inside the car at the Rib Shack didn't concern Janeen any longer. She had to decide which sister to invest her faith in. Time would tell whether she made the right choice or not.

# Chapter 4

# It's a Thin Line

Several hours after Sissy left that night, Ray stumbled in through the front door. Janeen thought it was odd because he usually parked his Rolls Royce in the garage. After she heard the alarm system activate the front door chime, warning that someone had entered the house, she made her way to the staircase landing and peered over the railing. Her left hand warmed the .38-caliber automatic pistol tucked inside the pocket of her full-length cotton housecoat, just in case it wasn't Ray who had tripped the alarm. Fortunately for him, his first inclination was to hit the light switch and announce who he was.

"Hey, baby, I'm home," he declared drunkenly as he stumbled over his own two feet. "What you still doing up this time of morning? All good wives are s'posed to be sleepin'."

Janeen sneered, then retired to an upstairs guest bedroom. The clock read 5:19 but she hadn't slept a wink. Ray often stayed out much later than married men are supposed to, but it had never kept her up before. She'd let it slide all those years because her mother explained to her during the first year of her marriage that men need time to bond and trade lies with each other "cause that's what menfolk do." Lately his clothes smelled more like baby powder and Similac than bourbon when he did make it home before daybreak.

For the better part of Sunday, Janeen rummaged through rows of clothes hanging in her luxurious walk-in closet to make note of business suits and dresses that still had department store tags dangling from their sleeves. Her mother used to say, "When a woman says she has nothing to wear, you best believe she's got too many darn clothes in the first place."

Janeen laughed to herself at the thought of her mother getting an eyeful of her obsessively collected wardrobe, and shook her head slowly, as Joyce had while viewing

her new kitchen accessories.

Sunday's mood was low and slow like an old black-and-white film that ended with the hero meeting his death over the woman he loved unselfishly. Accompanied by an Etta James CD that included a splendidly soothing rendition of Billie Holiday's "You've Changed," Janeen entrenched herself in busywork while Ray slept off his hard night of drinking and Lord knows what else the night's watchful eye saw him do. Busywork is what her mother called spending time actively doing nothing when a woman was worried about her man's affairs, business or otherwise. When Janeen's father became involved with the Black Panthers only months after they moved to Dallas back in the 1970s, her mother had once sewed enough quilts to keep every family in the neighborhood warm through the most unrelenting Texas winters.

Hours passed and a long somber Sunday had come and gone without so much as a single word from Ray as to his whereabouts the night before. Actually, the only time she heard his voice was the echo of his empty words ringing off the halls of their broad foyer on his way out the door. "Hey, I'm'a be at the office. Got some thangs to look after today." And he was

gone, with no acceptable excuse to speak of.

Janeen wondered where the love that sustained them year after year had disappeared to. If she could have gone there and dragged it back, kicking and screaming, she would have. His love was all she'd known. For her, there had never been anyone else.

Monday morning came much too fast for Janeen's taste after dreading its arrival since Friday. The bright yellow sun offered no mercy when it flung its stinging rays through the thin horizontal slits of the Venetian blinds in her favorite guest bedroom. After crying half the night, she awakened with one thought tattooed on her brain. It was the title to an old Ray Charles hit, "Don't Let the Sun Catch You Cryin'." She was well aware that big girls didn't cry, or at least they didn't let anyone know it when they did.

Lying underneath the covers, which held her closely like the comforting arms of a loving friend, she hated herself for getting emotional enough to shed tears over her anemic marriage. Saturday night's series of events opened the floodgates to accusations, suspicions, and fears. She pondered life without him, the only man she'd ever

loved or made love to. Surprisingly, she hoped she'd be woman enough to leave him if it ever came to that.

A few years before, a line had been drawn in the sand when Ray fathered a son by one of his former employees, but Janeen washed that line away with pain and trials of forgiveness. She probably would never have found out about the boy if he hadn't died of complications stemming from sickle cell anemia. Funny thing was, mourning some other woman's child is what held her marriage together. Come to think of it, that was the only other time she cried for any reason since she was a child. There was a soft spot deep within her for anything that died before its time, like the innocence lost in a child or the premature death of one or even the passing of the love for her husband that she once hoped would be never ending. Now she wasn't so sure about that.

With so much trouble brewing in her own life, she was growing weary and bitterly tired of being everyone else's rock. Val, Sissy, Kyla, and even Joyce sought her sensible, levelheaded advice and strong shoulders to lean on in their intermittent times of need. Her world was falling down around her like the walls of Jericho, with thousands of defiant soldiers marching around on her nerves trying to topple everything in their sight, and she couldn't think of one person she trusted to help her through it. It would have been unacceptable to turn to the women who looked to her for support, much like a preacher asking the congregation to counsel him on his sinful ways. It just wasn't done.

Years of suppressing her feelings had finally come back to haunt her. Janeen didn't have the foggiest idea of what to do next as she stood facing the wall mirror in her bathroom, surveying her half-naked body. Before she slid her long arms through the straps of her bra, she ran her fingertips along the rim of matching emerald green panties that clung to her smooth caramel-colored skin, then she moved them up slowly until they met her supple breasts. *They still look good,* she thought. *All y'all need is a little attention. Ain't that right, girls?* She playfully pinched her pointed nipples with her thumb and forefingers.

"So, that's what you've been doing up here all weekend?" Raymond asked from the bathroom doorway. At the sound of his voice, Janeen found herself recoiling toward the shower. The abruptness of it startled her. She instinctively threw her hands over her breasts to cover them from his sight, as if he were a stranger.

Ray was a good-looking man with a deep earth-toned complexion and solid build. He was dressed in a cocoa brown designer business suit with his briefcase in one hand and car keys dangling from the other. He enjoyed having fine things and fine women around him. His office was regularly staffed by ex–beauty pageant hopefuls and attractive female entertainer types.

"How long have you been standing there?" she answered, with a question of her own. Her snotty tone held an equal amount of rudeness.

"Long enough, just like you've been up here long enough. What's the deal anyways? Did I say or do something wrong? It ain't like you to retreat and hide yourself like this."

Without looking in his direction, Janeen reached for her housecoat hanging off the back of the vanity chair. She turned her back to him while wrapping herself in it and securing the belt around her waist. After pulling it tightly she responded calmly, "Oh no? Then who *is* it like . . . to retreat and hide herself . . . like this, Raymond?"

He tossed her a devilishly sly smirk and lowered his head. "What do you mean, who? Are you tripping because I came home a little late and a little intoxicated the other night?" He paused briefly, then glanced down to admire his pecan-colored hand-woven Italian loafers. "Besides, I've come home a lot later than that before and didn't get the cold treatment."

Janeen sat down on the vanity chair and gathered one thigh-high stocking between her fingers while positioning it to slip her leg into it. "Ray, look, for almost two days, you knew I was bothered by something enough to give up my own bed for the guest room, and you didn't think enough of me to come up and ask what was wrong." Her sentiment was accentuated by a loud snap when the elastic trim smacked against her midthigh.

His mouth watered when he caught himself eyeing the area of her upper thigh that the hose didn't cover. "Well, you know . . . I've been really busy lately and if I've been unavailable then I, uh, apologize."

"Unavailable? Ray, I haven't had a decent conversation with you in weeks. You're home late, gone early, and when you are here, it's 'Can you get me this,' or 'Baby, I need that.' I could have had another head growing out of my shoulders and you wouldn't have noticed. I need a lot more than you've been giving lately. A lot more."

She slid her other leg into the second stocking, then stood to see if they rested evenly on her thighs. Raymond was looking too but for another reason. *Damn, he looks good in that suit,* entered her mind before she could chase that double-crossing thought away.

"Oh, I see. It's an attention thang," he reasoned aloud, while noting the time on his diamond-studded Rolex with disdain. "We got to talk about this now? I am on my way out the door."

Janeen finally turned to face him. "Uh-uh, Raymond, don't . . . There will be no further discussion about this and you're terribly incorrect about the 'attention thang' as you so ineptly put it. It's a 'love thang.' And don't play me crazy. I know about your little 'something else' and I'll be living in the guest room until I decide how to deal with how I'm feeling about it."

Of course she didn't have the goods on him but her sixth sense had kicked in to overdrive. A woman's intuition should be her best friend when she's got man troubles. It'll never leave her when she needs an amen in her corner. And Janeen's intuition was standing firmly between her and her man.

The sober smile that had rested on Janeen's face forced Ray to pause but before he could get a word in edgewise, she stopped him cold with a resistant extended flat palm. "Uh-uh . . . don't . . . don't lie, it's very unbecoming and it's bad enough that I've allowed your so-called indiscretions to go on behind my back but *I will not have you lying to my face.*"

She'd spat out her objections venomously before composing herself. "Don't worry, though. Further on up the road, all of your transgressions will come to the light and karma will set things straight."

His lips twisted then. "Are you threatening me? I mean, what's this karma shit?"

"Oh no. I can't do anything to you that you haven't already brought on yourself. You'll see." Another thought came over her. "Muh'dear always said you were the kind of man who'd never cherish the kind of woman I am. You'd always be reaching out for someone or something else. Psssh, was she ever wrong about you," she added, sarcastically.

Ray attempted to soften the argument. He took a step forward. "Janeen, let's go away for a couple of days and talk about what you *think is going on behind your back.*"

Before he could cross the threshold, Janeen stuck her leg out to close the door in his face. "I don't think so, Ray," she said plainly from the other side of the door. "I'll be tied up for the next month. Got thangs on the job to look after," she teased, using the somewhat watered down King's English that Ray couldn't shake no matter how profitable his construction company and other shady enterprises were.

Ray shook his head and walked away mumbling, "She trippin'. Ain't no woman ever left me and she won't be the first." He figured she'd get over what ever she was pissed off about because it had been inconceivable for her to hold a grudge.

While driving in to the office, Janeen thought of all the things she should have asked Ray before slamming the door on him. She wanted to know why he had stopped kissing her deeply just because she was there, and what happened to the lovemaking interludes so passionate they'd do it until somebody passed out, gave in, gave up, or just plain quit from exhaustion? When was the last time he noticed a new pair of shoes she'd bought or commented when she changed her hairstyle? Why did he ever stop telling her how beautiful she was, how pretty she smelled, and how privileged he was to share the same bed with her?

She missed who they used to be, but none of that was of any consequence now. That had all but escaped her memory by the time she reached her building's parking garage. Her yesterdays had passed her by and they seemed so very far away.

# Chapter 5

# *Don't Say
What You Won't Do*

At just about 7:55 a.m., laughter poured out of the president's office at Rayjan Construction's main building. The office staff didn't usually begin to file in until almost 8:30, opening time for Ray's most profitable endeavor. The headquarters was decorated with fine woods and genuine crystal knick-knacks, flashy thingamajigs, and impressive plaques hanging on the walls to help legitimize it to customers and potential business partners. Ray had been an entrepreneur of some sort since he was a nineteen-year-old pimp, so he understood operating a black-owned business from the street to the balance sheet.

He'd witnessed on several occasions people being extremely suspicious of black businesses. Once, he'd heard that a very wealthy man changed his mind about starting the first black airline. The man said he couldn't get the idea "off the ground" because too many people had wanted to see the plane first. They'd said it had better look like it could "fly" before they'd buy tickets. Ray made sure his business looked as if it could soar with the eagles.

Sissy pulled her car around in front of the beige brick office building. She noticed two cars parked in the employee section. One she recognized immediately. It was Ray's Rolls, but the other one she hadn't seen before. The dirty Plymouth Duster had more than twenty years on it and looked as though it had never been washed. You'd have to guess the original color was burnt orange, but now it was just plain rusty. Typically, Ray's construction workers drove crappy cars like that, so Sissy didn't think twice about it. She was just delighted to have hers back from Kelvin's shop.

Humming a carefree hip-hop tune that had just played on her car stereo, Sissy bobbed her head to the beat going on inside it. Passing by the rusty car, she was vehemently repulsed when she noticed several greasy McDonald's and Burger King bags huddling up on the floor and backseat. *That is* so *nasty,* she thought as she made her way to the front door. While twisting the doorknob, she cringed again at the thought of someone's house being as filthy as the car parked in the lot.

Just as Sissy pushed the door open, the sound of cooing and laughter drew her attention to the president's office. Since she had complete freedom around her brother-in-law's company, she never considered knocking before barging in through the half-closed office door.

"Good morn—," she managed to get out before her eyes told her mouth to hurry up and close. All she could do was cross her arms and stare them down. Ray almost dropped the newborn baby he'd cradled in his arms when he turned and realized Sissy stood a few feet behind him. A pretty young girl hardly old enough to be considered a woman, except for that bundle of joy she'd recently pushed out of her womb, stood close enough to demand that he give back the lipstick that she'd laid on him earlier.

Despite having been busted, Ray still attempted to make the incident seem totally on the level. "Oh! Uh-uh . . . This is, uh . . . Sissy, uh, I mean Janeese, my sistah'n-law I told you people say you favor."

Ray watched Sissy squint in the girl's direction with contempt. She was thinking how young Ray's visitor appeared. She couldn't have been more than eighteen.

"Heyyy, Sissy," Ray said, in a backpedaling tone, followed by an over-eager although uncomfortable cheese-eating grin.

Sissy and the young girl locked eyes and continued looking each other over while Ray tried feverishly to place the infant back in her child-carrying seat. The young girl had a smile bright enough to cast a rainbow in the middle of a darkened sky and did resemble Sissy in many ways. They shared the same body type, approximate height, and complexion. At a glance, they could have passed for sisters. At a distance, they could have easily been mistaken for each other.

"Hey, yourself, Ray," Sissy spat with a quick glint of suspicion. "I see you have company this morning." She didn't excuse herself or apologize for interrupting in the least. Her eyes narrowed more like a woman catching her own man with his hand in someone else's cookie jar.

"Heyyy, Janeese," the girl offered naively, while sauntering up to Sissy to get a closer look. "Uhhh-huh. You was right, Rayyymond. She do' look like me. We could be suuuztahs. She's almost as light-skinned'd as I am. You mixed too, girlll?"

Sissy reserved her words despite the girl's ghetto approach at making her acquaintance. Instead, she watched Ray hover over the carrying seat as he buckled the child in as though he'd done it before, several times, and recently. All the feelings flashing through her were as confusing as the girl's grammar, but there were questions that had to be answered.

"All right, now, Tina," Ray sputtered, before backpedaling to the other side of the office. "You and this precious little baby girl will just have to run along so I can open the office."

As soon as the girl began packing up her things to exit, Sissy headed her off by blocking the doorway. "Uhh-uhhhh," she said, with a great deal of animosity. "Heyyyll, naw! You think you're just going to leave here without somebody explaining to me what this early-morning rendezvous is about?"

Before the girl could work her neck and get a thing or two off her chest still filled with nature's milk, Ray shot an eye dart Sissy's way that shouted loud and clear, "Let it go, please!"

Sissy declined to let him off the hook so easily. " 'Cause I don't like the looks of this at all," she added, with the demeanor of a prosecuting attorney. "Somebody'd better tell me something or I'm just going to have to draw my own conclusions, and neither one of y'all are gonna like it if I do."

Ray rolled his lips tightly between his teeth in an act to hold his temper in. The phone rang but no one moved. Sissy still blocked the doorway and any possible exit that Tina had from the office. The girl looked at Ray, who was watching the two of them, then she sat the baby seat down on the floor and slowly pulled off her earrings. "Look, Janeese," Tina announced rudely, with her jaws tight and shoulders pulled back, "I ain't got no problem wit' you but I'm going out that door with my child, and if I have to hurt you to do it I will."

Sissy noticed Tina reaching into her purse. She shuddered when she imagined what the young girl might come out of it with. The thought of going toe to toe with a person who had nothing to lose won out over her foolish pride. Tina voiced Sissy's thoughts as she tossed her earrings into her purse and hoisted the bundle of joy, wrapped in a pink swaddling smock. "Your fight ain't wit' me, no way," was all she said as she sidestepped Sissy to get through the door. The girl's illuminating smile was gone and in another blink of an eye so was the girl.

Ray dropped into the black leather chair stationed behind his desk. His head fell in his hands, then he began contemplating how to deal with the embarrassment he immediately attempted to lie about.

Turning back toward Ray after she'd watched the girl lug her new baby out of the building, Sissy had to laugh off her frustration. "Psssh. So, when were you going to tell Janeen about this Brenda-had-a-baby thing?"

"Her name is Tina," Ray stated matter-of-factly, without looking up.

"Brenda-Tina-Medina-whutehvah. When were you going to tell my sistah that you're out here running around making babies on the side?"

The outer door slammed shut. Sissy assumed that employees began to come in so she walked over to close the door to his office. When she approached the door, it suddenly flew open against her. "Hey!" she yelled. "What the —"

Tina stood there fuming with arms folded and her lips still pursed like a pouting kindergartener. "Oh yeah, Raymond, I need to know when you're going to help with that transportation thang we talked about Saturday night."

Ray's eyes revealed his utter disbelief. He jumped up off his perch and tore into the situation with pointed teeth. "Enuff!" he shouted. "I have had enough of this bullshit and I ain't having no more of it in my office." He took steps around his desk to get closer to the girl. His eyes were glazed over. "Tina, you know I don't handle my business like this," he huffed. "Now, I told you that I was going to take care of it, so get your *ass* out of my office!"

Tina's eyes fell toward the ground. She exhaled bitterly, shot a cold stare up at Sissy, then quickly trounced off in a tantrum. Sissy had never seen Ray act as if he could hurt a woman. She was now worried about Janeen's well-being more than the pain she'd feel once she found out about his baby-mama-drama.

Shaking her head slowly, Sissy could hardly speak. "Raaay . . . what are you going to do about this? I'm not sure if Janeen can take this right now. She's concerned about her career and just the other night she accused *me* of having a thing with you. Now this — I don't think she can bear it."

His eyes were burning red now and his breathing was deeply exaggerated. "So, what did you tell her *about you and me?*"

She raised her brow at the question. "What do you mean, what did I tell her? I told her that she must be out of her mind to think that. What was I supposed to have told her? Huh? Ray, I told her the truth."

A sinister grin slowly appeared on his face. "Yep . . . I bet you didn't tell her the whole truth, did you? I bet she doesn't know about your private little madame business, huh? Yeah, you keep that in mind before you go off thinking about telling mine. Looks like this'll be our little secret. Uh-huh, I like the sound of that. And by the time she does find out, I'll be a very rich man and won't none of this matter then anyhow."

Of course Sissy knew exactly what he was alluding to. There was this other thing they had between them and it would have been just as detrimental for him as for Sissy if the whole truth ever made its way back to Janeen. Defeated, Sissy collected a client's file off the top of Ray's desk and turned toward the door to leave.

"Hey," he called out, to get her attention, "if you don't scream, I won't holluh."

Her hand trembled as she fumbled with the car keys to get the door opened. White smoke from the spinning tires followed her out of the parking lot's exit. Thick black tire marks documented her hurried departure but the car she sped away in wasn't nearly fast enough to outrun the trouble she'd spawned for herself, or the demonic lies she lived with.

# Chapter 6

# *Be Careful What You Pray For*

The fact that someone had parked a company car in Janeen's reserved space didn't get her workday off to a roaring start. A brand new Champagne-toned Cadillac DeVille rested where she had parked her Cadillac of the same color for over three years. All of the executives who worked at First World Mortgage drove the same make of car. It was a much-appreciated perk to be awarded a luxury company car in any color, shade, or style that the automobile company offered. Janeen figured the car in her space belonged to the new senior-level executive who'd robbed her of the position she'd worked so hard for. It had to be his. *At least he shares my taste . . . Champagne,* she thought. But that didn't come close to being enough to deter her bitterness toward a man she'd never met. All she could think about was Mr. Bragg's voice message stating that the new senior VP would officially begin work that Monday.

Throughout the morning, Janeen stared out of the office window thinking. Memories of her very first position there, in the marketing department, skated through her mind. After she'd run her own small mortgage company for four years, Mr. Bragg courted her for months to come and join his team. It wasn't that she took enough of a market share to stall his success but she had earned the respect of Dallas Real Estate Group, which was the governing body of Dallas area realty and mortgage companies.

The company she previously owned was small but very successful and her father's dream for her had come true. He'd hoped that each of his girls would graduate from college and someday start their own business. Janeen realized quickly that her presence wasn't readily accepted in large white communities but as long as she stayed near her own people, the real-estate group gave her all the praise and support she could stand. Helping the underprivileged and disenfranchised, single parents, and low-income families to buy homes made her feel as though she was really giving something back to the neighborhood she had grown up in. Seeing small children playing in their own yards and jumping rope on the sidewalks in front of houses they could call theirs was well worth the hurdles of many a minority borrower's bad credit ratings and suspect employment records. But somehow, she managed to get over four hundred families out of overpriced rental slums. A Citation of Community Excellence from the mayor was the highlight of her short stint as an entrepreneur.

Letting go of a sure thing did have its advantages. Mr. Bragg offered her a salary three times what she cleared on her own, and promised to roll her "fair lending" program into his business matrix. She marketed it to all of her customers' co-workers and family members. Within the next year, First World became the largest lender to minorities in the state, making Mr. Bragg a much wealthier man. It also allowed Janeen to help more families than she could have ever dreamed possible to get a piece of the American dream.

All those fond memories forced her to

come full circle. A swift kick in the pants was waiting for her when she came back to reality, as well as a big fat thanks for nothing. All that hard work was wasted, she feared, putting up with backhanded compliments from people who had more clout than she did. She'd seen more than her share of improprieties at First World too, embezzlement, highly questionable management decisions, wife swapping, drug abuse, alcoholism, and everyday run-of-the-mill lazy executives making a king's ransom in exchange for little or no actual work to speak of. What she didn't know then was that Mr. Bragg felt responsible for his high-level associates when they overindulged themselves in costly exploits. Likewise, he had been good to her, too. He had never made decisions before that seemed remotely dubious, but his latest maneuver was killing her. Why had he changed horses in midstream?

Val saw Janeen when she arrived earlier in the day ranting about someone parking in her space, so she knew to steer clear of a woman trying to keep her head up, especially the kind of woman who didn't normally allow adversity of any kind to get in her way. Something had to give, and soon.

Janeen copied important document files from her office computer to a disk she'd stored in the locked top drawer of her desk. She downloaded corporate memos, minutes from important executive meetings and management production reports that she had access to from the database. After adding eleven more files to the twelve she already had, she popped the disk out and scribbled the word "Insurance" on it, then immediately slid it into the compact compartment of her Coach bag. Insurance was just what she needed after getting an inadequate explanation from Mr. Bragg as to why her life was being sucked into the Twilight Zone. She didn't know how the next four weeks would pan out. Too much was at stake to go down without some kind of a fight, but what if this situation rapidly deteriorated into quicksand? What if the harder she fought it the faster she sank? The mood was so unsettling. Company associates, who used to speak to her with the respect due a high-ranking military officer, had already begun looking away when she passed their workstations. *What was really going on?*

Where was the tall fine conventioneer Janeen had been so enamored with in New York when she needed him? Although they never actually met, she felt down to her toes that he could do something about the black hole swallowing her up. He had to be the kind of man, if there ever was one, who could wrap his strong arms around her and make it all better somehow. She smiled at the thought of him putting his foot in Ray's behind, on general principle, for being less than the man he was supposed to be. Lord knows somebody needed to. "I must be dreaming," she heard herself saying aloud, "to think I'll ever lay eyes on that man again."

Val had just returned from a smoking break in the underground parking garage, and Janeen summoned her in to discuss her marching orders for when the new senior VP came calling for an introduction.

"Yeah, Val, I just hung up with Mr. Bragg. He told me the new executive would be coming by to meet me around noon, and get this." She smirked devilishly. "The old man actually asked me to be on my best behavior because *he knows how I can get sometimes.*"

"I bet you're gonna show out, aren't you?" Val questioned, hoping she would do just that. "I know I would if I had the chance. Humph, I'd make sure he knew not to expect any cooperation out of me.

You know, they're probably going to want you to train him too, girl."

Janeen folded her arms as a sign of rebellion. "I hope they don't think I'm that stupid. I promised I would stick around for a month, and I will help out like I promised, but I will not, and I repeat, I will *not* take any more than the necessary steps to help him get acclimated in the company. I don't care if I ever see him but once and *that* might be one time too many. As a matter of fact, I've just decided to take the low road on this one. He'd better hope I don't slam the door in his face before giving him a piece of my mind. He could probably use it. I bet he's some twenty-five-year-old pimply-faced mama's boy not even worth my time or worse; some washed-up over-the-hill degenerate with a lot of years at the top and no other place to go."

"Go on, sistah!" Val co-signed. "Superwoman!"

"Suuuperrrwoman!" Janeen repeated, with exuberance. "You bet I'm a superwoman. Thanks, Val. I needed this little pep talk to get the fires burning again. I'm a take-the-bull-by-the-horns kind of woman, aren't I?"

"Yeah, girl, and I've even seen you kick

the bull in the nuts a time or two for good measure."

"You're damned straight I have. Just wait until he gets here. He'll be sorry he ever came around and took something that didn't belong to him. When he arrives, you let me know right away. Then you make his ass wait for fifteen minutes." Janeen was drunk with power. "Yeah, that ought to show him."

Upon returning to her desk, Val had a sense that something strange was happening on the customer service floor she worked near. Ordinarily background chatter filled the air from rows of mostly female customer service reps dealing with disgruntled callers wanting to know why their mortgage payment was going up again. And when it all halted suddenly, she gave up rummaging for a lipstick in the depths of her large purse. The silence was deadening like a horror movie when the killer is on the other side of the door, just before the movie audience begins yelling at the screen for the woman to run the other way.

Feeling the hairs rise up on the back of her neck, Val's instincts screamed for her to look up. When she lifted her head, something unusual caught her attention. In the distance, casually strolling directly toward her from the elevator, was a fascinating figure of a man in an exquisitely tailored three-button dark gray business suit. Her eyes were so affixed to the tall man's sturdy frame and confident swagger that she failed to notice more than eighty women peeking over their cubicles to steal a glance at him.

Her mouth dried up like Egyptian cotton while at the same time her palms moistened with perspiration. With each step that the stranger took, drawing nearer to her desk, she grew more anxious. The mere sight of him caused a tingle deep within her. This obviously refined gentleman was black, as black as the winter nights are long. And everything on him was well defined, from the tapered, coal black, wavy hair crowning his head down to the stylish Gucci lace-up dress shoes.

A sexy cleft in his pointed chin and the silkiest eyebrows ever put atop a man's eyes accompanied a thick mustache, all complemented his almond-shaped eyes. He more than fit the bill of a leading man from a best-selling lustful romance novel. And from the way many of the women fanned themselves while getting an eyeful, he appeared to be the kind of man who handled himself well in the bedroom, shower, bathtub, kitchen countertop, backseat or wherever else he chose to please his woman. He was most certainly a vision from someone's intimate dream.

Thinking that the exceptionally well-put-together brother must be lost, Val prepared herself to meet this fine gentleman and be gracious enough to personally escort him to wherever he needed to go. "Ooooh," she moaned quietly, "he's bowlegged, too. Meet me somewhere after dark," she mouthed wishfully, just under her breath.

After reaching her desk, the distinguished stranger paused, then smiled cordially. "Hello, I'm Rollin Hanes." Val watched his mouth as his name rolled off the tip of his tongue. "Is this the correct place to meet with Mrs. Janeen Hampton-Gilliam?"

The man stood there waiting for a response to his question. He was extremely handsome and seemed quite used to women ogling him, but Val didn't mind having her name added to that long list. She had a strong feeling that she'd seen this man somewhere before, maybe on television or perhaps in a fashion magazine. She was sure of it, and a woman doesn't forget men like him.

"Excuse me, miss," he whispered, sneaking a peak at the nameplate resting on the right forward corner of her desk. "Am I . . . Ms. Valorie Winston . . . in the right place to meet with Mrs. Gilliam?"

Val looked him up and down all over again without realizing she was undressing him with her eyes, not really hearing or comprehending what he'd said. "Who?" was all she could muster in the way of a response.

He was exceptionally easy on the eyes and his naturally charming persona was what most women would love to wake up lying next to every morning. And, as an unsuspecting fish is lured by the glow of a fisherman's tackle, Val was swimming downstream fast, with her mouth wide open. Never underestimate easygoing charm.

Rollin was embarrassed for her. He slid his large hands into the pockets of his trousers and jiggled car keys with one hand and loose change with the other one before removing one of them to point toward Janeen's office door. "Mrs. Gilliam," he repeated. "I do believe that's her office . . . right behind you."

Blinking her eyes rapidly to regain the composure that had somehow slipped and fallen between her legs, Val cleared her throat while avoiding eye contact with him. "Uh-hmm. I'm sorry, uh . . . Mr. Hanes. I'll let her know you're here."

In an instant, she popped up from her chair and turned to approach her manager with worrisome news. Before she turned the knob to enter the closed door, she exhaled deeply. *Whewww . . . I need a cigarette,* she heard herself say.

The door opened slowly. Val peeked her head in through the crack. Janeen sat behind her desk with her legs casually crossed. She listened to a jazzy CD while running an emery board across her fingernails.

"Yes?" she said casually with an air of aristocracy.

Val tried diligently to calm herself down. "Janeen, I mean, Mrs. Gilliam. He's here."

Janeen continued filing away as if she hadn't carefully planned for this confrontation. "He who? The man I'm about to reduce to nothing? Is that who you're referring to?"

"Uhhh . . ." Val's eyes danced from side to side. There was so much she wanted to convey, but the man *was* waiting, after all.

"Well, you tell him to sit down, turn flips, or roll over until I'm ready to deal

with him," Janeen quipped. "I'm indis-
posed at the moment."

Val's forehead wrinkled as she frowned
her way through a precarious good news/
bad news dilemma. She ducked her head
out of the doorway momentarily to get a
sense of Rollin's patience, hoping she'd
figure out what steps to take in order to
bring this potentially dicey situation under
control.

Rollin rocked on the soles of his shoes
patiently while Val's rear end wiggled at
him from the doorway. He had reservations about this supposed meeting but decided not to attempt to figure out why the
assistant didn't simply buzz her manager
to inform her that he had arrived. He was,
in fact, in Mr. Bragg's office when the old
man had instructed Janeen how he wanted
things to fly regarding her introduction to
the company's newest member.

Suddenly, Val turned toward him and
brandished an awkward smile. "Excuse
me. I'll . . . be right back," she stated
hastily, then disappeared behind the closed
door.

Janeen's fingers were now interlocked
and idle on her lap. She hummed along
with a tune coming from her portable CD
player. Val nodded her head to the tune

briefly, then dove right into the good news/ bad news.

"Heyyy, Janeen," she offered, excitedly. "I told the man to wait for a moment but I don't think he's accustomed to waiting on anything."

Janeen twisted her lips. "So? What are you saying? Is he too good to wait? I hope he does think that much of himself. It'll be much more exciting if he thinks he's a match for Superwoman."

"No . . . what I'm trying to say is . . . Well, he's not what I expected and damned sho' wasn't what you expected." Just as Val opened her mouth to expound on it, a faint tap on the door stifled her thoughts. Val hunched her shoulders as the door opened slowly from the other side. "Superwoman," she announced through slightly clenched teeth, "get ready to meet Mr. Kryptonite."

Janeen was still puzzled. "What are you talking about?"

Rollin leaned in just as Val had moments before. "Excuse me, but is everything okay in here, ladies?" he asked. "If now isn't the best time, I could come back later."

Val bit her lip when Janeen's pupils dilated to the size of quarters. "I guess an introduction is in order, huh?" she suggested as she pulled the door completely open so that Rollin would feel comfortable enough to come all the way in. "Janeen Hampton-Gilliam, meet Rollin Hanes."

Rollin smiled and offered Janeen a cordial handshake. "Hello, Mrs. Hampton-Gilliam. It's a real pleasure to meet you after hearing so much about you. Mr. Bragg has raved about your work since I met him. First World is very fortunate to have you."

Standing between the two of them, Val carefully watched them while they watched each other. Janeen seemed amazed, shocked. She studied his face and noted his smooth and even dark complexion. Not one mark nor blemish. Not one hair was out of place. She wondered how a man could be so elegant and yet as masculine as a street brawler, all at once. Being face-to-face with him after so many nights of having him share her dreams took all the restraint she could muster to contain her unsettled emotions.

Behind several moments of silence, Janeen sighed humbly. She almost laughed at the thoughts of how rudely she'd planned to act danced shameful circles around her, mocking all the salty comments she expected to nail him with. Then in walked the one person she needed in her life. *And I'll be,* she thought, *he has the nerve to have the cutest dimples, too.*

"Mr. Hanes, I am also pleased to meet you," Janeen replied finally, accepting his hand. When their hands touched, she felt her heart skip a beat. "Uhh . . . Mr. Bragg instructed me to be on my best behavior, but I'll just have to see about that," she added in a coy tone.

With Val still in the middle of things, Rollin conveyed his thanks to her, expecting Janeen to send her assistant away, but instead she asked him if he wouldn't mind stepping outside for a minute.

"Certainly. I'll be . . . right out there," he replied, quite perplexed.

After he graciously bowed out, both women stole a glimpse of him from the back. Val took one extra peek before closing the door.

"Janeen, where did that man come from? I mean, who makes a man like that, 'cause I want a whole six-pack of 'em for myself."

Janeen was holding herself still. She seemed to have seen a ghost. Both women were right about one thing. The brother was fine, plain and simple. And not the kind of fine normally manufactured by long hours spent in a gym but the kind of fine his mother and father would be proud of. No mistake about it, Mr. Rollin Hanes had been sho' nuff fine for a long time.

Val's emotion spilled out disbelief. "There is no way you're gonna be rude or mean to *that* man. No way. Janeen, he has to be just as dreamy as the man you've been thinking about and losing sleep over since you've been back home from New York."

Inhaling deeply into her open hands cupped over her mouth and nose, Janeen breathed in the scent of the cologne subtly transferred from his hands to hers. "No, he's not 'just as dreamy' as the man I've been losing sleep over since I've been home. He *is* the man I've been losing sleep over, and oddly enough missing, since I've been back."

"You're kidding? That's him? That's the tall, dark, and handsome mystery man that had you all twisted like a virgin who couldn't *wait* to give it up?"

Janeen nodded, confirming the astonishing truth. "Yes, Rollin Hanes is *that* man."

"Well, what are you going to do about it? I mean . . . I know you're married and all, but, uh . . ."

"Let's just see where this train goes. Although it will be a real trip to see how a dream plays out."

Suddenly Janeen took a step back, then peered down at the floor where she previously stood. Val thought it strange but couldn't help following her boss's eyes, too.

"Uh, what are you looking for?" Val inquired with concern.

"Oh, just making sure he didn't see my panties hit the floor before he left."

"Oooh, you're crazy, girl! But that exquisite specimen of a black man will have you packing an extra pair of 'drawz' in your briefcase."

Janeen giggled like a young girl talking about boys for the first time as she held up two fingers. "Two pair," she argued suggestively.

Rollin overheard the laughter coming from the other side of the door. He slid both hands back into his trouser pockets again and realized that whatever they found so amusing had something to do with him. He didn't seem to mind being laughed at or pushed out and made to wait. Hearing black women enjoying themselves for any reason was worth it. Actually, his concerned expression dissolved into a light chuckle all by itself.

And just like that, Janeen was back to her typically wonderful high-spirited, hot-natured, adorable self. The man she longed to know better was right outside her office. Now she'd have to decide what she was going to do about it.

"Open that door, Val, and ask the man in, please," Janeen ordered with a straight face. "We've got some serious things to discuss."

# Chapter 7

# *In the Meantime*

Rolling down Metropolitan Avenue in the middle of the day with the hot sun beaming down on her car, Sissy felt chills run through her. The depressed south Dallas neighborhood that stared back at her with a squinted eye was a far cry from the prosperous back streets she grew up learning to roller skate and play hopscotch in. Both drug abuse and apathy had removed all traces of better times only twenty-five years earlier. Despair and desperation successfully replaced the desires and dreams that once dwelled there.

Most of the local businesses had packed up and gone, but some diehard faithfuls refused to let go, where the land value was resurging like a phoenix above a battlefield of broken crack pipes and paper-bagged forty-ounce bottles. As a result, hoards of developers had recently descended on the wounded neighborhood to pick away at its fleshy carcass. Two years ago, the city began granting tax breaks to any company willing to relocate their operations or build there. That's when the land grab began.

Rows of abandoned old wood-framed houses were typically being utilized for drug deals or other unlawful undertakings. The decrepit homes were pushed over by the city's bulldozers and swept away. Many community leaders celebrated each one's fall and blessed the city council's efforts to rid them of the eyesores. But common sense should have alarmed them to beware of bureaucrats jam-packed inside that Trojan horse; especially after begging for that very action to take place themselves for more than seven years running. Just like taking candy from a baby, developers bought entire blocks at a time and began throwing drugstores, yogurt shops, gated high-priced luxury apartment buildings and parking lots at those same community leaders, who gave up the booty on the first date, before they knew what hit them.

Subsequently, those very same community leaders began waging one protest after another down at city hall, crying about the rise in taxes squeezing them out of their own homes in the southern Dallas sector.

Sissy knew very well what was going on and how she played a major role in getting unsuspecting black folks to take an additional $50,000 above current market value to sell their property. Her brother-in-law Ray had established a limited partnership with high-profile downtown businessmen through his construction company. The plan had been laid and Sissy was paid exceptionally well to bait the traps. Unbelievably, in less than a year, she managed to convince residents from two neighboring blocks to sell out on their homes.

Feelings of deep-seated guilt arose whenever she made an appointment to visit with another unsuspecting victim of their scheme. Posing as a representative from an honest real-estate developer, she perfected a sales pitch that all but promised a "first dibs" opportunity to repurchase a newly built brick house on the same lot when columns of them were expected to spring up out of the ground the following year. Unfortunately, the fine print didn't substantiate any of her claims. Sissy rationalized the unscrupulous deed by telling herself that the sellers were getting more than any other developer was willing to pay and a minimum of $80,000 would ultimately buy a much nicer home in a community they *could* afford taxes in. Doing the right thing with the money would be their responsibility. Unfortunately, most of the sellers were flat broke again within months of selling out.

As pleasantly as she could, Sissy knocked three times on the wooden plank holding the address nailed vertically against the front of the small shotgun house. That type of long narrow house was called shotgun because a blast through the front door would surely hit the back one.

The house had once been painted white, although just how long ago was a mystery. It was leaning to the side like an old pimp. It seemed that it would only take one good huff-and-I'll-puff before the withered frame gave way to the pissed-off wolf.

Just as she contemplated knocking again against the paint-chipped plank resembling a rather large band-aid for the ailing house, Sissy heard someone's voice from inside.

"Ye-es," the faint voice called out with an accentuated southern drawl. "I'm comin'. I'm comin'," the voice added, as if answering the door was too much to ask.

When Sissy felt slight rumblings of footsteps getting nearer to where she stood, it was clear that the porch she stood on was merely an extension of the same flooring the person inside the house walked along. "Why would anyone want to live like this?" she thought aloud.

"I'm comin'," someone called out again, while jiggling on the doorknob to work the door open.

Sissy stepped inside the screen door, which held no screen, and worked the doorknob from the outside. With a final and almost comical duet of pushes and pulls, the front door suddenly popped open. Sissy's hands flew back as if she had walked up on a rattlesnake. Someone stepped into the shadows of the partially opened door, where they felt safe and obstructed from total view.

When Sissy could not make out the small-framed person standing only three feet away from her, she asked apprehensively, "Is this Mrs. Mary Lee Jackson's residence?"

Upon hearing the cordial tone in the visitor's words, the door was pulled all the way open from the inside. Standing inside was an old woman in a thick, faded pink terry-cloth bathrobe and matted matching house shoes. She was hardly five feet tall. Her hair was silver and plaited with long extensions dangling like thick ropes. Looking at her hands, Sissy figured the woman to be at least eighty years old but she couldn't be sure.

Looking at the old woman gazing up at her with clenched fists parked on her narrow hips, Sissy hesitated before speaking. "Uh . . . hi," she offered, with an outstretched hand. "I'm Janeese Hampton from the Rayjan Real Estate office."

The woman didn't accept her hand. Instead she smacked her lips in opposition to the offer. "Humph, you tricked me good. Had I known they'd be sending a pretty girl down here, you'd still be standing on the other side of a closed do'."

As she moved back to slam the door, Sissy begged her for a few moments of her time. "Ma'am, I know you don't want to see me or anybody else offering to buy your house, but please give me a few minutes and I promise I'll never come back unless you ask me to. Five minutes, no more. Promise."

She looked Sissy over thoroughly for the first time. "You seem like a nice enough girl and I'll bet someone else would just come behind you to bother me all over again. So you may as well come on in," she said. The offer was halfhearted. "Not too many people make it by here like they used to. Most everybody's packed up and moved away," the old woman added, while nodding her head as she stepped aside to let Sissy pass.

The unnerving creaking of the old rusted door hinges took Sissy back to her childhood. Their house wasn't all that different from this one. Whoever had put up all those low-quality tract houses had only one thing in mind, take the money and run.

Inside, the rickety old house held little lighting at all. The windows were covered by thick gray drapes stained with age, which probably used to be ivory in color but now showed only the faded tones of dust and time. The thin plywood walls, painted a tangerine shade, enveloped something freshly baked from the kitchen. Surprisingly, everything else in the house was neat, considering the looks of it from the outside, and well arranged as if it had been that way for decades. Strong wooden furniture held its place. Antiques of all kinds, including a Victrola phonograph and a rather extensive collection of crystal trinkets, poised themselves to be admired.

Upon further surveying the front room, which was meant for family gatherings or company, Sissy felt a sense of calmness. The lady asked her to sit, so she chose the loveseat, hoping the woman would join her there. She'd learned that the closer a sales-person got in proximity to the prospective client, the better chance they'd have of closing the deal. When the lady collapsed on a hand-carved rocking chair across from her, Sissy realized this would not be a quick sale at all, just as it hadn't been for the other developers who came before her. Ironically, Sissy did let a relaxed giggle slip out when the old lady's feet flew up, un-characteristically for a woman her age, as soon as her bony behind hit the padded chair.

"Whew!" the woman sighed. "This old rocker here seems to get further and fur-ther away from me."

Without another moment wasted, Sissy got down to business. "Okay, Mrs. Jackson."

"May'Lee, call me May'Lee," she inter-rupted. "Everybody's called me that for years." The woman's southern drawl re-minded Sissy that many older south-erners dropped consonants from their names in speech. Besides, Mrs. Mary Lee sounded too proper among friends anyhow.

"All right Mrs. May . . . Lee," Sissy repeated agreeably.

"Naw, that's not what I said," she corrected further. "Not Mrs. May Lee. Just plain ol' May'Lee," the woman huffed without contempt. "The mister has been gone now for more than forty years and if you attach missus to my name, I'll just be reminded of him, and I could do just fine without that today."

"I'm sorry, ma'am, but that's just how I was raised, to respect my elders. Please forgive me." *Score one for Sissy.*

The woman nodded that she understood and Sissy quickly jumped back into her salesman role. "You know . . . Ms. May'Lee, all of the other people on the block have sold their property, for a lot more money than they could get on the seller's market. Some of them have already purchased nice brick homes in other communities and they couldn't be happier. Now, I know you've been made other offers but I really think you should consider selling and moving on. All of your neighbors are gone and —"

"Move on to where, young lady?" she snapped matter-of-factly. "This is the only home I can remember and this is the home I'm gon' meet my Maker in. Shoot, the good Reverend Jackson, God rest his soul, gave me this home as an anniversary present in nineteen hundred and forty-seven, and it was good enough for me then and still is."

Looking down at the papers Sissy had brought with her for signature, the woman smirked. "What exactly do those papers you got on your lap say anyhow?"

"Well, they say that you are prepared to sell this property to my company and in return we'll give you eighty thousand dollars," Sissy answered, letting the word "thousand" roll off her lips slowly to make it sound more enticing, but the lady wasn't moved by the offer.

"Ooo-wee, that sounds like a lotta money," she said, pretending to marvel at the amount. "What would I do with all that? We only paid twenty-nine hundred for it." She wrinkled her brow as if a revelation just came to her. "You know something. I smell a rat. Don't mean to offend you, now . . . What's your name again?"

"Janeese Hampton," Sissy replied, as if it were wasted breath.

"Yeah, like I was saying, Ms. Hampton, don't nobody overpay for nothing in this world if'n they don't have ta. So, why would y'all want to buy this old house, what don't mean nothing to nobody but me?"

She was right and Sissy knew that she knew it too. For a few brief moments, they sat in silence while the woman expected a response. Sissy tried to reason with her. "Well, actually, you're correct. The property is worth a lot more to us than it would be to the normal person. To be honest —"

"Don't you worry about being honest," Ms. Jackson quipped. "I'll settle for the truth. See, I've been around too long to go by someone else's idea of what honesty is because it tends to waver from person to person, but *the truth*, now, that's something all together different."

Faced with the one thing that continually plagued her when she visited the old neighborhood, Sissy felt compelled to render it. "The truth is, we'll make a lot more on your property when you're off of it," Sissy answered with a proud smile. "Ms. May'Lee, that's the truth."

For the first time, Ms. Jackson let out a triumphant laugh. "Now, didn't that feel good to you? And it didn't cost you nothing." Before Sissy could tell her just how right she was, the woman rose up out of the chair and headed toward another room off to the side. "You like peach cobbler or apple cobbler best?" resounded from the other side of the walled-off kitchen area.

"Excuse me . . . uh, peach, I like peach best," Sissy shouted back.

While Ms. Jackson tinkered around in the kitchen, Sissy sat uncomfortably until she took it upon herself to stand up and get a closer view of the items that any museum would have coveted dearly. Rows of photos encased in antique frames lined the dusty bookshelves and sat atop the upright piano against the far wall.

Ms. Jackson returned with two healthy scoops of peach cobbler on fine china plates with two silver-plated soup spoons tucked in her apron pocket, which she'd placed over her housecoat. She immediately set the plates on the coffee table and joined Sissy in viewing her shrine of friends and family.

"Ms. May'Lee, you have so many wonderful things here. It must have taken a lifetime to collect all of these beautiful pieces of crystal and all of these photos."

Ms. Jackson placed both of her fists on what could hardly be considered hips and leaned her head back in deep contemplation. "I do believe I got this one here at my wedding, then I just had to have more of them." She was referring to a charming little ballerina gracing the top of a fabulously crafted crystal music box. The surface, on which the ballerina stood, was made of mirrored glass, giving it the appearance of ice. The woman turned it over and twisted the key underneath. As soon as she set it back, the ballerina began to dance to a slow but happy tune that forced Sissy to smile and hum along with it.

"I have always liked that tune, too," Ms. Mary Lee commented. "It's a Chopin nocturne, I forget which, but it sho' is pretty."

"It is pretty," Sissy agreed. "When did you get it? In the forties?"

"Heh-hehhh!" she laughed. "Forties, no ma'am. I was wed in nineteen hundred and twenty-two. Long before you were even thought of."

"Wow! Nineteen twenty-two? You must have been a child bride."

"Nah, but I felt like one. I married the good reverend when I made twenty-one and graduated from Teachers College."

Sissy began doing the math in her head. "Let's see . . . so that would make you . . ."

"That'll make me one hundred years young next month, on the second," Ms. Jackson boasted, flashing a full mouth of her original teeth. "To be in the business of money, you sho' do figure slow."

Despite the harmless insult, Sissy felt privileged and honored to spend time with the woman who just a short time ago was nothing but a name on a deed of land to be acquired. Now she stood taller in her visitor's eyes than all the famous women she'd read about in schoolbooks while growing up. Sissy was in awe and wanted to know more about the things the woman had seen, experienced, and probably tried hard to forget, though this was still supposed to be a sales call.

Just before returning to the loveseat to bring up business again, one of the photos on the piano caught Sissy's attention. It was a slightly faded black-and-white picture but something about it was strikingly clear and familiar. "May I pick this one up, Mrs. Jackson . . . uh, Ms. May'Lee?"

"Sho', child, go on ahead."

She walked over to it slowly and studied every square inch of the nine-by-six photograph just to be sure. Her inclination proved correct. "Ma'am," she said nervously as she turned to face the old woman, "is this you in the picture with the taxi driver?"

"Well, let me see that." She stepped closer to the photo but not too close, due to her far-sightedness, and grinned. "Yes, it is. I had this picture made years ago. This here is the fellow what came to mind when you called out your last name. Hampton was his family name, too. He was my cab driver for years until he passed. Very nice fella." She flashed another smile at Sissy. "I thought maybe y'all might be kin but you don't seem to favor him none."

Sissy's heart fluttered. "Yes, ma'am, you're right. I've been told all of my life that I . . . favor my mama's side of the family. I never did think about it before but I didn't get any of my facial features from my father at all."

Ms. Jackson looked up at Sissy, who appeared as if she were about to faint. The old woman caught on to what her much younger guest was getting at. "Well, I'll be. You say Julian Hampton was your daddy? Then I know you're good people. Your daddy was a kind and loving man. He talked about his girls every time he carried me someplace in that old cab of his."

Sissy's emotions swelled until she could barely hold herself together. The coincidence became overwhelming. Ms. Jackson raised her right hand and rested the back side of it on her forehead as if it hurt a little to reach back that far in her memory. "Hampton is what I usually called him but he told me that each of his daughters' names stood for something. Yeah, I remember now. There was Joyce, named for his mother, and Janeen, after his sistah. Yeah, yeah, then there was Janeese, a baby girl, named by his middle daughter." The old woman slapped her knee with delight. "I'll be. What was the pet name he used to call you by?"

"Sissy," she said, nodding proudly.

"That's right. That's it. Sissy! He would say, 'Sustah Jackson, Sissy's crawling,' or 'Sissy's cooing now.' I could tell that he really enjoyed having a baby in the house again. Boy, he sho' did love y'all girls and that pretty wife of his."

Sissy felt even more ridiculous now. Ms. Jackson seemed like a long-lost grandmother to her already, and if she didn't run out of there immediately, she feared she might vomit up the shame rumbling in her stomach.

There stood a wealth of knowledge about the world, the community, and most of all, Sissy's father. And since he had been killed in a car accident before Sissy could even walk, she'd never had a chance to know him at all.

Receiving a stiff nudge from behind startled her. Sissy jumped and almost knocked the cool glass of water from Ms. Jackson's frail hands. "Oh! I'm sorry, Ms. May'Lee. Please forgive me. I just haven't met anyone who knew him, outside my family, I mean."

After the cool water was gone and hours of talking about her father in detail passed, Sissy left Ms. Mary Lee Jackson's humble home with a new respect for old friends and new ones too. She also learned that her newest acquaintance was a matriarch of the community and the oldest living graduate of Texas's Black Teachers College. The woman *was* black history.

Leaving was difficult but the delightful old woman told Sissy that she had a standing invitation for pie or conversation about old times. She even agreed to think about selling, once Sissy convinced her that the neighborhood wasn't safe anymore and that retirement facilities in the city were well equipped and willing to take in a real prize like her. The friendship kiss Sissy planted on her cheek to say thank you so much for more than just the peach cobbler sealed a bond between them. She handed Ms. Jackson a business card and walked away slowly, trying not to trip over the tangled mass of conflicting emotions before her.

Explaining to Raymond why the deed had not yet been signed by the area's last holdout wouldn't be pleasant but Sissy could care less about that now. She had decided, before her car pulled away from the curb, to break ties with Raymond and his shady dealings. The visit made her proud to be her father's daughter. From then on, she'd refuse any longer to trade in his memory for deeds best done in the dark.

# Chapter 8

# *Barbecued Fingertips*

Rollin waited outside Janeen's office until he was summoned. Within the first five minutes that he reentered the office, he overtly sought to get her undivided attention. "If it's not too short notice, Mrs. Gilliam, I would love to take you to lunch." His tone was deep and soothing. "After all I've heard about you, I can't wait to find out if everyone exaggerated a bit about your talents and long list of achievements. Actually, you're much younger than I expected you to be."

Janeen was likewise impressed with Rollin's presence and poise, while caught up in a moral dilemma. Her well-laid plans to annihilate the opposition as soon as he arrived were lost in the shuffle somehow. She'd given too many thoughts to this man to be cruel to him. But more than that, he was there now in the flesh.

Rollin's words sounded good to her. They seemed to be honest and considerate, two adjectives that she hadn't saddled her husband with for quite some time. Maybe just talking wasn't such a bad idea after all. Janeen had prepared herself to take a stand against the establishment and be as difficult as the law allowed when the man who'd taken her job arrived, but now the time for all her posturing was over. This was her moment of truth. She looked him in the eyes and prepared to make that stand. Unfortunately, "Let me get my purse" was the only thing that came out of her mouth.

Within minutes, his shiny Cadillac pulled in front of the valet stand at Gershwin's, a posh restaurant on the north side. The menu was reasonably priced for lunch and the food nicely prepared. Being at the top of the list of luncheon spots given to Rollin by other senior-level managers, it should have been no surprise to discover many of them halfway through their entrees at a quarter past noon.

Janeen did notice that Rollin was out of the car to open her door before the valet attendant had a chance to work for a larger tip. She didn't mind it at all that the restaurant's foyer was overcrowded, which allowed Rollin to stand closely behind his date without anyone who knew them raising a brow.

While they steadily advanced on the waiting list, Rollin caught a whiff of her perfume. He slowly breathed it in. A nice citrus fragrance, worn by the right lady was tempting but he remembered to keep his head on straight and on the business at hand. He couldn't afford to get too close too soon. That would have ruined everything he'd trained for and ultimately compromise his position. And there was no way he could allow that to happen. He'd worked much too diligently to make a mistake that early in the game.

Janeen's mind strayed off its usual rigid course as well. She rather enjoyed their brief encounter of close proximity more than she cared to admit. Having him that near to her was comforting somehow. Rollin was a few inches taller than her husband, Ray, and carried about twenty more pounds of muscle in all the right places. Rollin was all man, in every way imaginable, and Janeen was a woman inching toward the last step off the marriage bus from hell anyway. What harm could one lunch do? The same harm as *just talking*.

After they were seated across from each other, Janeen wrestled to contain her smile. It was a refreshing change of pace when he fussed over her by pulling her chair out before the waiter could offer to do the same. At least chivalry was still alive.

She couldn't help wondering if Rollin was the kind of man who would remain that way, long after the first romantic kiss and all the sinful delights that usually followed it. Another smile had to be caged when she surmised, in a single beat, that he was definitely *that* kind of man.

Moments later, Janeen found herself staring across the table again. This time Rollin was staring back. "What's on your mind, Mrs. Gilliam?" he asked, as if he already knew the answer.

"Nothing really," she replied eventually, behind a thick shadow of doubt. "And it's probably about time you started calling me Janeen, since I did promise Mr. Bragg to show you the ropes."

"Okay, Janeen," Rollin agreed, and then began perusing the menu. "So . . . Janeen, what's for lunch? The blackened snapper looks good. You into fish?"

"Oh yeah, I love seafood. Can't hide my

Louisiana roots, I guess, and I'll eat just about *anything* blackened." Immediately after she'd said it, she wanted to take back the provocative package she'd sent the comment in but it was too late. Wincing, Janeen noticed that his eyebrows were already on the upswing. "I mean," she said, avoiding his eyes by looking down at her menu, "well, you know what I mean."

What he was more than certain of were his interests in more than First World Mortgage business. Only if it were another place and time, he reasoned, things would be different. Unfortunately, reality stopped by to remind him to play with the cards dealt him. Because of his situation, this woman was off limits for more reasons than the obvious.

Rollin decided to make some of his intentions known before the situation became any more awkward. "Listen, Janeen, I know you're uncomfortable with me taking a position that in all rights should be yours, and believe me, if it all works out like I think it will, it'll be yours when the time comes. Just like it was meant to be. Trust me."

That was the second time in three days Janeen had heard that prophesy. Mr. Bragg had said the same thing when he convinced her to stick around for at least a month. What she couldn't understand was what motivated Rollin. He didn't seem all that attached to his new position, although she would have relished it greatly.

"Thanks . . . Rollin," was her barely audible reply. "That's very kind of you to say so." She was smart enough to leave it at that, although burning questions persisted regarding how he was selected for the coveted $113,000 position. Some questions had to be answered in their own time. An initial lunch outing was not the appropriate venue to probe for those answers.

Despite all the cognitive dissonance Janeen experienced, she took time to note that he was obviously thoughtful too, lessening her sense of stress. Just like that, he'd taken control of the situation without patronizing her or threatening the pride he knew she needed to keep.

Their waiter appeared with lunch, then made himself scarce. Janeen watched Rollin carve away at his delicious meal while she only nibbled at hers. Still a bundle of nerves, Janeen found it hard to come up with other stimulating topics to discuss because everything she considered bringing up related to where he'd come from and how he ended up there, with her job and in her life.

By Thursday morning, Janeen felt more comfortable in her new role in the company. Besides, she had enjoyed Rollin's company during lunch every day since they formally met. Each time he suggested a reputable eating establishment, showcasing a well-dressed wait staff and valet parking. By ten each morning, Janeen had received a call from Rollin's executive assistant, Scarlett Dun'ker. The calls came like clockwork. Val answered them, Janeen accepted them, and lunch was served.

Ten o'clock had come and gone. No call. Janeen tried hard not to be concerned but the truth of it was, she had already grown accustomed to the idea of sharing her midday meal with Rollin and it didn't take long before withdrawal set in.

After staring hopelessly at the phone for what seemed like forever, she tried to get a bit of work done on her computer. Thinking of Rollin's charm and wit ruined her ability to focus no matter how much effort she put into it. Although chasing a man was out of the question, she was getting hungry and there was nothing wrong with a woman showing her gratitude for all the meals. *Right?* she thought. *I mean, 'cause it is good manners to say please and thank you. And when you're thankful for something, you should offer an in-kind gift to reciprocate. Right?* Go on, girl. Rationalize . . . rationalize.

When it appeared that no lunch invitation was forthcoming, Janeen had a notion of her own. As the elevator doors opened on the seventeenth floor, she stepped off slowly, contemplating whether she should turn around and go back or not. Too late, the doors had already closed. Cautiously she ventured past the first set of offices and followed the directions that Val had supplied, to the end of the hall. The old furniture, which sat outside of the last two executive suites, had not yet been replaced. The standard gold leather and ebony wood chairs came with each office and it was at the executive-level manager's discretion to order something new, if they had varying taste. All of the other executives employed an interior decorator to create a comfortable working environment to suit their individual taste. Another perk, which Janeen viewed as needless and costly, but she couldn't wait to get promoted and throw down money at the furniture store for her new office digs. It was a *perk* after all, needless, costly, or otherwise.

A glance at her watch informed her it was eleven-fifteen but there was no sign of Rollin's assistant, Scarlett, the overprotective gatekeeper Val had warned her about, nor the man himself. Caught between cowardice and compromise, she walked around to the business side of the assistant's desk and pulled open the top drawer. Pencils, pens, and paper clips were scattered about inside. A stack of yellow Post-it notepads sat atop a large stack of brown letter-sized hanging folders.

There was still no one in sight when Janeen decided to leave a message for him. After pulling a couple of blank notes off the pad, she wrote: "Hey, you. Thought I'd offer lunch but you were out. Next time . . . my treat. Call me." Once she'd signed her initials, she realized how personal this note sounded. Thinking better of it, she decided to leave him a voice mail instead.

After balling up the note she'd written, she tossed it in a wastepaper basket along with the idea. When Janeen bent over the desk to return the notepad to its rightful place, she heard the door being opened just behind her. In her haste to get the drawer closed, she neglected to notice that the notepad had fallen on the floor. Before she could step to the other side of the desk to avoid being mistaken for a snoop, an attractive woman with an athletic build emerged from the office with a stack of brown folders cradled in her arms. They were identical to the ones in the desk drawer. In a move to close the door behind her, the woman paused when her eyes found Janeen standing behind her desk next to a slightly opened drawer and a notepad from it resting on the floor.

Janeen grinned cordially. "Hi. I'm . . . Janeen Hampton-Gilliam," she stated, with uneasiness, sensing that the woman thought she had trespassed into her personal space. "I was looking for Rollin Hanes but he doesn't seem to be . . . around. So I'll just go," she added with embarrassment.

"Oh, I'm glad to finally meet you," was the woman's response. "Rollin, uh, Mr. Hanes, speaks of you often. I'm Scarlett Dun'ker, his assistant."

Noticing that Scarlett was well built and very beautiful, Janeen began wondering how long Rollin had had such a pretty young thing working closely by his side and probably attending to his every whim. Scarlett looked her trespasser over thoroughly as well. She scanned Janeen from head to toe as if she was casually sizing up the competition, then returned the same knowing smirk Janeen had tossed her way.

Scarlett rested the folders on her chair before suddenly picking up the notepad Janeen dropped. She looked at it peculiarly, then at her trespasser again. "It seems that you've dropped something, *Mrs.* Gilliam," she stated quite smugly.

Janeen pretended to be clueless. "I'm sorry, I don't know what —"

"Heyyy, Janeen," Rollin announced from the door leading to the other office. "I see you've met Scarlett, good. As a matter of fact, I've been running very late all morning but I was just about to call you."

Janeen and Scarlett continued the stare-down until the assistant broke eye contact first and went about her secretarial duties.

"Hi, Rollin," Janeen replied, after her brief sparring session with the help. "I wasn't sure if you were tied up so I decided to stop by and visit your office for a change." She surveyed the waiting area and discovered Scarlett taking in every word. "I had planned on leaving an invitation for you to join *me*, but if you're busy —"

"No, not at all." He offered a friendly

handshake. "Looks like my schedule just opened up."

Janeen was delighted. "Good, I'm starved," she said in Scarlett's direction. *And I got what I came for. A sistah named Scarlett. What were her folks thinking?*

With Rollin following closely behind, she headed toward the elevators and shot Scarlett a Got-my-eye-on-you wink as she strolled by. Scarlett's shrewd expression warned Janeen that she wouldn't be the only one winking.

Watching Mr. Salley push small pieces of trash into a receptacle using a short-handled broom, Val puffed on a cigarette while concealed in the shadows of the parking garage. She looked on suspiciously as Janeen and Rollin casually strolled to her manager's car.

As a friendly gesture, Janeen offered to open his car door. His blushing gesture of gratitude fell flat when he noticed that her rear tire on the passenger side was mashed against the hard concrete.

"Uh-oh," Rollin said, bending over to inspect the mishap. "It seems that you've got yourself a flat here. I'll take care of it."

Smiling as if the man had just laid his suit coat over a mud puddle or something

141

equally chivalrous, Janeen was a heartbeat away from saying something goofy in appreciation when instead of taking off his jacket he merely pulled out his cell phone and dialed up his assistant, who was at her desk thumbing through *Cosmo*.

"Hey, Scarlett. Yes, it's me, Rollin. No, we were about to exit the garage but discovered that Mrs. Gilliam has a flat tire. Please call my people and have it attended to. Thank you. All right, 'bye."

Glancing at her watch, Scarlett immediately picked up the phone and dialed the number. "It's time," she said into the receiver. Then as if nothing happened at all, she calmly returned to her magazine.

No sooner had Scarlett ended the call than a white nondescript wrecker truck that had been idling next to the curb a few blocks from the First World Mortgage building pulled away slowly and headed toward the parking garage.

Although Rollin didn't lift the car with one hand while changing the tire with the other, it was indicative of how that kind of man got things done. He didn't wait to ask Janeen what she thought or how he should handle it. He took control of the situation, made a call, and voilà, her deflated tire was dealt with accordingly. He was a man of

142

action, immediate action no less, just as she knew he would be.

While Rollin took another look at the flat tire, he spread his long arms apart wide, turned his palms upward, and hunched his shoulders. "I guess this means lunch is canceled, that is, unless you don't mind riding with me again."

"I did have my heart set on chauffeuring you around since you've been such a sweetheart to me, considering . . . you know." Of course he knew what she meant. He had made a concerted effort to assure her that his position with the company remained as much of a nonissue as possible. "I've got an idea. What if we take your car and I'll drive?"

Rollin nodded his consent. "I get to enjoy your company and I get to watch you. . . . Well, it sounds like a winner."

*What was that I-get-to-watch-you comment all about? Don't tell me he's finally getting around to noticing that I'm fine, too,* Janeen thought, as she reached at the foot pedals after her outstretched legs fell short. She made herself comfortable in his driver's seat by adjusting the mirrors and steering wheel while Rollin looked on with a warm chuckle. "Don't laugh at me," she ordered in her most coy voice. "Not everyone is as tall as you. It's not funny."

"I'm not laughing at you. I'm laughing with you. And it's just that you look quite adorable reaching for the floorboard like that. Reminds me of my younger sister when I agreed to give driving lessons years ago." During the last part of his sentence, his words trailed off as if they shouldn't have been spoken aloud. "Old times," he added, merely to punctuate his thoughts.

Janeen glanced his way, then back at the road. Rollin's eyes were glossed over enough to prove positively that he had taken a mental trip to a far-away place. Janeen knew that look all too well. It had secrets painted all over it, in broad strokes and many coats too. Of course she wanted to know where he'd mentally escaped to and wanted even more to ask if she could join him there. Too many questions loomed about this man with the perfect manners, face, taste, and just about perfect everything else. As sure as breathing, Janeen was faced with the question of whether her marriage warranted saving as she contemplated her desire to step inside Rollin's life somehow and discover what made this man just so perfect. And, besides the obvious, what made her adore him so much. Until they reached their destination he remained quiet, undoubtedly contemplating that life behind his far-away gaze.

Cautiously pulling the car up as close to the metal bumper guard as she could in front of a neighborhood restaurant, which surely had to have been a McDonald's or Burger King in its previous life, Janeen thought of all the cars she'd seen over the years get their rear ends tapped by other motorists who made the sharp turn into the parking lot while driving too fast. She didn't want to be the next one. Rollin sat in the passenger seat with a happy smirk masking his handsome face.

"What?" she asked loudly, while looking his way. "You think you're too good for the Rib Hut? Is that it?"

"No, no," he answered, with his hands up to block a would-be wisecrack to follow. "I was thinking just this morning how I'd love to have a plate of ribs, chicken, potato salad, and 'fixins.'"

Janeen didn't overlook his attempt at sounding Texan, nor did she know whether or not to feel relieved that he wasn't too perfect to get his fingers covered with sauce or be insulted while he made light of her restaurant selection, so she did what felt natural. She climbed out of the car and slammed the door. Rollin laughed even harder as she stormed away in a mock huff, looking over her shoulder with a quick I'm-not-sure-what-to-make-of-you glance in his direction before hastily going inside the place.

She studied the order board like a Rib Hut rookie who'd never eaten there, viewing it line by line. An older salt-and-pepper-haired cook watched impatiently from the kitchen window, shaking his head. Janeen could tell what he was thinking.

The tension mounted. Janeen decided that there was no way she was going to allow herself to look like a novice when Rollin finally made his way into the famous neighborhood landmark. "Oh, shoot," she mumbled. "Here he comes." She peeked over her shoulder to get another look at the front door. Rollin was holding it open for an elderly couple to enter before him. The man in the kitchen window had taken a seat by then because he'd grown tired of waiting for Janeen to order.

"What do you suggest for today, sistah?" Janeen asked of the heavy-set bleached blond woman working a relic of a cash register.

"Rib plate," the woman responded

matter-of-factly before crudely sucking her teeth.

What a big help she was. Imagine that, someone suggesting a rib plate in a Rib Hut. How original. No sooner had Rollin made his way inside where Janeen stood, than the older man from the kitchen window bounced up from his seat, yelling, "Mistah Hanes, Mistah Hanes! Glad to see you again." That auspicious greeting caused a raise of Janeen's brow. "Don't even slow down over there, that menu board is for folks who *don't know* what they want. Can I get your usual for you this afternoon?"

"Usual," Janeen restated in disbelief. "And what is your *usual*, might I ask, Mistuh Hanes?"

"Rib plate," Rollin answered in a whisper before walking away to return the cook's overzealous salutation.

"Mistah Hanes, how have you been? That tip you gave me on the game was worth its weight in gold. I owe you for that one. San Fran beat the Rangers like they stole something from church on a Sunday."

"Brisket," Rollin greeted warmly, "you know money can't come between us, but you *can* do that other thing for me, though."

The older man nodded gleefully, then yelled, "Two usuals coming up!"

Before Janeen could hold up the serving line any longer, Rollin rescued the cashier from his date's indecisiveness. "I just thought for once I would try something other than a rib plate," Janeen argued. "And how do you know that man Brisket anyway? Mr. Groves has run this place for forty years and now some Brisket fella' is doing the cooking? Humph, I know they'd better not change the sauce." She pretended to fume but it was not a very convincing act. Her cheeks kept revealing the smile she couldn't conceal.

When the plates were delivered to the table, Rollin looked the food over and sighed. "It looks great. And smells good, too." Suddenly he placed his hand over Janeen's and squeezed softly. "You mind if I do the honors?"

Janeen bowed her head and closed her eyes to give thanks as Rollin openly blessed their meals. He was certainly a man who knew God, trusted Him, and believed in Him, too. But all of her tranquil thoughts dissolved into thin air after Rollin's first bite of lunch. Watching him chew his way into a generous helping of well-seasoned meat heated things up for Janeen. She

148

noted how his strong jawline flexed with each bite. And when he licked the barbecue sauce from his strong fingers, she thought for sure she'd scream out loud.

"Whooo-wee," she whispered to herself during a deep exhale. "Yeh-es, it does look good." An attempt to eat her own meal proved futile because she didn't want to miss anything on the other side of the table. Not that Rollin was a sloppy eater but he did have the cutest little dab of sauce in the corner of his mouth after the ribs had vanished. Without thinking, Janeen picked up her napkin and carefully wiped the sauce away. Immediately after she'd done it, internal dissonance forced her to rationalize whether or not she had any business taking such liberties. *What was I thinking? Now he'll be concerned that I'm trying to get close to him, or maybe that I'm some kind of kook.* "Rollin, I'm sorry. I . . . I shouldn't have."

Rollin was more than accepting of her kind gesture. "Hey, it's okay. Thanks for thinking enough of me not to let me walk around all day with special sauce on my face." Janeen returned his thanks with a timid smile. She had begun to care for Rollin despite feeling guilty for not resolving issues with her husband before allowing herself to drift into thoughts of getting closer to another man, considering all the years she'd invested in her marriage. She felt that she owed Ray at least that much, in spite of his recent shortcomings or the fact that their relationship left her wanting more than he was willing to give. A decision to get past the hold Ray cast over Janeen was close at hand but letting go of the only man she knew would be easier said than done.

When they were finished with lunch, Rollin said his good-byes to Brisket. Janeen and the lady cashier exchanged similar fake so-longs as she and Rollin left.

Rollin paused when Janeen opened the car door for him with exuberance.

"Don't you think you're carrying this reverse chivalry thing a bit too far?" he half-heartedly complained after being tucked into his seat.

Without warning, intuition prodded Janeen just then to turn around. After giving in to her sixth sense, she was almost sorry that she had. Sitting in the very next parking space was an all-too-familiar silver Rolls Royce whose driver and passenger eyed her every move with a shocked glare as he and the woman in his car both feverishly attempted to cleanse their mouths from the residue of a guilty act. Initially, Janeen thought the young fair-skinned woman was Sissy behind the tinted windows but the woman's eyes were very different from the ones she knew well. Although the scene caused a knot to form in her throat, Janeen was relieved that at least her man's indiscretions didn't involve her younger sister.

Refusing to give it another thought or surrender her dignity, Janeen settled into Rollin's car, then grabbed the gearshift to back away from the building when Rollin noticed the passengers from the next car were still gawking his way. His eyes drifted toward Janeen. She looked dazed, confused, and ashamed, a heap of emotions all jumbled together.

Despite the bad timing, Rollin felt compelled to ask Janeen who that man was and whether she knew the much younger lady. With a stoic expression, Janeen looked in the rearview mirror before moving the car. "No one important," she answered calmly. "Just some woman I've never seen before and my husband unsuccessfully trying to wipe her cheap lipstick off his face."

It was difficult to decipher whether Janeen was more hurt or pissed off by Ray's adulterous actions, done in broad daylight no less. Her man had resumed his wicked ways, forcing her to admit to herself once and for all that a woman can't change a man's nature, no matter how hard she tries. The man has to change his mind in order to change his ways if he wants to become a better man.

At that precise moment, she also realized that regardless of how much she still loved her husband, her dignity was the one thing she'd vow not to let him take from her. Not then, not ever.

# Chapter 9

# *Changes*

Sissy slept half the morning away after enduring her girlfriend Morgan's disturbing news late into the night before. Amidst sobbing babble, she'd informed Sissy that she was pregnant. Two different early pregnancy tests confirmed it and since Morgan hadn't had unprotected sex with anyone but Brewster, she assured herself that the baby had to be his.

Upon hearing the details, Sissy verbally assaulted her protégé about sleeping with any man without using a condom, much less someone else's man. After shouting "How could you be so stupid?" several times into the phone, then immediately regretting it, Sissy sank deep into the fluffy pillows until they comforted her. She contemplated how she'd handle playing the role of part-time pimptress and full-time friend. More than anything else, she wanted to remain objective and be supportive, but Morgan was a real money-maker and rule number two in the call-girl's handbook outlawed getting pregnant, directly behind the number-one cardinal sin of the game prohibiting falling in love with a client. Within the first three minutes of their conversation, Sissy learned that Morgan had transgressed both numbers one and two.

Sissy wanted to further reprimand her working girl's lack of professionalism and utter stupidity but the woman deep within ultimately compelled her to just shut up, listen, and empathize.

When the painful sobbing was over, Morgan asked Sissy for some direction, after making it clear that she didn't want to be another minority single-mother statistic, and abortion was out of the question because of her religious beliefs.

Since advice was about as cheap as the back end of a buy-one-get-one-free offer, Sissy did the best she could while thinking at the same time how she'd want someone to advise her if she were in the same situation. Inform the father-to-be and make the decision together was Sissy's heartfelt suggestion, but Morgan had limited her options. She was jammed up in more ways than one. Loving a married man carried consequences of its own. Carrying the child of a powerful married man presented dangers in the gravest sense.

Guilt wrapped itself around Sissy so tightly that she slept the dwindling hours of the night with labored breath as if the trouble Morgan was caught up in had plopped itself down on her chest, too.

When morning came right on schedule, Sissy was woken up by a ringing telephone. While feeling her way around in the king-size bed it finally occurred to her that the annoying rings were coming from the floor, where the phone had fallen amidst her troubled tossing and turning. She rubbed her eyes and gave a long stretch and yawn before placing the receiver to her ear. "Hello. Yeah, this is Janeese."

A woman's voice spoke back. It was coarse and full of the painful intonations of a woman scorned. "I'm Clair. You know, your boyfriend's wife."

Sissy searched her memory quickly but came up blank. "Who? I don't know what you're talking about."

"You don't, huh?" the voice shot back.

"But it's obvious that you know my husband well enough."

Sissy recognized the salty sentiment in the woman's words. She was hurting something awful and intended on lessening the hurt with that phone call, but Sissy fired back.

"Uh, you must have the wrong number because I don't know *what* the hell you're implying or why you'd think I have anything to do with your husband." The woman's name still hadn't rung clear enough in Sissy's head to make a dent. "Furthermore," Sissy shouted, stalling as she checked for a number on the caller ID box, "I'll have the police hunt you down if you ever call here again." Unfortunately, caller ID displayed Anonymous in large distressing letters. It was a valiant attempt to bluff her way out of a compromising position that didn't find its mark.

"Listen to me, *nigger bitch!*" the caller berated her. "I found your number in the same bag with some condoms and hotel receipts at my husband's office and I know who you are. Maybe you screw so many men that you don't bother to remember their names or take the time to think of their wives and children in the process, but I'll say this, keep away from Brewster or

I'll have you violated in so many ways it'll make the front page."

*Brewster,* Sissy mouthed silently while thinking back on Morgan's dilemma. Now it was clear that the woman had her wires slightly crossed: right sin, wrong girl. Before Sissy could respond, the caller abruptly hung up. "Hello? Hello?" fell on deaf ears. The woman was gone but she left behind the impact of her rage. Terrified by the woman's threatening tone, Sissy began to hyperventilate when it dawned on her that she had never once given a thought to her clients' wife and kids.

She leaped off the elevated bed with a miscalculated step and nearly met the floor face first. After breaking the fall with her left hand, she bounced up with catlike agility and headed for the den of her spacious loft apartment, rapidly tearing through documents in several desk drawers until she came up with the item that she needed. A folder labeled Business Opportunities trembled in her hands. She managed to flip it open and steady herself enough to concentrate. While scanning down the first of five pages of names with the tip of her forefinger, her eyes widened when one name seemed to jump right off the paper. Councilman Brewster Wilks appeared halfway down on a long list of powerful men whom she'd arranged extracurricular activities for. Suddenly the trembling stopped. At least now she knew who wanted to scare her out of her mind and probably wished her dead.

Brewster Wilks was the same man Morgan had kept Sissy up crying over. *What luck. What rotten luck.* Among all the men whose names appeared on the list, Brewster Wilks had the worst luck of all. He had a raving wife who was more than likely dangerously close to a nervous breakdown and at least one pregnant girlfriend to deal with.

Sissy couldn't help wondering which of those headaches would hurt him more when and if his private business hit the fan. Either way, the entire ugly situation was sure to stink up the place and sling excrement all over everyone involved, including her. There would be no getting around it. She was sure of that.

While getting dressed as quickly as humanly possible, Sissy decided to take a drive and clear her dizzy head. Nothing made sense anymore, not the dealings she had entered in with Ray and certainly not

the sex-for-profit business she was ill prepared to manage in the first place. A week
ago, she was making good money peddling
flesh and facilitating mortgage deals. Now,
coming up with enough nerve to face either of them seemed virtually impossible.

After driving aimlessly around the city,
she eventually pulled over from a busy
thoroughfare and took a side street to
Malcolm X Boulevard. With only her
frayed wits to accompany her, Sissy parked
her car against a curb on the fringes of
Ginger Park, the very park in which she'd
spent countless hours playing as a child.
Out of nowhere it occurred to her that she
was in her old neighborhood. The same
neighborhood she'd avoided like the
plague because of the suffering she knew
her cunning and treachery would cause the
people she'd helped to uproot and sell
their houses.

Afraid to move, she remembered ac-
quiring a natural sedative recently that just
might be what she needed. Shuffling items
around in her designer handbag, she came
across the gift that dread-head had hooked
her up with when she endured the long bus
ride home. She hoped there would be
matches somewhere in reach because her
cell-phone battery charger was plugged in

to the cigarette lighter outlet.

Poking through the glove box, she found a collection of matchbooks from various restaurants she frequented. With sharp pains shooting through her left arm, Sissy held the match flame against the tightly rolled marijuana joint. When she inhaled deeply, she heard the crackling of dried weed as the fire made its warm acquaintance. Blocking out everything other than the wicked spliff held between the tips of her index finger and thumb, she readily welcomed the euphoric state of mind that quickly began to replace the trouble-ridden one.

As the familiar aroma filled the car, she mellowed slowly. No stems, no seeds, no sticks, no stress. One hit after another uncovered additional layers of freedom. Free from woes, cares, and reality.

"Ooooh, lah-lah-lah-lahhh," she began to sing, along with a song on the oldies radio station — KOLD or something like that. "I did you wronnng, ahh-ahh ahh-ahh, ahh-ahh," she added, trying to remember the words. "I made mis-takes tooo-ooh-ooh-ooooh." Giggles came pouring out of her mouth. "That's right, nigga bitch! You've made some mistakes all right. You've made plenty of 'em. Ha-

hahh. I'm cryyyy-in'. Ooh-ooh-oooh," she chimed in again, although more off beat and off pitch than before. The drug had clearly taken effect and obscured her mind as well as her ability to hold a tune.

Standing on the grass a few feet away from Sissy's car, a small brown-skinned girl about five years old held a large green-and-white beach ball with both hands. The girl's head appeared to be twice the size of a normal child's her age. Sissy shook her head slowly to ward off the evil buzz fairies floating around her but the child's head didn't shrink at all. After repeating the shaking a second time, Sissy looked at the small child again before bursting into laughter as she pointed the little girl's way, figuring she must have been hallucinating on some mighty potent herb.

In midgiggle Sissy noticed a thin neatly shaven man with an even dark complexion who appeared to be twenty-something, standing behind the small girl. His faded jeans were worn and tattered but the look of contempt shrouding his face was brand-new. And there was no mistaking who it was meant for. When Sissy realized what was happening, she took a long befuddled look at the half-smoked spliff before tossing it out of the window, still lit. The next thing she saw was the girl being whisked away by the hand, literally snatched from the bad lady's presence, who'd laughed and pointed at the child with an obvious birth defect.

"Wait, waaait!" Sissy screamed from the open window of her car. "I'm sorry. I didn't knowww! Wait!" But they didn't wait. The man and child disappeared into the distance, leaving Sissy to ponder why she often seemed to hurt other people, even when she didn't set out to.

Tearing out of the park as fast as she could, Sissy jumped on the freeway and weaved in and out of traffic like an ambulance-chasing attorney in hot pursuit of his next whiplash client. Battling the paranoia she encountered, rearview mirror checks became all too frequent. Every other block, she'd look to see if she were being followed. At first, she was suspicious of the faded blue plumbing van, then a young kid on a motorcycle, and then a woman in a white convertible. It seemed that each of them was following her at one time or another. She concluded that the marijuana had her tripping, and swore to rip dread-head's lips off if they ever crossed paths again.

Sissy's nephew Kelvin leaned against the

doorjamb while sipping on a red cream soda with one hand and soothing his protruding belly with an open-palm rub using his other one when she drove up. The transit area that held cars that had been serviced was stacked deeply. The mechanics must have been working overtime, Sissy thought when maneuvering her car through its maze like a kid playing a Pacman video game.

Watching her differently from the last time she visited his shop, Kelvin sucked on his teeth as though something about her annoyed him.

"Hey, Kelvin," she offered cordially. "How have you been? Looks like business is really picking up. Good for you. Is Cooper here?"

Kelvin didn't move an inch. He wasn't sure what to say because he didn't recognize the woman behind the brown Anne Klein sunglasses. The expression he returned in place of an answer bordered on disbelief and distrust. What was her angle this time? Pleasant hellos and "How have you been" were not her normal greetings. To err on the side of caution, he simply nodded his head to the side of the garage where Cooper was having a late lunch.

Sissy noted his cue and slowly headed in

163

that direction. "Thanks neph— I mean, Kelvin," she corrected herself as an afterthought.

With apprehension, she approached the large galvanized iron table where Cooper sat on a matching metal chair gazing at an oily auto-mechanic handbook. Sissy wasn't sure why she was really there. Not having thanked him properly for repairing her air-conditioner served as a suitable excuse.

Cooper turned page after page of the manual as if he were caught up in a thrilling crime novel. He looked so sweet, she thought, hardly like a big strong man at all as he took small bites from a supersized Subway sandwich and methodically eating one potato chip at a time. *He always did like taking his time,* she remembered fondly while blushing about it.

"Hey, you," she offered calmly as Cooper remained engrossed in his reading. Actually, he had to pull himself away from the grease-stained pages in order to look up. "Hey, yourself," he replied, using the same quiet tone that she had. "To what do I owe this visit? Your air-conditioner on the blink again?" he scoffed before returning to his book.

"No, my car is fine. It's probably the only thing in my life that's not jacked up right now," she answered. "But I'm a big girl. I'll work it out."

He nodded, still avoiding eye contact. "I have no doubt that you will do just that."

Sissy got the message loud and clear and knew that she had it coming. Cooper may have been excited to see her but he refused to show it, assuming that she must have needed something from him. He was right, she did.

Holding her left hand awkwardly, Sissy tried to sooth it by rubbing it gingerly with her right one. "Do you mind if I sit a minute?"

Without looking up, he mumbled, "If it suits you," then let out a sigh of frustration. "Wait, I'm better than that," he apologized. "Please have a seat, Janeese."

He extended his hand but Sissy hesitated to sit, frowning at the dusty chair she was offered. Immediately assessing what the problem was, Cooper quickly pulled a red cloth from his back pocket and wiped the chair clean. "Now there's a throne fit for a queen," he exclaimed through a half smile.

Sissy was almost too embarrassed to say thank you to the man she had known over ten years and had once been in love with. Cooper had hoped that an opportunity to get to know her all over again and catch up on lost time would present itself.

There was a long bout of silence. Both of them felt the awkward strain of remembering a love that never properly lived out all of its days. Cooper turned his face away as her eyes drifted up to rest on him. "Hey, Coop, this isn't easy for me either," she said eventually, after a wealth of emotion had finally worked its way to her mouth. "I don't know why it's so hard for me to see you again. Maybe it's because a woman who's been missing her husband without a damn reason why he pulled one hell of a disappearing act is just a bit pissed off. Three long years, Cooper! Then presto, you're in town again, and to make matters worse I just happen to stumble into your ass. You could have at least called me to say that you were back. What happened, Coop? Was it something I said, something I did? 'Cause I need some answers."

Cooper slowly turned toward Sissy after she had tossed her monologue off the back of his head. His eyes locked on her saddened face. Half lost in a thought, he hesitated before speaking. "Uh . . . I knew this moment would come and I feared it as much as I counted every second for it to arrive. I know that I have a lot of explaining to do but I can't right now."

"What do you mean, you can't? Even if you didn't take our marriage seriously, I did. I mean . . . we were old enough to make that decision, even if we did promise to keep it a secret until after you graduated. I got one call saying that you were in some kind of trouble, then nothing. I figured you'd found someone else but I thought you were man enough to at least tell me about her."

He almost laughed at the mere mention of the ridiculous possibility of there being anyone else for him other than Sissy. "I know . . . I know it may not sound fair but I promise you that there has not been anyone else for me. I still love you very much . . . never dreamed of stopping."

That revelation made her feel better but it didn't come close to being enough. "I just don't get it. My life has been on hold all this time, just hoping that . . . you'd be working through whatever it was that made you walk out of it. I feel foolish now but I hoped that somehow you were working your way back to me and . . . well, that maybe we'd pick up where we left off." Her words were serious and to the point but they came out in a much softer voice than she had rehearsed them in her head.

"Janeese, thinking about getting back to

you saved my life and right now my world is upside down but I can't begin to get into it. Just promise me that when the time comes to sort all of this out, that you'll try to understand why I did what I had to do. That might not sound like an apology, but it is. I am so sorry. I'll just have to work it out on my own."

His words were soft and thoughtful, although there was still too much of a thick gray cloud to make Sissy feel better about their situation. Cooper knew it, too. He'd only hoped that his words would be accepted in the spirit in which they were offered. He had said all that he was allowed to. Any more and he would have risked compromising his future, and theirs together.

He exhaled wearily to try and rid himself of the mountain of penned-up anxiety while battling with his conscience. When he realized that his silence and freedom were intertwined, he clenched his teeth together, then sought an avenue to get his mind going in another less taxing direction.

After watching Cooper's disjointed attempt to redirect his attention to his whale of a sandwich and the oily pages of the auto manual, Sissy felt like an outsider who'd overstepped her bounds. She could tell that he wanted to say more but for whatever reason he wouldn't. She felt the unshakable and desperate need to push forward and decided to attack that need for more information by chipping away at it around the edges.

"That, uh, looks like a great sub you have there," Sissy said awkwardly. "Mind if I have a bite? I mean, it does look big enough to share."

Cooper eventually peered up from his lunch with suspicious eyes that narrowed when something didn't feel right. The Sissy he remembered would never have let go of a discussion in which she didn't get all that she'd come for. Her tenacity was a quality he greatly admired. Suddenly he lifted his hand closer to Sissy and reached for her sunshades. Instinctively she jerked her head back like a small child refusing to take her medicine.

"Funny, but I would swear it's too dim in this old garage to need those."

When Sissy offered no response, he made another attempt to remove her designer frames. That time, she didn't move a muscle. Using his middle finger to nudge the glasses down just enough to see over them, Cooper sighed. Sissy's eyes were as red as the rag he used to clean her chair. "I don't believe it, Janeese. You're zooted." She couldn't deny it and he didn't want to believe it. "How long have you been getting high?"

She tilted her head back, then pushed up on the bridge of the frames. "Not long," was her feeble reply. "And after what happened today I won't ever mess with it again, believe me."

"Humph, so you have the munchies? But that's not why you came by here at the risk of getting your clothes dirty, is it?"

Contemplating the inevitable, Sissy began to slowly rock back and forth on the chair. She wanted to run but she needed to stay. Uncharacteristically, a tear rolled from underneath her sunshades, streaking her right cheek. Before Cooper could make sense of it, she sprang up from her chair and turned to leave. "Look, Coop, if I'm bothering you, I'll just go."

"No, wait a minute," he demanded while grabbing her left hand. "Wait just one minute."

"Ouccccccch!" she screamed. "That hurts!"

Cooper immediately loosened his grip on her arm. Realizing that he hadn't grabbed it tightly enough to cause that kind of pain, he held it in a way that allowed him to inspect it. "Ah-ah-ah, just hold on," he whispered softly. "Move your fingers."

She tried to move them but they hardly complied. When he asked Sissy to roll her wrist, she screamed louder than before, then recoiled, nearly falling over her seat. The second scream was followed by a host of onlookers. Kelvin pushed through them to get a closer look. His initial glare of concern was replaced by an expression of wonder.

"What the hell is going on over here?" Kelvin barked.

"Looks like her wrist is broken," Cooper surmised. "Yep, I'd bet my last nickel. It's broken."

Sissy moaned with intense pain as a trail of tears followed the first one from her bloodshot eyes. Cooper kneeled down to look into them. His eyes were warm and forgiving for the first time since she arrived.

"You need to see a doctor right away," Cooper insisted.

Kelvin stood there taking it all in. He started to speak but decided to reserve his comments.

"Don't worry, Mr. Clark, she didn't hurt

it here," Cooper answered, knowing the question hiding behind his employer's frown.

"Wheww." Kelvin was relieved. "Then get her to the hospital. What y'all waiting for? Go'on, now!"

As Cooper lead Sissy away by the other hand, she turned back to get another gander at his half-eaten sandwich. "J.R. . . ." she affectionately called him for the first time, "do we have time for lunch?"

Cooper smiled at their private joke. "You still got the munchies, huh? Sure, we'll stop and pick up something for you along the way."

Just like old times, he was still looking out for her best interest. And, just like old times, he was still her man. She just hadn't figured it out yet.

# Chapter 10

# Spilled Milk

During the somber trip back to the office, Janeen managed to keep a stiff upper lip but silence accompanied her and Rollin all the while. There was so much for both of them to consider. After seeing Janeen's dilemma firsthand, Rollin wanted to comfort her and offer a strong shoulder to lean on but he knew it wasn't his place to do so. The last thing he needed to do was jeopardize his professional position, no matter how much he wanted to hold her close to him long enough to make her forget about what she'd just witnessed. Realizing that a woman's heart can be the most fragile thing God has ever created and knowing that her love can run deeper than the ocean's floor, Rollin was forced to stand aside and watch her go through it alone. That's the way it had to be.

When they pulled into the parking garage, Rollin wisely suggested that she take the remainder of the day off to collect herself. Janeen agreed as she parked his car alongside hers. Slowly making her way around the back of the automobile, she looked at the tire, which had previously been deflated. The tire looked normal now and she felt good about it. Now she could get away from there, away from everything that could possibly cause her more grief.

Without saying good-bye, Janeen climbed into her car and made her way beneath the heavy steel-barred parking gate. Rollin leaned against the trunk of his identical automobile and crossed his arms in deep thought, keeping in mind what he had been sent to do. No matter how his assignment panned out, he thought, Janeen couldn't make it through without getting caught up in the middle of it. She was too close to the eye of the storm not to get sucked in. There was no way to avoid it and by the time it was all said and done, she'd probably hate Rollin for the rest of her life.

When Rollin reached the seventeenth floor, he frowned as several well-dressed government suit types milled about, waiting for his return. He waved his hand subtly as he marched passed them. The dark-suited clean-cut men saluted one another with knowing expressions, then quickly followed him into his large office. After the last one entered, Rollin promptly closed the door behind them.

Scarlett collected her notebook and brown file folders, got up from her desk, and walked into the adjoining office, too; the same one that Rollin had come out of when Janeen came up to offer him lunch.

After all the suits were comfortably seated inside, a slim-built white man who seemed to be forty-something in age and appeared to be the leader was obviously irritated. He paced back and forth near the window. "How was lunch?" he asked Rollin plainly.

"Lunch was great, but that's not why you're here, so let's get down to it." Rollin was a bit out of sorts, too, though not for the same reason the head suit was.

"You're right. That's not a bad idea," acknowledged the head suit. "One question, though; how in the hell did you end up at the rib place at the same time as Janeen's peach of a husband?"

"Like I had anything to do with that. She

insisted that she drive my car after somebody decided it was a good idea to flatten her tire," Rollin answered, in a tone that screamed *I told you so*. "I've been steering clear of that place. You know I'm well aware that's where Ray Gilliam takes most of his lady friends. I never could have guessed that's where she'd want to take me."

Out of nowhere, one of the younger men, who reminded Rollin of a Harvard grad he couldn't stand, commented, "I thought she'd put two bullets in him when she spotted him with that pretty young thing of his. I know my wife would have had me for lunch if I'd —" Rollin shot him a nasty glare, freezing him in the middle of his sentence and letting him know just how little the comment was appreciated.

Everyone in the room sensed what Rollin was dealing with. The head suit said, "Okay, fellas, let's keep our focus. We're all on the same team." He looked at Rollin peculiarly. "You've come highly recommended but this thing is coming apart and I can't have the operation unraveling on me. And I hope you're not getting too close to stay objective on this one. I know that you two have been spending a lot of time together."

As Rollin slammed his large hand down on the desk, his expression became more venomous. "Make that the last time you question my commitment or professionalism, Lieutenant Drennon. I've been doing this for eighteen years and that's why you brought me down here, because I'm the best at what I do. You were getting nowhere when I got involved four months ago, so do us all a favor and let me do what I do best." No one moved, out of respect for Rollin's credentials and fearing possible reprisal if they dared to challenge him.

A knock at the door broke the heated spell. Everyone avoided eye contact with one another. The investigation was moving well behind schedule, making everyone a bit uneasy. With an uncontrollable turn of events, they had to handle matters as they came up, instead of mapping out the details as they had initially intended.

"Come on in!" Lieutenant Drennon yelled at the door.

Two secret-service types lingered on the other side of the door when it opened. They surveyed the office, then stepped aside. A tall fair-skinned man with distinguished features strolled inside.

"Hello, Mayor," Drennon greeted, with a faint smile. "We're all glad you could make it. There's some things you'll want to hear right away."

Drennon shook the mayor's hand, made introductions all around, then closed the door and locked it.

On the other side of town, Janeen parked her car outside of Joyce's Joy Day-care Center. Sitting there for what seemed like days on end, she continued watching the children at play on the other side of a tall chain-link fence. They ran, skipped and jumped to their hearts' content, laughing and singing out loud. Her brief childhood memories called out to her but she shrugged them off. Her past was *not* the place she wanted her mind to travel. Too many new problems existed to go speeding down yesterday's unpleasant highways.

She looked at her face in the rearview mirror to see if the pain shown through her new masquerade. She sneered back at a sad expression when her misery was apparent. If the eyes are the windows of our souls, then it was apparent that her soul was wounded and crying out. Joyce would surely catch that right off the bat if Janeen went in for a short visit. Also, she decided that Joyce's persistent threats to pray for her would be too much to bear. She couldn't stand to have people feeling sorry for her, not even her own sister. For Janeen, the only thing worse than being pitied were people who spent too much time pitying themselves. That part of her came from her daddy. Because of his distaste for weakness, pity was a stranger to their home. If anyone in his immediate family made a mistake, no matter how grave, they were expected to deal with it the best way they knew how. One clear-cut rule existed, no moaning was allowed. "Wasted tears ain't gon' stop the spilled milk from spoiling," he would preach.

"Spilled milk," she heard herself say as she turned on the ignition. "Humph, after all these years, I'm still my daddy's girl."

"Hey, Janeen!" Joyce shouted from the front door of her child-care facility. "Where'r you going?"

Busted! There was nothing she could do then but turn the engine off and get out to face the music. Janeen marveled at how much Joyce reminded her of their mother while holding the door open and calling out to her. Dinnertime and bedtime had both been administered by an open door front-porch holler. Suddenly Janeen didn't feel so bad at all. Actually she was quite glad to be discovered in her failed attempt at leaving.

"Heyyy, Joyce, your center looks great. I think I like this green trim better, too."

"Thanks for noticing. It does suit the place," Joyce agreed after a hug. "I thought I saw your car out front. Where were you running off to?"

"Nowhere and anywhere, girl," Janeen replied with a gusty sigh of relief. "I came by to see you, then I started watching the kids play. You know how I get when I overdose on little giggles."

Of course Joyce knew the scoop. Her sister's inability to have children had caused several fights between Janeen and Ray, one of which was so violent that Janeen threatened to kill her husband if he ever put his hands on her again or opened his mouth to ridicule her inability to reproduce. Three days after their last big fight, Janeen had applied for a handgun permit. For two full weeks following the fight, Ray had spent his nights at the Holiday Inn. At least that's what his credit card receipts stated. By the time he'd crawled back home, Janeen had received the permit and practiced several evenings at the gun range. She surprised herself by how proficient she was at shooting targets. But using the gun to save her life was a different matter altogether. Silhouetted targets didn't have hearts, didn't share the same last name.

Noticing that Joyce's face was lit up like a Christmas tree, Janeen looked around to see what all the joy was about. She didn't recognize anything out of the ordinary so she playfully pushed Joyce into the nearest restroom, which happened to be the men's.

"Janeeeen," Joyce chuckled, "what's gotten into you? Do you know this is the men's room?"

"I don't care what room this is. I know that look!" Janeen's smile grew as grand as her sister's. "There's something you've been keeping secret. Sommmmebody's in luh-uv. And look at those pants. You can hardly breathe they're so tight."

"Hush your mouth, ain't nobody in love." Joyce was so giddy she could barely contain herself.

"You might not be in love yet but I bet you've been in somebody's bed." Janeen dodged Joyce's playful punch, then began singing, "Joycee's got a boyfriend, Joycee's got a boyfriend."

Both women were elated and laughing at the top of their lungs. It had been a long time since they acted like sisters, so care-free, sharing, and close. To their surprise, the door opened. A young father stepped inside to find them acting half their age. Embarrassed, they straightened their faces and quickly made their way out of the boys' room only to begin laughing all over again in the laundry room.

"So, who is he? What does he do? How'd you meet?" Janeen prodded. "Come on. Give — give."

Instinctively, Joyce began separating and folding clothes, which had been donated for the church's clothing drive. "I'm not telling you anything. Besides, there isn't anything to tell." She continued folding and separating with little success convincing Janeen that a man hadn't found his way to her sister's heart, as well as between her sheets.

"Yeah, there's something, all right," Janeen reasoned. "But I'll let you hold on to it until you're ready to give it up." She began folding and separating along with her big sister. "Attending to these clothes and standing here like this . . . well, it just takes me back to when we were younger."

Staring starry eyed out into space, Joyce concurred with a playful hip bump against Janeen's side. "It does feel good," she admitted, as her smile dissipated.

While walking another large bag of

clothes to the folding table, Joyce felt something of a different nature to get off her chest. "Janeen, I've been thinking . . . thinking about the last conversation we had at your house that didn't do anything but drive us further apart. No matter how it looked to me, I should have stayed out of your business. I guess I'm trying to say I'm sorry and I was wrong."

Janeen reached across the table and hugged her sister as tightly as her arms would allow. "I don't want you to concern yourself with that," Janeen advised. "Doesn't matter anyway. It would only be wasted concern. Like spilled milk." Joyce knew exactly what that meant; don't bother.

Suddenly Janeen's smile disappeared. "Guess who I saw today?" she asked soberly.

"I bet you're gonna tell me who."

Janeen put her hands on her hips and stuck her neck out like a peacock. "Some extremely young woman, who I ain't nev-uh seen before today, sticking her tongue down my husband's throat."

Caught with her guard down, Joyce assumed she was kidding. "Uhhh-uh! You did not. Don't go lying on that ol' no-account husband of yours. He can do bad all by himself without you making up stuff to slight him."

"It's the truth, I swear it," Janeen re-affirmed. She appeared well adjusted while discussing her husband's infidelity, as if she were recapping a weekly soap opera. "I was shocked, then I remembered what you told me about seeing him at the Rib Hut, having a lover's quarrel with Sissy. After that, I was actually okay with it."

"How's that? You sure you're okay? Love him or not, he is still your husband."

"I was okay because I saw the woman. She was barely out of her teens, if at all. At first glance, she could have been mistaken for Sissy, unless you looked real close." A thought came to Janeen, like an itch that had to be scratched. "Uh, Joyce, did you have on your glasses the day you saw the argument?"

Joyce thought back. Before a full range of contemplation could exhaust itself, her facial expression gave her away. "Naw, I didn't. Come to think of it, my glasses *were* broken. I just got them back from the re-pair shop yesterday." Her demeanor pleaded for forgiveness. Instead, she was awarded another long hug.

# Chapter 11

# How Come?

While reflecting on his and Sissy's last kiss, which had taken place over three years ago, Cooper got a sinking feeling in the pit of his stomach. And because of his present situation, he could not afford to wine and dine the woman sleeping a few feet away from the chair he lounged in at her apartment. Also, he wasn't sure if she would want him to re-enter her life when she found that he'd had some unpleasant issues of his own to contend with during their time apart, stemming from an unfortunate incident.

Sissy did enjoy the brief intimate moments that they shared before she'd quickly drifted off to sleep. The sedatives, which the doctor prescribed while setting her left arm in a cast, had taken effect before they pulled into her apartment garage. Cooper had taken great pleasure in cradling her tired body in his capable arms when he carried her from the car to her welcoming bedroom. The way he watched her resting was painfully sorrowful, like a desperate man who cared for a woman he used to know. So many things had changed. So many lies between them existed. Six and a half years previously, they'd shared bright ideas and hopes of a long life together. Then, without explanation, Cooper disappeared three years later and reneged on his part of their secret marriage, which had never been spoken of aloud. Now she'd have to learn everything if he planned on patching up their past, although he wished none of it ever happened. At least his silence was almost over, he reasoned. And if he could just keep from damaging their relationship further before all was said and done, he might possibly still have a place in her life.

Two hours later, back-to-back *Good Times* reruns alleviated most of Cooper's tension. Ordinarily television had no place in his life. He chose to pass his time reading novels, engineering textbooks, and just about anything else he could get his hands on. Mindless hours of laugh tracks and overdone sitcom subplots held no interest for him.

As the evening sun began its slow dissolve into the horizon, Cooper's restlessness multiplied with each passing moment. Standing up from a comfortable chair to stretch his legs, a wide-mouthed yawn came over him. It was almost 8:00 p.m. and he was running late for another destination but couldn't see himself leaving her sedated like that. What if something happened? What if she didn't wake up? What if she needed him?

Pacing back and forth slowly at the foot of Sissy's bed, he began to run different scenarios over and over in his head, scenarios that included him providing interference for some very powerful people. The pressure was getting to him. He wasn't adequately prepared to be that involved in someone else's business or sure if he could keep up the facade another day. Unfortunately, a deal was a deal and he'd made it in good faith. He was a man of his word, after all, a man who would see it through to the end, although it twisted him deep inside to do so.

Suddenly, the cell phone in his pants pocket rang. It startled him. Sissy stirred a bit when Cooper attempted to answer the annoying ringing. Hurrying to the other room, he answered the call in a low voice. "This is Coop. Yeah, I'm here now. No, she's still out. Right, right. No, she hasn't asked me anything yet."

Cooper continued to speak cautiously while occasionally looking behind him to make sure that Sissy was still asleep. Nervous doesn't begin to describe how jumpy he had become, considering his usual cool, tough exterior. "I know I'm late," he retorted into the phone. "What do y'all expect me to do, leave her here by herself?"

Cooper wearily wandered over to Sissy's home office area. He held the phone to his ear as he moved papers out of the way to make a clearing to sit down. "I know how this works, you've told me enough times. No, I don't have a problem with our arrangement. I'm just tired is all, just plain tired."

Hearing Sissy stir again, Cooper made his way back to her bedroom. He peeked his head in. She was still very much in dreamland so he returned to his seat on the corner of her desk.

"What would it look like?" he asked the caller. "Then how should I know? I'm not cut out for this espionage stuff. Okay, okay, I'm looking."

As he turned to face the desk, he shook his head. It was hard to believe that he had actually agreed to go through with this whole sordid business. There had to be a better way to make up for all the lost time. There had to be.

Fumbling through her desk drawers, he couldn't locate anything that remotely resembled the information he needed to obtain until suddenly a red glossy folder grabbed his attention. He picked it up and opened it. "Wait a minute, I think I might have something here."

After briefly viewing the papers inside the folder, he knew it was much ado about nothing and started to replace the folder. "No, false alarm. There wasn't anything to write home about." He continued fingering the documents, scanning each one. "Oh, wait!" his voice rang, with excitement. "Hold on a sec. . . . Okay, shoot me some of the names and I'll match them against this list I just found." Running his finger down the page, just as Sissy had done earlier in the day, Cooper nodded to each name he heard. "That's all of 'em. Yes sir, they're all here, present and accounted for, and several more. All right, I'll copy it."

Cooper figured that the piece of letter-sized paper that he held between his fingers would be more powerful if he could have realized its full potential. Making an extra copy for himself seemed smart at the time so he did just that and hid it in her apartment. No sooner had he stepped away from the hiding place he chose than he heard a knock at the door.

As Cooper looked through the peephole in the door, Sissy called out to him from the other room. Two very handsome women, who appeared to be very anxious, stood side by side in the hallway. With reluctance, he opened the door and introduced himself in the most sincere voice he could project. "Hello, ladies, I'm J. R. Cooper . . . Janeese's, uh, Sissy's friend."

Both women took their time looking him over apprehensively before accepting his handshake and salutations. "Hi, I'm Janeen and this is Joyce. We're *Janeese's* sisters."

"Is she in the bedroom?" Joyce asked, staring too long at the front of his oil-stained navy blue work pants.

"Yes ma'am, she is," he replied.

" 'Ma'am'?" Janeen repeated with a broadened smile. "Looks like Sissy found herself a southern gentleman." She also noted that he was a fine young southern gentleman but failed to recall that she had met him through Sissy years before.

"Well, at least he is southern," Joyce quipped with a rude smirk before making her way to the bedroom to check on Sissy.

Janeen extended her appreciation to the gallant young man standing guard over her little sister. "Well, Mr. Cooper, we thank you for seeing to Sissy for us but I think we'll take it from here."

Quickly catching the hint that he had just been dismissed, Cooper moved through the doorway and smiled back at Janeen. "Please tell Janeese that I'm sorry but I have to go now. I think she'll understand."

"Is there anything else, Mr. Cooper?" Janeen asked in her best business voice.

"No ma'am. I'll catch up with her later. Thank you."

By the time Janeen joined her sisters in the bedroom, Sissy was rubbing her eyes and mumbling something about a six-foot Subway sandwich chasing her in her dreams. Both of her older sisters laughed but before the last chuckle was spent, Joyce twisted her lips while inquiring suspiciously, "Did that young man who just left have anything to do with that cast on your arm?"

Janeen nudged her for the untimely and

rude comment. "Don't be nudging me," Joyce challenged. "I love this girl, too, and I care about her well-being."

Sissy tried to sit up in bed. Janeen rushed to aid her uncomfortable endeavor. "Take it easy," she insisted, while eyeing the prescription bottle on the nightstand. "I'm sure the doctor doesn't want you to exert yourself."

"I just broke my wrist, I didn't have *heart* surgery," Sissy argued. Then she proceeded to cough repeatedly. "And no, J.R. didn't have nothing to —"

"Anything," Janeen corrected.

"*Anything* to do with it," Sissy continued with a resentful glare. "I fell from this ridiculously too-high bed running for the phone. J.R. is an old friend who was in the right place at the right time to help me out." She began to cough again, this time violently.

Janeen jumped up and headed for the kitchen. "I'll get you some water. I'll bet the drugs you're on made your throat dry." She had no idea that her little sister was dealing with the cottonmouth aftereffects of smoking marijuana.

While Janeen was out of the room, Sissy adjusted her body to get more comfortable on the pillows. "Whoooo, I'm out of it. I sure did need that nap. Sleep hasn't come easy lately."

Meddling wasn't Joyce's strong suit but she did want to know what Sissy was dealing with. Grown-up or not, Sissy was still Joyce's little sister.

Janeen returned with a glass of water and handed it to the somewhat dazed and distraught bad girl. After a few labored sips, Sissy sank back into the pillows as if a monstrous weight had been lifted off her. "Thank you, Neen," she said, feeling better already. Janeen smiled at the use of the affectionate childhood name. Many years had passed since she'd heard the name that warmed her body throughout.

"Don't mention it. We just have to get you back on your feet. Me and Joyce have better things to do than sit around here baby-sitting your rusty butt," Janeen replied playfully.

"I know that's right," Joyce chimed in, giving Janeen a jovial high-five hand slap.

"Rusty?" Sissy protested. "Uh-uhh, I know y'all didn't. First of all, my butt hasn't been rusty since I could pee off myself, and secondly, Neen, it's *'Joyce and I* have better things to do than sit around here and baby-sit your *fine self.'*" That last comment caused the sisters to erupt with laughter.

"Oooooh, look who thinks she's something." Joyce postured before standing up to show off her own wares. "It ain't never gonna be finer than mine." She began strutting around like a prostitute on parade, shaking everything she had in Sissy's face.

"Go on, girl, work it!" Janeen added, dancing along with Joyce from the edge of her chair.

"It takes years to get this fine and you have at least another ten to put in before you can even be considered," Joyce joked.

While the room was in a joyful tizzy, Sissy suddenly found the strength to sit up and dance along with them while snapping the fingers on her good hand to a syncopated beat. "Heyyyyy! . . . Go, Joycee. Get busy. Shake your booty. Go, Joycee . . . go Joycee . . . go Joycee . . . go Joycee. It ain't your birthday, get busy anyway. It ain't your birthday, get busy anyway. With your tight pants on."

After several minutes of unbridled tomfoolery, Sissy lay back in her bed and wiped the tears of joy from her eyes. "Wow, we haven't acted this silly in years," she said. "Boy, it sure does feel good."

Janeen nodded, holding her stomach as Joyce struggled to catch her breath. "Ye-es, it does," both older sisters agreed.

When a thought came to Janeen that she couldn't shake, she giggled while attempting to get it out. "Reee-member," she said, looking at Sissy, "when you would come home after learning the latest dance at school and me . . . uh, Joyce, Muh'dear, and I, would all line up and try to follow your lead?"

"Uhhh-huh, I know I do." Joyce laughed out loud. "I never could get those steps right."

"You sure couldn't," concurred Sissy to more glee as Joyce stood up again and unleashed her best attempt to nail the cabbage patch and prep dance steps from the mid-1980s.

In the midst of the merriment, Sissy's face grew sad. "Seems like we never get together anymore and just be sisters, have fun and enjoy each other's company like this." Joyce and Janeen both signaled their agreement as Sissy continued. "Joyce is always busy with the day care and Janeen, you're busy making money hand over fist, but you both have the book club to share and I never did find time to get involved. That's my fault, I know, but I'm going to do something about it." Sissy took a second to reflect further before resuming. "And Joyce, I know you're not going to want to hear this, but Janeen and I go to church every Sunday and catch a brunch somewhere, but . . . you don't do church for some reason, though I've never heard why not."

Joyce was quiet momentarily. She had always regretted not having a closer sisterly relationship with Sissy but because of some old family skeletons and her own part in it, she couldn't allow herself to foster one. After pondering Sissy's comment, she searched Janeen's eyes for an answer but none came forth, and instead Janeen's eyes floated toward the floor. "Well, I love the Lord more than anyone, Sissy, you know that," Joyce offered, in her own defense. "There's just some things too deep to season with reason. Things are just the way they are, that's all. Maybe someday they'll be different. That's why I pray so much for all of us. Only God can heal the old wounds haunting our family. He'll make it right someday, somehow. Trust in that."

A more than curious expression latched itself on Sissy's face. "What are you talking about, Joyce?" she asked as if it hurt her to.

Joyce shot a quick glance at Janeen again. This time, it was returned with a Please-Joyce-not-now plea for clemency.

"If there's something I should know, somebody needs to tell me," Sissy begged. "I'm not a child anymore. And I'm a sister too, just like y'all."

Janeen shook her head in defiance. "Uhh-uhh. Joyce is right about one thing. This isn't the time. Not now. Soon."

"Okay, y'all, *keep* your little secrets from me. I'll find out anyhow. Just the other day I was making sales calls for Ray in the old neighborhood and met this sweet old lady named Mary Lee Jackson, and she knew Daddy. She even had a framed picture of them together on her piano."

The name sounded familiar to both of the older sisters. Joyce squinted her eyes as if she were trying to force the memory to the front of her mind.

"Ms. May'Lee?" Janeen whispered. Her surprise was overwhelming. "That old woman can't be still alive! She must be a hundred years old by now."

Sissy was happy to inform them that she was. "Uh-huh, but she's alive and kicking. She had some nice things to say about Daddy helping her out after her husband died and how Muh'dear was somewhat of a

Renaissance woman with the beautiful quilts she sewed by hand and those candles she sold. It made me so proud. You know, I'd forgotten what great parents we had. Yeah, I was glad to meet Ms. May'Lee. She'll be one hundred years young next month. I say we throw her a big party and invite everyone whose name she puts on her list."

Joyce frowned in wonder while listening to the discussion about someone she should have known. "May'Lee who?"

Touching Joyce's shoulder, Janeen whispered, "You knowww, old Peach Cobbler."

"Ohhhh yeahhh," Joyce remembered, now also whispering. "Old Peach Cobbler."

Amazement and joy returned to Sissy's tired face. "Y'all really do know her?"

"Mmmm-hmm," the older sisters acknowledged.

Janeen couldn't wait to get it out and enlighten Sissy with some family history she did feel good about sharing. "Old Peach Cobbler is what Joyce and I had to call her or mama would get so mad, so we'd whisper her name. Muh'dear worried herself sick that Daddy may have had himself another woman stashed away somewhere in town because he'd work overtime and do odd favors for this 'special customer' of his. Muh'dear was cool with it at first until Daddy let it slip that the special customer was a her, not a him. He said she was no competition, but Muh'dear refused to believe him."

Joyce had to place her hand over her mouth to stifle the punch line from slipping out before the joke had completely been told. "Oh, how they argued for days," she added. "Muh'dear actually stopped speaking to Daddy for a while and forced his hand."

Sissy's eyes were big as saucers and filled with anticipation. "So what happened then?"

"Well, one day Daddy came home from work early," Janeen explained. "He had a deep pan of the best peach cobbler we'd ever eaten. Muh'dear started speaking to him again for being thoughtful enough to bring home dessert, giving her a break from the kitchen. But paradise restored was not long-lived, not at all. When she did get around to asking him who had made such a wonderful dish, he rubbed his belly and told her that his special customer named Mary Lee Jackson had baked it."

"No, Daddy didn't. I know he didn't," Sissy said in disbelief.

Joyce snickered like a child listening in on a grown-folks' conversation. "Yes, he did too. As proud and as stupid as it sounded, Daddy actually said her name for the first time."

Sissy was more captivated than ever and couldn't wait to hear Janeen tell more. "Come on, now, what happened next?"

"Muh'dear was so upset, she snatched Joyce and I up by our collars and dragged both of us to the bathroom and locked it, like we had something to do with it. After we watched her push her fingers down her throat to throw up all the food in her stomach, she came after us with the weirdest look on her face. We ran around that tiny bathroom screaming and dodging for our lives. We didn't know what came over her. Pssh . . . we were scared as hell. When Daddy finally busted the bathroom door down, Muh'dear had Joyce by the neck with one arm, trying to stick her hand in Joyce's mouth, and had me pinned down on the floor with her knee in the middle of my back to hold me still, planning to get to me next. When I tell you that I thought Daddy would kill Muh'dear for the way she had us fearing for our own safety . . . Then all of a sudden, he stepped back and braced himself against the doorjamb when his knees got weak. I didn't know what to make of it but I was glad that Muh'dear took her knee out of my back." Janeen hesitated in order to get herself together because of what followed next in the story.

At the same time, Joyce began to wipe the tears away from her eyes, but her smile had not abandoned her. Janeen placed her hand on Joyce's back to soothe her nerves before going on.

"This is a great story," Sissy admitted happily. "Come on, Janeen, finish it. Where was I?"

"Okay. There we all were. You were still a baby, sleeping through it in your crib while Muh'dear was going crazy. Daddy stood there, tall but broken, with tears rolling down his face. It was the only time I ever saw him cry. That terrified me 'cause he was always such a strong man. He said, 'Magnolia, you're gonna let your jealousy make you harm your own daughters?' And without hesitation, Muh'dear snapped back, 'I'll be damned at Jesus' feet 'foe I let some woman poison 'em to death in my own home. Neither your sins nor your whore is gonna send my children to early graves.'" Janeen stopped briefly to state her mind. "I thought for sure we were all about to meet Jesus firsthand then. I didn't know Muh'dear even knew words like that, much less how to use them. It shocked Daddy, too. Guess he didn't know she knew them either."

"Huh, I know I didn't," Joyce said, vividly remembering the horrible scene.

"Daddy took one hard step toward Muh'dear, so hard that I expected his foot to go clean through the floor. We all jumped back and cringed. The idea that we were afraid of him must have been too much to deal with because he tore out of there so fast that he knocked the screen door off the hinges on his way out the house. We all cried for about an hour and weren't sure where he went or if he'd ever come back. Next thing you know, that old cab he drove came roaring up to the front of the house. Joyce and I hid in our bedroom and peeked out through the curtains. Daddy hopped out of the car and ran over to the rear passenger door. He whipped it open and helped this petite little piece of a much older woman out of the car and marched up the walkway with her trying to keep pace behind his long strides. After seeing the woman for herself, Mama was never sorrier for anything than she was for accusing him of cheating on her with old

Peach Cobbler. To think that sweet little old lady could poison anyone was ridiculous. We all knew it by the time he introduced her to us. After that day, we never heard an unkind word spoken between Muh'dear and Daddy again."

Joyce wiped the last fallen tear away. "Spilled milk," was all she had to offer, and it was more than enough to help Sissy understand what Ms. Mary Lee Jackson had meant to their family. She was as much a part of it as anyone not born into it could have been. It was then they began planning to meet with the older woman to discuss a celebration for her one hundredth birthday party.

# Chapter 12

# *Eight More Days*

Cooper stepped off the elevator in the parking garage beneath Sissy's apartment building. It was 8:30 p.m. and he was already running unforgivably late. Sissy's health troubled him but thinking of a way to get back to his jeep, still parked at the auto shop, was the only thing that mattered now. Before he could get to the street-level exit, the urgent sounds of squealing tires from a shiny black Chevrolet Tahoe made him hesitate before taking another step. In an instant, the automobile slammed on the brakes directly in front of where Cooper was hugging the wall and fearing for his life. Something was alarming about the way the Tahoe appeared out of the night like an apparition.

The windows of the SUV were heavily

tinted, which prevented him from seeing who drove the car. Everything about the incident warned him to be cautious but he had already admitted to himself that he'd lost control of his life in a little redneck bar in Virginia four years ago. Now some menacing vehicle was idling, probably waiting for him to make the next move. When he did take a calculated step toward the exit, the Tahoe inched up slowly, matching his pace. It was a wicked game of cat and mouse — a game the big black cat was winning.

Cooper grew more concerned that someone from his past was there to hurt him, and enjoying themselves while doing it. His heart raced furiously as he sized up his formidable foe. Adrenaline pumped throughout his muscular frame until he could no longer stand being stalked.

Suddenly Cooper took off in a flash for the street just outside the garage exit, then pushed his body at top speed for twenty meters. He sprinted as fast as his legs could carry him, drawing ever so near to the garage exit, his gateway to freedom. But the menacing SUV sped up just enough to beat him to the exit.

Exasperated and winded, Cooper surrendered any hope of making it out of there on his terms. There was nothing left to do but throw his hands up in defeat as his broad chest heaved in and out in a mad search for oxygen.

As he panted, the window on the passenger side slid down a few inches. A man's voice called out, summoning him through the small slit of the cracked window, "Hey! Get in!"

Obstinate, Cooper stood motionless with his jaws locked as the crude voice demanded again, "Mr. Cooper, get in the vehicle! Now!"

In the time it took him to think, the back door was pushed open from the inside. A clean-shaven well-dressed man pointed the biggest gun Cooper had ever laid eyes on at his face and beckoned him to get in once more. The game was over.

Once inside the SUV, Cooper felt a calm presence roll through him. Three of the biggest secret service–types imaginable, each dressed in dark suits, wore matching condescending grins. The cat-and-mouse maneuver was simply a pastime to them and their game was at Cooper's expense. One thing was clearer then: if they had wanted to hurt him, it would already have been done.

The two men seated in the front seats

casually turned around face forward, then the Tahoe began to move. The third man in the backseat with Cooper holstered his gun and held out his hand for the list of names from Sissy's desk. After he looked it over, the list was placed inside his coat pocket. Until they reached their destination, Cooper was asked a laundry list of questions regarding Sissy, Janeen, and everything else he may have learned about the sisters over the past week. He reported what he knew, which wasn't much, before being reminded of how important it was for him to keep his mouth shut or the consequences wouldn't be favorable.

At 9:15, the black Tahoe pulled up in front of Kelvin's automotive shop. The back door opened slowly. Cooper stepped out with his lips pressed tightly together. As his second foot hit the ground, the large vehicle burned rubber to flee the scene. The sudden jerk sent him reeling to the hard concrete. In spite of his bruised ego, he was glad to be alive and relatively unharmed.

"Underground parking," Cooper murmured with hostility while entering yet another subterannean garage. Maneuvering his jeep through rows of parked police cruisers, he backed his old Wrangler against a cement wall near the far end of the garage. Even though he usually felt relatively safe in his domain, insecurity overwhelmed him now because he knew that the sorts of people who drove the Tahoe could get to him anywhere, if they wanted to.

While striding through the first security checkpoint, Cooper noticed an officer nodding at him familiarly. If the officer had known his current status in life, he wouldn't have given any form of salutation.

As he approached the second security checkpoint, another officer passed him by, scoffing at him. That cop did know Cooper's status in life and reminded him of it with contemptuous sneers.

"Signing in, J. R. Cooper," he announced to the desk officer, whose nose was deep in a box of doughnuts. That officer glared, too, from the opposite side of a thick bulletproof window.

"You're late!" the doughnut cop announced in return.

"Tell me about it," was all that Cooper could say. He was being pulled from both sides and in the middle, all at once.

Twenty minutes later, all the treacheries

of the day swirled in J. R. Cooper's head as he stared through cell bars while anchored to the bunk bed and dressed in a white cotton county-issued jailhouse jumpsuit. Jeremiah Reynoldston Cooper III, convict number 129107, had had a very trying day, one that wasn't over yet. Not by a long shot.

After opening his palms upward, convict number 129107 bowed his head and prayed earnestly for forgiveness for all the sins that he and everyone he had ever known might have committed. He was sorry and repentant, both equally so. Sadly enough, J. R. Cooper was incarcerated for the sins committed against him.

After a heartfelt amen, Cooper opened his eyes to find a distinguished well-dressed suit standing casually outside his cell door. This one was different from all the others he'd come in contact with over his last month of captivity. This suit was a black man. His demeanor was different from the others', too. He was, most assuredly, a man who handed out orders instead of taking them. He was unmistakably the man.

"You think he heard you?" asked the man wearing a navy pinstripe suit.

"Excuse me, sir?" Cooper questioned

with a clueless expression.

"Your prayers. Do you think the man upstairs heard your prayers?"

Cooper thought a bit before answering. "I have a distinct feeling that I'm about to find out, one way or another."

Without hesitation, the man shouted, "Gate!"

Upon his command, the cell door opened as if he'd just waved his hand and made it so. Thousands of times, Cooper wished he had those kinds of powers, powers that made people jump at his command. The powers that would allow him to wave his hand, open the cell door, and disappear into the life he'd planned for himself and worked so diligently for, graduating from college in three years in order to have. But the reality of incarceration for attempted murder rendered him powerless. Prayer and solitude were his cellmates, both equally so. He became strengthened by one and controlled by the other.

Staring at the man who stared back at him, Cooper waited patiently. He waited to be told what to do. Having served more than three years of hard time in a maximum-security facility in Virginia, he was well versed on waiting, watching, and listening for the next cue. His behavior behind those bars was orchestrated down to the time in which he was allowed to shower, eat, and exercise.

The man backed away from the cell door and motioned for him to come forth. Cooper bounced from his metal bunk and stood at attention, which was a customary act of compliance. When two uniformed detention officers appeared with iron shackles to constrict his movement, they were casually waved off. Immediately and without question, both men did an about-face and returned from whence they came.

"We need to talk. You may not be coming back here. Is there something you want to bring with you?" the man asked, in such a way that sounded more like a demand than a question.

"No sir," Cooper responded solemnly, feeling like a disobedient child.

Together they marched down the long corridor. Convicts from both sides of the cellblock looked on curiously as their comrade, known only to them as Coop, made his way past them. Respectful stares followed the best-dressed brother who had ever graced their temporary domiciles.

Once inside a small investigation room, Cooper was offered a seat at a small wooden table. His first thought was to wonder how many confessions had actually been pulled, beaten, or tricked out of the accused previously sitting at that very table in that same tiny room reeking of dried sweat and urine. No doubt the room had absorbed years of sorrowful stories and rivers of salty moisture pouring from the brows of repentant souls. Wondering what they would be expecting him to repent of was Cooper's second thought.

With his back to the suspicious inmate, the man adjusted his necktie in the large two-way mirror as he started in with the business at hand. "Mr. Cooper, I'm Rollin Hanes, the reason you're here. I know there must be a million questions you want to ask me but they can wait. What I need you to do is listen to what I have to say. Your life and many others depend on it."

Cooper nodded and nervously scratched his head while adjusting his posture in the chair. "Yes sir," he answered out of habit.

"I personally asked that you be re-manded here, to the Dallas County lockup for safekeeping and for whatever else you can do to assist in our investigation. When I discovered that you were property of the state of Virginia, I had a private conversation with the governor. And, after persuading him to do the right thing, he was more than happy to make a phone call to set the wheels in motion."

Cooper almost leaped out of his seat after hearing who was involved in his transfer. The governor was ultimately responsible for having him locked up and the key conveniently misplaced. Cooper was sentenced to a thirty-five-year term for being in the wrong place at the wrong time. It had all happened on the night he celebrated his early graduation from Virginia Tech.

Rollin was well aware of *all* the details that had transpired during that unfortunate incident. He noted Cooper's anxiety when hearing the governor's name, then he continued. "And I also learned of your prior connection to Janeese Hampton," Rollin told him. "You know what I'm talking about, don't you?"

Of course Cooper knew. He thought the secret he shared with Sissy was theirs to keep. Now it was being used to turn him against her. Puzzled at how Mr. Hanes knew about it, Cooper lowered his head in shame. He just kept telling himself that he could help her if he knew the true source of her troubles. Maybe he could uncover what they had on Sissy, warn her, and still get the help he was promised in Virginia, when they snatched him from his cell in the middle of the night and threw him on a Dallas-bound private jet.

"Good. Then we're on the same page," Rollin stated, somewhat relieved, while taking the time to examine the list of names Cooper had copied from Sissy's red folder and handed over to one of his men in the black Tahoe. "So far you've done everything we've asked of you and we thank you for that. I know it must be difficult, considering your relationship, but some things can't be avoided. It's like snow falling in April — it happens. Sometimes that's how it goes."

Several people watched Rollin work his magic from outside of the investigation room on the opposite side of the two-way mirror. The mayor of Dallas was among them, along with Lieutenant Drennon.

Amazed at Rollin's skill, a young observer whispered, "He's good. Very good."

Scarlett corrected him. "He's the best," she declared. Her tone was deliberate and sure. Watching Rollin's smooth technique time and time again was as enjoyable to her as it was educational.

Back inside the small poorly ventilated room, Rollin briefed Cooper on additional details and explained that everything else would be divulged on a need-to-know basis. Rollin then shook Cooper's hand before informing him that a temporary safe house would be his new home for the next eight days.

# Chapter 13

# *No More Pretending*

Ray stepped out of the master bedroom whistling a carefree tune as he headed for the kitchen to begin his morning ritual of guzzling orange juice laced with a shot of cognac and chomping on toast while listening to his favorite AM radio news broadcast. As he rounded the corner from the living room to the breakfast nook, his catchy whistle was cut short when Janeen surprised him. She was dressed for corporate combat in a stylish rust-colored pantsuit with matching pumps, and was finishing off the last glass of OJ. What Ray was thirty seconds too late to witness was his wife disposing of a brand-new half gallon of her husband's morning juice by gleefully pouring all but three ounces down the sink drain.

"Oh, Janeen," he said, with a hint of uneasiness. "I thought you'd already left for work."

"No, not yet. I thought I'd take my time for once and enjoy the last glass of this Florida squeezed." Her tongue slid out between her lips and ran a complete lap around them.

Disregarding what she said, Ray walked past her as she leaned casually against the counter with her legs crossed at the ankles. He immediately discovered that she wasn't joking. There was no juice in sight.

Ray laughed uncomfortably. "I know for sure that there was one full carton of orange juice in this fridge last night," he stated while closing the refrigerator door in disappointment. "You want me to believe that you drank every bit of it yourself?"

"Uh-huh, like water down a drain. You should have been here to watch me. It really went fast. I couldn't even taste it, disappeared so fast."

Ray scratched his cheek. He was obviously annoyed and suspicious. Besides, Janeen was never one to drink a great quantity of fruit juice, especially OJ, because the acid irritated her stomach. It seemed that Ray's morning was going downhill already. Just the way Janeen had planned it.

Standing in the pantry doorway, Ray exercised an executive decision. He chose not to attempt a halfhearted effort to follow through with the ritual he enacted every day. What he couldn't do was let *her* get away with it uncontested.

"So you think that's how you'll get back at me for the woman you saw me with, by throwing out my juice? You know how I love to start my mornings off with it. That's mean, just plain mean."

"Mean? You've got some nerve," she spat back. Janeen's tone was sharp but lacked her signature dose of stinging attitude. "It's been days since I caught you and —"

"Caught me?" said Ray in a loud, strained pitch.

"You heard me, I didn't stutter. Yeah, caught you! What else would you call being busted outside a rib joint with a girl less than half your age?"

Ray didn't have a leg to stand on. Since the Rib Hut incident, which occurred two weeks earlier, he'd chosen to avoid Janeen around the house, if he came home at all. He figured that an uncomfortable conversation had to be fast approaching. He should have realized that there was no escaping the inevitable. After all, he was witnessed committing a sin against his marriage, tried, and convicted by the court of love in the first five seconds that she saw him and his girlfriend getting cozy. The sentencing phase was the last stage of the process and Janeen held powers of both judge and jury in her hands. Ray's transgression was morally wrong. His lack of discretion was inexcusable. For that, he would have to pay dearly.

As he stood on the corner of Speechless and Don't Even Try It, Ray had no plausible answer or explanation for his actions. Janeen thought he'd at least make an attempt to pacify her but the thought never crossed his mind.

With her briefcase handle clutched firmly in her hand and wishing that she held Ray's neck just as tightly, Janeen pivoted on her heel and headed for the back door. Pausing to unlock the dead bolt, she turned to face the guilty man with the stupid look on his face. "You know what, Ray," she said, flashing her teeth, "you didn't even have the decency to say you were sorry. Pssh . . . and believe me, you *are* sorry — a sorry excuse for a man.

Come to think of it, I'm sorry that I allowed you to rent space in my life for as long as I have."

"Yeah, whatever." Ray smirked in displeasure and disbelief that Janeen was standing up for herself.

"By the way," she huffed, tossing him a likewise smirk of her own, "you can take that trifling expression of yours with you when you pack up your things and find some other place to be sorry. That's right, Ray, I'm not asking you to leave. I'm mandating it. And, just in case your vocabulary can't grasp what that means, I'll make it plain. Get the hell out of my house!" With that, she'd said her piece knowing there was nothing left to say. The back door shook when she slammed it behind her.

Janeen settled into the driver's seat of the car with her dignity still intact. It may have been bruised but it certainly was not broken. While driving in to the office, all thoughts of Ray and his trifling ways were extinguished. Etta James breathed life into "At Last" with every sultry note. That transported Janeen to a better place mentally, though not having laid eyes on Rollin's fine exterior or relishing his charm for more than a week, Janeen had become weary of showing up at First World every morning. She pretended that she hadn't been affected by the fact that he had suddenly become tied up in all-day meetings and was too busy to return her calls.

Throughout the morning, nothing moved in her office. No quasi-important documents were reviewed, no daily reports were studied. Time, it seemed, even plotted against her and unconscionably stood still, so she took a notepad from her drawer, informed Val that she'd be unavailable for a while, then caught an elevator down to the basement. There she traveled along storage aisles while staring at hundreds of boxes of archived reports from executive board meetings.

She collected boxes dating back to the hiring of Edward Greathouse and Rick Wells, two of her contemporaries whom she'd suspected of skimming money from the company for quite some time. Hours of sifting through mountains of paper, which completely covered two large tables, helped Janeen see a pattern that both men utilized to hide their lies and greed. She took notes and listed the reports in question but there still wasn't enough evidence to hang the culprits. Everything she gathered was circumstantial. She needed a peek at their original expense ledgers to compare with the doctored reports, and unfortunately the ledgers happened to be locked in the crooks' respective offices. She was sure that neither of them would be willing to grant her access to them. She'd just have to bide her time and wait.

Val stared at her curiously when she returned to her office with a worn-out expression. "Hey, Janeen, you all right?"

"As all right as I'm going to be. Do me a favor and get these notes to Daniel Koster as soon as you can and tell him that we need to meet after he's had a chance to look them over." Her assistant noted Janeen's stern look and knew immediately that she meant business, so Val took the notebook, excused herself, and darted off to handle the task as directed.

Janeen paced the floors of her office pondering how serious her accusations were of two of her contemporaries. There would come a time to show Mr. Bragg just how valuable she would be as a senior manager, if for no other reason than to prove her prowess for sniffing out the company's sludge. She tried to push the thoughts of company corruption out of her head but she couldn't. She had to get them,

Greathouse and Wells, she'd decided, and with Daniel Koster's help she would.

She sought a mental break and perused her e-mail in-box to pass the time. There were several interoffice memos but not one message from Rollin as she'd hoped. Nothing was clear regarding his intentions concerning her. Unwittingly, the desire to be in his company had become an obsession for her. Many of her nights had been filled with speculation of where he was spending his evenings, wondering if someone special had captivated him as she imagined doing herself. When the reality of her dilemma set in, she realized she was caught up in a tidal wave of emotion, and there could be no more pretending. The woman was utterly, hopelessly, and indubitably falling in love with Rollin, and she had to come to grips with it.

Confronting her true feelings for another man was too much to bear, as she sat in her office. She had to get out of there before imploding and losing her wits. After pressing the button on the office phone to contact Val, Janeen stretched out her long fingers, looking her nails over for possible scuffs in the polish. "Yes, ladies, you could use some work," she said.

"Who are you talking to, Janeen?" Val asked over the phone.

"Oh, I didn't know you had picked up. I was just apologizing to my poor fingers. Been neglecting them something fierce. Hey, I just had a thought. What do you think about taking the rest of the day off to hit the spa, do a long lunch and catch up on some power shopping with the boss?"

"I don't know. The spa sounds cool, a long lunch is always my kind of party, but the shopping thing is way out of my league. I've been saving some money to get back into school, since you'll probably be leaving the company in a week or so and this girl needs to move right on along with her cheese. You know what I'm sayin'?"

Janeen was quiet for a hot second. Something was cooking inside that busy head of hers. "Val, don't worry about a thing. Get your purse, sign off of your computer, and forward your calls. I've got this covered. Give me five minutes."

One extremely compliant executive assistant took great pleasure in following those instructions to the letter. When Janeen emerged from her office, Val was standing patiently near her desk with purse in hand. "I's ready, Ms. Daisy," Val teased, in her best pre–politically correct minstrel dialect.

Janeen handed her an envelope with a personal check of $1,000 enclosed. "Consider this your summer bonus. Now let's hit the pavement before they make me lose my mind."

Val didn't think twice about accepting the summer bonus, although she had never heard of such a thing. She knew that Janeen had a big heart and after she opened the envelope, she was assured Janeen's personal bank account was just as large.

Their first stop was Magnolia's, a plush upscale nail salon and body spa on the north side of town, which served complimentary espressos and wine spritzers while their clients waited to be serviced. Val's eyes lit up when two very attractive young black women, wearing matching black body suits and nylon aprons, approached them upon entering the nicely decorated spa.

"Hello, Janeen," one of them saluted as the other offered her a cocktail.

"No, thank you, Naomi," Janeen refused, "it's a little early for me, but I would like herbal tea if you have some."

"And you, ma'am?" the other woman asked of Val.

Wasting no time in gladly accepting the drink offered to her boss, Val unleashed a grin that indicated she could really use one. "Oh, me? How kind of you. This will do nicely, thank you." She snatched the glass out of the woman's hand so fast that the unsuspecting salon worker nearly fell over trying to hold on to it. "Oooh! You okay, honey?" Val asked insincerely. "Good. Can you be a dear and get me another one of these when you get the chance. Toodles."

Janeen couldn't do anything but laugh as she winked at the attendants before they dashed off to prepare a private room for their favorite customer and her thirsty associate.

Val sipped her concoction and people-watched. She got an eyeful of the local celebrities rubbing elbows with one another. "Janeen, there's Shuna Jamison, the Channel Five anchor woman. I'm going over to get her autograph."

"Uh-uh, Val, don't." Janeen pointed at a sign over the door. It read NO AUTO-GRAPHS, PLEASE. AT MAGNOLIA'S, EVERYONE IS A STAR. "These people come here to get away from all that notoriety. This is the one place they can come when they want to feel normal, like every one else and —"

Before Janeen could complete her statement, the anchorwoman glanced their way and immediately began making her way over to them. "Heyyy, girl," Shuna hollered from across the room. "Janeen, you missed my birthday party last weekend. Everyone asked about you. I had to lie and say that you were ill and couldn't make it. Now tell me what's really going on. I needed my partner in crime."

Val was blown away. Hey, girl? Did Janeen have another life she didn't know about, Val wondered, as she excitedly watched their exchange while sipping away at her beverage until the straw sucked air. It made an annoying slurping noise at the bottom of her glass but Val could care less.

"Uh, excuse me, Shuna," Janeen said with a perky expression. "This is my friend Val. She wanted to meet you but I know the shop's policy on that."

The ebony-skinned cover girl of an anchorwoman flashed her bleached white teeth in Val's direction before extending her hand. "Val, any friend of Janeen's is a friend I need to have, too. Don't concern yourself with that sign or this ol' stick-in-the-mud. Janeen is always trying to observe protocol. I keep telling her to live life long *and wide*."

"Yeah, girl, that's what I keep telling her, too," Val advised, jokingly. "But she don't listen."

Before they could further the conversation, Naomi reappeared with two thick neatly folded white bathrobes and announced that their room was now available. Never before having the nerve nor the money to fall into such a cosmopolitan wellness center like Magnolia's, Val followed Janeen's lead.

They undressed in individual stalls that had mirrors on every wall that only lit up if the on button was touched because not everyone was ready for such glaring exposure with all the lights on.

Val called out softly, "Janeen, can you hear me?"

"Yeah, Val, you finding everything okay?"

"Uh-huh. I just wanted to say thank you for introducing me to Shuna Jamison and all. I mean, not as your assistant but as your friend."

"Outside that building, you *are* my friend, and a lot of times inside that building, too. Besides, Shuna and I go way back." Both women stepped out of the stalls simultaneously as Janeen continued her thought. "We were in college together but both of us have been too busy trying to make our mark on society to spend the kind of time it takes to be real close, like you and I are."

Hearing those words from Janeen was worth more gratification to Val than the one-thousand-dollar check, or almost. Neither of the women had ever given their friendship much thought before then. They both knew it existed and that had been good enough. But like all friendships, no one ever knows how deep the roots are, until someone comes along and tries to pull them up. Their friendship had yet to be tested.

With their heads wrapped in large white towels, Janeen and Val laid side by side on matching massage tables. The two blond female masseuses, who could have easily passed for Swedish Olympic weight lifters, completed their tasks. As they worked, they casually made humorous comments in their native European tongue about their clients, who were still relaxing on the tables. Janeen didn't like the idea of being the butt of anybody's jokes, in anybody's language; not when she was paying good money for their services.

"English! English!" she demanded, so loudly that even Val was made uncomfortable by it. "I told both of you about this before. If you want to continue doing business here, you'll only speak English in the presence of other English-speaking clients. I'm sick and tired of your thoughtlessness. Even if you weren't joking about us, it's not a good feeling to think that you might have been."

Janeen's hostility had built up over the years while visiting many Asian-operated nail salons, where the workers rarely spoke English except when they were asking for her money. One day she said No more, and refused to take it from anyone any longer, regardless of what country they came from.

"So sorry, ma'am," one of the women apologized, with her head down. "Please forgive us, it was very inconsiderate."

"*Da*, please to forgive," the other one said, likewise.

They immediately gathered their things and left the private room with their shame in tow. They also left with a new understanding and respect for black women.

"*Da*," Janeen repeated, in disgust. "*Da* just won't cut it."

Satisfied with the way Janeen handled the talented body crackers, Val was proud to have witnessed it firsthand. "Damn, Sistah Souljah. Remind me to stay on your good side. Humph, I'm glad you didn't speak their language or you might have really given them a piece of your mind."

"I knew what they said but I didn't want to take it to the next level and call them on it only to have them attempt to deny it. It was German and not even textbook either. I've heard kids begging in the streets of Berlin use better diction."

Now Val was almost sad, thinking of all the places her friend had visited and the many wondrous things she knew compared to her own infrequent travels outside U.S. borders. "So what were they joking about?" Val asked, not sure if she wanted to know the answer.

They were laughing at the way Val's behind jiggled during most of the massage but Janeen couldn't bring herself to say it. Instead she spared her friend's feelings.

"Nothing important enough to repeat. Forget about it."

Val may not have had the where-with-all to pick up on foreign dialect but she was more than street-wise enough to surmise that the joke was on her. Knowing that she could have stood to lose more than a few pounds, she figured the argument had something to do with her voluptuous behind but that was all right with her. Good help, which is what they were, is always hard to find anyway. What took the sting out of it was the way that her friend stood up for her and didn't think anything about doing it. That's how Janeen was every day of the week and Val could count on it like bill collectors calling her house for overdue credit card payments; nothing would ever change about that.

Naomi entered the room with worried eyes. "Is everything okay in here?"

"Just fine now," Janeen answered, wrapping herself in the luxurious robe.

" 'Cause both of them left here crying, speaking broken English and afraid of losing their jobs," added Naomi, seemingly overly concerned with Janeen's satisfaction.

"No, that won't be necessary. We just had to set 'em straight, huh, girlfriend?"

Instantly, Val perked up. "That's right, just an etiquette lesson is all. Some ho's ain't got no class."

"Ohhh-kay," Naomi responded. She was at a temporary loss for words, trying to get over the blatant contradiction in Val's awkward comment. "Glad . . . we could clear that up. Now, then, why don't you ladies get ready to enjoy your pretty feet and hands treatment?"

Naomi ran water into two five-gallon foot soakers and added cuticle softener, then left the room. After settling in to the deep cushioned chairs while their toes stretched enjoying the heated bubbles dancing around in the water, the ladies chatted about trivia until Val noticed Janeen had stopped talking altogether. "Hey," she said in a soothing tone. "What's got you looking like you just broke one of the heels on your favorite pair of shoes? Is it First World business?"

Janeen raised her head enough to show the troubles and uncertainty her worrisome expression couldn't hide. "Val, why did you and Terance call it quits?"

Caught off guard by the question, Val's forehead wrinkled awkwardly. She thought back to what had actually transpired and ultimately ended her marriage with her second husband.

"Where'd that come from? Whewww . . . Uh, Terance and I were good friends for a long time before we got something going. You know, I needed a certain type brotha and he wasn't even close. I wanted the degreed, corporate, dick-slinger type."

Janeen chuckled, "Aim high, girl. Humph, sounds good to me, especially that dick-slinger part."

"Well, I talked him into working harder and going to City College at night. It was so much fun helping him to study for his exams. It was almost as if I was in school with him somehow. But I didn't have the drive to do what I was asking of him."

Janeen nodded. "So far, sounds like a match made in heaven to me."

"Yeah, it was good, for a while at least." Val looked into the water, wiggled her toes and reflected back on the turning of the tide. "We got married right after he graduated because Terance wanted to wait so he could feel better about his situation. You know how some brothas get. They want to have the right job, an education, and a home before they feel ready to settle down. It sounds good but it doesn't always work out that way."

There was a light tap on the door. Naomi's assistant pushed a cart holding assorted gels, lotions, and cremes into the room. Janeen asked if she could come back in twenty minutes. The assistant happily obliged and as suddenly as she appeared, she vanished.

"Yeah, I had to learn the hard way," Val continued. "Sometimes you can push a man too far and he'll become another person on you altogether."

"How do you mean?"

"It didn't take long before he'd earned himself a promotion and adapted to the corporate structure. He started buying expensive suits when we could hardly make the new car payments, and to make matters worse, he joined a gym. He said it was necessary so he could start making the right connections. He made some connections all right. After he lost over forty pounds and his clothes started hanging right, he went and lost his mind. Suddenly our cute little starter home wasn't good enough, my cooking wasn't good enough, and I guess he came home one day and decided that I wasn't good enough anymore, neither."

"That's nonsense. I never knew he tripped on you like that. After all you helped him to become." Janeen shook her head while examining the remnants of a defeated friend's heartache. Love residue is what she called it when the fire from a tired affair burned down to nothing and all that remained was charred worthless crap to show for it.

"The hardest thing was missing the sex we used to have. I know that marriage is about a lot more, but without it, things started to fall apart. I mean, I could have dealt with a whole bunch of dirty boxers on the floor and breadcrumbs on the countertop if he was still hitting it right. Or better yet, if he was hitting it regularly."

"Whuuuut?" Janeen was astounded. She had never heard of a black man voluntarily shutting down the factory without having been forced to. "He was holding out on you, girl?"

"Holding out? Sheee-it, he was holding the dick hostage," Val confirmed with a riotous laugh. "He was too tired, too sleepy, too hungry, or too overworked. He would say, 'I'll give you some on Friday.' Then his butt would stay out all Friday night. And to think, I'm the one who taught his trifling tail how to use that big ol' brown thang in the first place. Before I knew it, some other chick was enjoying the fruits of my hard labor."

Although Val laughed at the misfortune she'd endured right along with Janeen, she was still sore about the life she could have had with a man she learned to love and groomed to become more than she bargained for.

Suddenly an impish grin perched on Val's lips. "He got what he deserved in the end, though."

"And what's that?"

"He started *dating* his young white assistant, if that's what you want to call it. She got pregnant and he was so proud. He wanted a quickie divorce, and said we grew apart. He was serious, too. Before the ink had dried good on our papers, they flew up to Las Vegas and got married right away. The whole thing was a mess. Her parents hated him, they said for ruining their daughter's life. It was ugly when the baby came and there wasn't one drop of Terance's blood in that child's entire body. The baby was white, girl! And so was the baby's daddy."

"No way!"

"Oh yeah. Terance was so hurt when he realized that his boss was also dipping his pen in the company's ink. The old man told the woman he was sterile, so the stupid chick put the baby on Terance. And there he was, a newlywed whose wife had a baby for another man. Ain't that some talk-show shit?"

"Sure is, Jerry Springer sweeps week. He can go on right after the man who married a goat."

Naomi heard the laughter emanating from the next room. She peeked her head in and shot a humorous pleading look at the ladies who couldn't control themselves. "Uh, ladies, could y'all keep it down to a light roar? We do have other guests."

"Please forgive us, Naomi," Janeen apologized, "we'll do better. Promise."

Both women playfully placed one hand over their mouths and the other up in the testifying position to signify Girl Scouts honor. Naomi played along. She pointed her finger at them and shook it like a salty troop leader, then she ducked out again.

"Oh . . . that's so triflin' of Terance. It served him right," Janeen said as she calmed down.

"I guess so, but in all honesty, I missed him until he tried to come crawling back after his Barbie doll's parents moved her out as soon as they learned what the real deal was. But it was too late then. There was nothing left. It's funny how shame can strip a man of all that makes him what he is. I thought about taking him back but I didn't want to end up like so many other sistahs I know in bad relationships. Unlike them, I'd rather *be* alone than wishing I was."

Suddenly quiet rolled into the small

room with them. Val wrinkled her nose at Janeen. "Why did the business with me and Terance come up anyway? You and Ray gonna finally call it quits?"

Janeen whipped her head around. There was something in the way Val said "finally" that didn't sit right with her, although Val had only moments before shared all of her dirty laundry. Perhaps Janeen was more of a boss than a friend when it really came down to it.

Janeen purposefully checked her attitude before the words could connect with it and reveal her true distaste. "What exactly do you mean by *'finally'*?"

Val was confused by the question. "Finally, I guess I figured you would have given up a long time ago."

Offended as well as concerned that someone outside her marriage was openly second-guessing it, Janeen leaned forward on the edge of her seat. Something inside forced her to consider how her relationship must have appeared to others. Her marriage was waning, true enough, but she didn't feel comfortable after hearing her subordinate calling her on it. She was almost too afraid to ask but she felt compelled to. "And what would make you think that?"

Val caught on that the topic was still too fresh to delve into any deeper. Her own marriage had ended two years ago and it was old news. Janeen's front-page story was still being written. The pain was definitely on the surface and the wounds had not yet begun to heal.

"Look, maybe this isn't the time to get into it." Val's tone was much stronger than it had been. She was not going to be taken lightly or forced into a discussion heading for the street. She knew all too well that women on the hot end of a friendly discussion gone bad couldn't control its pace or the damage it was sure to cause, especially when a man was involved. And Lord knows you can't tell a black woman *nothing* about her man, even if she's already seen the truth for herself.

Janeen fell into a daze as she relaxed into the oversized chair. A strange subdued expression displayed itself. Peace was restored. "Maybe now is the perfect time to talk about it, among friends."

She stretched out her hand toward Val. It was the best way she knew to say that she was sorry for the attitude, without really having to say it.

Val grasped her hand tightly and shook it. Val's kind and supportive words were barely audible but they were as clear as a bell. "I know," Val said softly. "Remember, I've been there too."

Nothing else was said about the recent husband troubles Janeen suffered through until they had finished lunch at the Blue Water Café. Val listened intently as her friendly boss shared some of the intimate details.

"When we met, Ray was as wild as Friday night. He taught me one hundred and one uses for *bobby-que* sauce. Uh-huh, one hundred and one. He was a lover man but I wasn't the only one he showed his little tricks to. I knew it, but I was young and dumb and couldn't see straight for pining over him." She neglected to share the fact that Ray had been a pimp in his younger days. He was forced to give up that occupation before Janeen would agree to marry him.

Val was surprised after hearing of his prowess in the sack. "Ooooh, Ray."

"Yeah, now he's too old to be pulling some of the same stunts that gave me second thoughts of marrying him. There's this other thing, too, but it's not that bad all the time. Enough of a head-ache, though, to make me tired of loving

241

him like I used to." Janeen considered revealing her demand that Ray move out of the house, but thought better of it. She hadn't grown used to the idea herself yet.

Rather abruptly, the waiter returned with Janeen's credit card receipt, thanked them, and disappeared. While Val was picking at her teeth and gathering her purse off the floor, concern forced her to cross the line. She hesitated while getting up from the table long enough to capture Janeen's full attention.

"Janeen, wait a minute. You said *it's* not that bad all the time. *What* isn't that bad all the time?"

"Oh, it's nothing. Just forget that I ever mentioned it."

"Okay, and I'm supposed to be stupid. You sound just like another woman that I used to know, a battered woman, Janeen. Has he ever hit you?"

Janeen seemed terrified that someone might know she had allowed Ray to get away with it and allowed him to stick around as if nothing happened. "Nahh-no," she stuttered. "It's nothing like that."

"I'll just say this and be done with it. My sister Marla let her husband knock her down one time too many and she never got up again. Listen to me, Janeen, even a broken clock is right twice a day, the rest of the time it's not worth keeping around."

# Chapter 14

# *Turn Tables*

The following workday, Val turned up her nose just before approaching the long hallway leading to Scarlett's desk and Rollin's offices. Her displeasure with Rollin's attractive administrative assistant was obvious. Each time Val stopped by Scarlett's desk to hand deliver agendas to GEMs (the name chosen for the group of executive managers) she had to promise herself to be nice. Val's initial meeting with Scarlett was destined to fail when she dropped in to introduce herself only to be blown off by the younger woman, who unmistakably had little respect for other women colleagues.

Scarlett did finally agree to attend the meetings but paid no attention to them. Instead, she flipped through the latest edition of *Oprah* magazine and circled the articles she planned to read when she would not be interrupted with what she considered trivial chitchat. That overt slap in the face didn't go unnoticed, nor was it appreciated by any of the thirteen members.

When Scarlett was nowhere to be seen, Val sighed in relief, figuring the young misfit had a change of heart and was sitting in the conference room upstairs already, eagerly awaiting the next GEMs meeting to begin. She figured wrong.

Hearing the second door to Rollin's adjoining office being opened from the inside, Val made ready for a possible confrontation. She never could have expected the next turn of events.

After making her way over to stand just on the other side of the second office door, Val flinched unavoidably when the mayor was the first person to leave the room. The award-winning smile that always accompanied him on television was absent. Instead, he glared at Val, neglected to speak, then quickly headed for the elevators with two bodyguard types in perfect step behind him, as if their hair was on fire. The door was left ajar just long enough for Val to get a glimpse inside. There were several suits, all of whom faced Rollin, who was turned toward a large bulletin board.

Immediately she recognized one of the men from his profile. She would have bet her salary that he was the same man who, then dressed in white overalls, had driven the wrecker truck the day Janeen's car had a flat tire. She wondered why he was dressed in an expensive suit now, meeting with the mayor and other important-looking men. Something was very strange about it . . . very strange.

A closer look at the bulletin board revealed what everyone's eyes were glued to. The large board was covered with blown-up photos. Val probably wouldn't have noticed them if she hadn't been drawn to her own picture among the collage of photos. The one she appeared in was taken outside Magnolia's just after she'd gotten out of the car with Janeen. Before she could ponder why someone would waste film by taking seemingly insignificant shots of her, someone pushed the door closed from the other side.

Too many questions flooded her mind to keep them sorted out. Although she was sure Rollin was handling business for the mortgage company and there had to be a simple explanation for the photographs, the most troubling question was why

Janeen happened to be in nearly all of the pictures on that board, except the ones with Ray in the company of some high-falutin' politician types and a very young lady, who at first glance appeared to be white.

All the possible scenarios to explain the mayor's presence and the tire changer businessman made her head hurt. And when it dawned on her that what she saw had to be surveillance photos of some kind, the realization made her shudder. To hell with the GEMs meeting, she decided. Val was a bundle of nerves.

She had a cigarette dangling from her full lips before she knew it. Her habit was begging to be fed as soon as the elevator doors opened on the garage level. *Ding,* the elevator bell sounded when she reached her destination. Giving less than a thought about city ordinances prohibiting lighting up cigarettes on elevators, a tremendous cloud of smoke emerged from the small elevator car before she could step out of it.

Pacing back and forth like a caged lioness, she tried to close her eyes and envision all of the pictures she got a look at before the closed door had shut her out. She remembered seeing Janeen on several of them. Sissy was photographed with some man she hadn't seen before, Ray with some white girl, she thought, and a lot of city hall types. Where Val personally fit in was as much a mystery as the role Rollin played. If he was there to spy on her boss, then why were all the other photos of people in Janeen's life taken? Too many questions and zero answers. Was Janeen into something big enough to involve the mayor? Not Janeen, not in a million years, she reasoned.

Trying to calm herself down, Val leaned against the brick wall nearest to the glass doors, outside the elevators. A thick stream of smoke blasted Mr. Salley in the face as he passed her by.

The elderly man was sweeping up cigarette butts and other loose pieces of trash, just as he had since Mr. Bragg opened the mortgage company in 1962. Thomas Salley held the longest tenure of any company employee. His loyalty allowed him the privilege to come and go throughout the building, as he pleased. His ability to go about, seen and not heard, made him nearly invisible, too. The fact that Val blew smoke in his face without realizing he was two feet in front of her sufficiently proved that point. Having been a fixture for so long, he often overheard things and made observations that no one gave him credit for.

After she apologized to the bent-over janitor, who should have long since been retired from his menial duties, Val pulled him aside for an impromptu interrogation.

"Heyyy, Mr. Salley," she said with a big smile. "You know, I've been meaning to talk to you for a while about some of the things that's been going on around here."

The old man hunched his shoulders and leaned his push broom against the wall to listen to the insistent woman's questions. "Oh yeah? What kinds of thangs?"

"You know, things that go on that ain't supposed to be noticed, things that don't add up."

Mr. Salley pushed the brand-new baseball cap back on his balding head far enough to reach the crown of it. "Hmmm," he moaned while scratching. "I can't see as to what you're getting at, but if you ask me some specificities, I'll sho' try to tell you what I know."

This might be harder than she thought. *Specificities?* "Okay. Take this, for instance. The other day when you were down here, and moments after Ms. Janeen and Mr. Hanes, that new handsome executive, left together, a white wrecker truck showed up to fix Ms. Janeen's tire. Didn't you think it was strange how fast they got here? I mean, Ms. Janeen and that Mr. Hanes weren't out of the garage good when the fix-it mobile rolled in."

Stroking his soft wrinkled chin, as if it helped him to recollect better, Mr. Salley shook his head. "Naw, can't say that I figured that to be odd. But what did strike me as kinda peculiar was the fact that the man didn't need neither jack nor tire iron to change the flat. Thangs gettin' to be too fast for me these days."

Val tried to make sense of his statement but failed. "What do you mean, Mr. Salley?" she asked finally.

"Well, I would say that had to be the only time I've seen a man, in all my years, fix a tire without having to change the flat one. He just looked it over and crawled underneath the car. Looked like he hooked something up to it, waited a little while, then drove away. It's like I said, things gettin' too fast for me these days. How'd they know the tire's really fixed if nobody takes the time to fix it?"

Since Val knew nothing about fixing flat tires, she could draw no conclusions from the old man's reasoning, that is, until he continued. "Ever since that Mr. Hanes showed up here four months ago, all sorts of thangs been happenin'."

She moved closer to the man to make sure she heard him correctly. "Mr. Salley, you must be mistaken. Mr. Hanes has only been employed by First World for the last month or so."

Too tired and too old to argue, Mr. Salley collected his push broom and dustpan from a resting position on the wall. "Well, my eyes might be old but they still good to me, my ears too. I can remember the day that Mr. Hanes had carpenters come in and knock a hole in the wall betwixt the two offices and put in a special door, so's he can hop between 'em when his big-time friends come callin'. I know for sho' that was four months ago, 'cause it was the day after my seventieth birthday."

Val considered the man's information. By the time another question came to mind, the old man had shuffled off and out of sight. He'd shared enough, then made himself scarce.

"Four months, not one," she repeated to herself over and over, "four months, not one." She found it difficult to wait for Janeen to get out of her board meeting to run all this by her. Val wondered how to tell someone that the man she'd fallen in love with seemed to be having her followed and photographed. *Very calmly . . . very calmly, that's how.*

Janeen peeked at her watch every time she thought the executive meeting was about to end. Two hours spent discussing projected earnings, disappointing production numbers, and lame excuses from incompetent fat-cat executives made for a nearly unbearable afternoon. The only other manager in addition to Janeen with their business in order was Daniel Koster. He was a likable man, a hard worker and a brilliant accountant. The highlight of each meeting for Janeen was his report detailing his department's successes. Janeen knew that his managerial skills and business savvy were both top-notch. Daniel was more than qualified to run the company if Mr. Bragg ever decided to step down. He was the best candidate but he would never get the chance. Too many overpaid gold-bricks stood in line ahead of him.

Edward Greathouse III was likely to receive the nod from the old man when the time came for a shift in leadership, although Janeen had suspicions that he was skimming money from the company via fraudulent expense accounts. It appeared that only a few thousand dollars per month were being embezzled, but if the white-collar thievery had gone on for at least fifteen years, that would turn out to be a sizable chunk of change. Janeen had stumbled on the supposed impropriety previously after she came across an error when reviewing one of his quarterly reports on a hunch. His reports always sounded too good to be true so she decided to research the accounts further. It irked her to keep silent, but until she had all her evidence, she'd have to wait to expose him.

Mr. Bragg was trusting to a fault and since the company was making more money than it ever had, he didn't audit any of his executives' accounts. Rick Wells was second in line for succession behind Greathouse. Rick was capable enough to manage a company the size of First World but one quick spot check into his shady reporting practices proved damaging as well. Janeen couldn't prove beyond a shadow of a doubt that Wells was padding his numbers to an illegal degree, but he'd probably caught on to Edward Greathouse's practices and decided to create a slush fund of his own.

If Janeen had anything to do with it, she'd nail them both and suggest Daniel Koster take over the helm, but it wasn't likely that she'd ever get the chance to use the dirt she had on them to benefit her worthy associate, since her time with the company was limited. She was on her way out, standing on principle, after being passed over for Rollin. Stricken with animosity, Janeen still felt drawn to Rollin and the mysterious way he disrupted her world while conveniently cementing himself in it.

The board meeting concluded eventually but the man Janeen dreamed of having as a more intimate part of her life neglected to show up and grace the room with his presence. Mr. Bragg didn't appear to be bothered by skipping over Rollin's property-recovery report but the old man did ask Janeen to hang around as the others filed out of the lavishly decorated conference room.

As instructed, Janeen gathered up the documents handed out during the meeting, then stood when the CEO approached her. "Mr. Bragg, you wanted to see me?" she asked, looking up from Greathouse's and Wells's doctored reports. She almost smiled, noticing that nothing had changed. They were both still taking money.

Mr. Bragg looked worried but tried hard to disguise his concern. "Janeen," he called out. "Janeen. How are you? I mean, how are things going?"

Knowing that he really wanted to know her thoughts on staying with the company, as her promise to stick around for the month was nearing expiration, Janeen answered kindly. "I'm doing as well as can be expected. Thanks for asking." Her voice was subdued but clear. "And you, Mr. Bragg, how are *you?*" This time her speech reeked of sarcasm.

"I've been better, that's for sure. I've been much better, thank you," he repeated himself, when it seemed he had difficulties finding additional words to say.

Feeling the awkwardness of the moment, Janeen helped him work through the rough spot he seemed to be stuck in. "Ohhh-kay," she offered, while making a move for the door. "I have things to do but I'll be moved out of my office by the end of business on Monday. Unless there is *something* you wanted to tell me." This was his chance to beg her to stay, despite the present uncomfortable situation he'd placed her in.

When her mentor's face drooped and his eyes declined to meet hers, she had her answer. What she didn't have was a place to go after Monday nor a definite career path.

Mr. Bragg had promised that things would be all right if she stuck it out. She'd held up her end of the deal but he was running out of time to make good on his. It was the first time in seven years she'd left him uncharacteristically speechless, apparently helpless, and unmistakably no longer in control of the situation at hand.

Janeen was now certain of two things: whatever back-room deals were being negotiated, they didn't include her, and they had to be much bigger than the honorable Jacobsen Bragg realized. It was getting clearer all the time that she was only days away from being out of a promising position and once again on her own in the business world.

# Chapter 15

# *Tangled Web*

Massaging her aching fingers, Val grimaced. Her writing hand began to cramp after scribbling two letter-sized pages of notes detailing her suspicions. Going over the strange coincidences, the conflicting reports of the dates of Rollin's employment, and all of those photographs, made her sick to think of what kind of trouble Janeen had gotten herself into. Val wished that she hadn't stepped into that office doorway thinking Scarlett was going to be the one to come out of it, because then she wouldn't have seen all of those troubling pictures. Everything else could have easily been explained away. But she had seen them. Now she was miserable and couldn't think straight from trying to make sense of it. She'd been rocking slowly back and forth at her desk for hours. The strain had grown more monstrous by the minute.

When the pressures from worrying about Janeen's woes became too overwhelming to sit on, Val sprang up from her desk. With both pages of notes clutched in her hands, she headed up the rows of cubicles for the ladies' room in hopes of finding solitude and maybe a place to hide with her convictions until Janeen returned. Each step she took pulled more energy from her anxiety-ridden body than she had to spare. Val would later swear that she could literally hear her troubled heart struggling to adequately pump blood.

On her way through the customer-service floor, her pulse raced faster and faster until she could no longer manage to put one foot in front of the other. Feeling faint and sinking slowly down to her knees, Val instinctively placed her left hand firmly over her heart in what felt like an attempt to muffle it and keep it quiet. Although she was surrounded by a battalion of workstation cubicles, no one seemed to notice her plight until she was nearly unconscious and sprawled out on the floor.

Eventually screams of "Help her!" mingled with shouts of "Call nine-one-one!"

filled the spacious service center. Panicked men and women circled about, milling over Val's still body with their terrified expressions of sorrow until additional co-workers, with the presence of mind to assist a woman in distress, arrived.

As the light faded from Val's fluttering eyes, the last thing she remembered seeing was Scarlett kneeling over her, firmly holding her hands. Val's frightened eyes closed with Scarlett repeating, "Just relax . . ." until Val could hear her no more.

Meanwhile Janeen waited patiently for the elevator to take her back to the eighth floor, to the comfortable refuge of her office. She had no idea of the drama going on just nine stories below. And since taking the stairs was out of the question, she simply had to wait it out.

"There must be something wrong with them," Rollin whispered, standing extremely closely behind her. "I had to take the stairs up two flights to get here."

Recognizing whose strong sultry voice that was, Janeen closed her eyes and relished the heated breath that had just tickled the back of her neck. She paused before turning to see his face, the face she'd been dying to see again. Him. Rollin.

She wanted to tell him how much his coming into her world forced her to re-evaluate her marriage and how the thought of being with him made her heart cry out. She hoped he would understand how important it was for her to *need* someone at that point in her life. Her fondness for Rollin had evolved well beyond merely talking, just as Janeen had feared. The drama that usually comes along for the ride was on the way.

Not sure where or how to start the conversation, Janeen merely sought to communicate what she felt. "If I turn around, do you promise to stay awhile?" She secretly crossed her fingers while awaiting his response.

"You sure you want that?" he asked in a low mellow voice.

Janeen almost melted on the spot. *Of course he's joking with me,* she thought. *But it feels so good that I'll go along with the game.* "Ye-yes, I'm sure," she answered softly. "I would like that very much." Now she was afraid to turn and face him. She was letting him inside her heart, openly and without apprehension. That's where she needed him. That's where he belonged.

"Hmmm. I don't know about this,"

Rollin replied. "I could get used to something that isn't mine. Then what?"

Suddenly she turned on her heels. "How many times does a girl have to say she's sure?"

"Okay. Tell you what, if you're still sure a week from now I could be prepared to stay a lifetime."

Janeen wanted to fall into his arms right then and there and give him some of what she hoped he wanted too but one thought ran a marathon through her brain in just seconds. *A lifetime! When did he decide this?* She stared deeply into his eyes trying to detect if he was serious. The sincerity flashing back at her was startling. His eyes convinced her that it hadn't been a game at all. Actually, he appeared more positive than she was that whatever had developed between them was real.

She moistened her lips with the tip of her tongue. "A lifetime, huh? Is that a threat?"

"Better than that, it's a promise."

The problem was, which Rollin Hanes was making the promise? Even if he didn't really mean all those words, they were strong enough to reach down into the essence of the woman she knew herself to be and pierce her soul. Rollin was that smooth, with a subtle arrogance that proved he didn't have to try to be. It's the way he was put together. He had it like that and she wanted every bit of it for herself.

With no reason now to bridle her emotions, and feeling the same yearning she had when she initially met Rollin returning, Janeen leaned in close enough to feel his chest against hers. *Ding.* The elevator suddenly arrived. As the doors opened, she took a slow, cautious step away from him so it would appear to be something other than what it was — a heated moment that was extinguished too soon.

"That should do it. I hope that nothing else gets in your eye," she said, loud enough to throw someone off, if they happened to catch a glimpse of the truth.

"Oh yeah, thanks a lot," Rollin said, playing along while rubbing his eye feverishly. "I'm glad you came along when you did, Janeen. I would have been lost without you."

Scarlett watched the ridiculous attempt at trickery. She shot both of them a sideways smirk. "Uh . . . excuse me, folks, but *Mrs.* Gilliam, everyone's looking for you. You should know that your assistant is on her way to the hospital. They're putting her in the ambulance now."

"No! Valorie?" Janeen was mortified at hearing the news.

"If you hurry, you can catch it. That's why the elevators were shut down," Scarlett explained.

Before Janeen could ask what happened, she was on her way down to the lobby floor. When Rollin attempted to follow her, his trusty assistant signaled to him not to with a convincing raised brow.

Janeen didn't wait around to question it. As she hurried through the lobby, she heard the sirens blaring before she reached the front doors. Unfortunately, the ambulance had already made the last turn out of the parking lot and hurried into traffic.

On the seventeenth floor, Rollin stood in his office reading the notes that Scarlett had pried out of Val's clutched fists. His beautiful assistant looked on with her lips drawn tightly and arms folded likewise against her chest as he read the last line of the two-page handwritten document. It stated in bold letters: *"Must Warn Janeen."*

Simultaneously both of them turned their attention toward the posted collection of photos and accompanying organizational charts naming all of the major players in their investigation. At the top of the chart was an old police mug shot of Janeen's husband, Ray. On the next level down were eleven-by-thirteen blowups of Janeen's and Sissy's driver license photos, placed side by side, which indicated they were also viewed as potential witnesses or worse. Beneath theirs was a row of unlikely suspects, all nicely dressed and each one a member of the Dallas city council.

J. W. Blake's photo was the first one. No matter how much makeup was applied to his sunken cheeks, the fact that he was a longtime heroin user was still apparent. Placed next to his picture was Luther Griffith's. Luther was a devout Baptist, but only on Sundays. On other days of the week, he was your typical run-of-the-mill kiddy-porn-distributing pedophile.

To the left of Griffith's was the council's only African-American member, Bernard Mecheaux, who had been a successful assemblyman for the state before winning his local post. Unfortunately for him, he had not been as successful hiding his profound sexual preference for white women and white men too. His deep-seated case of self-hatred knew no bounds. Any race other than his own suited him just fine in the bedroom.

Kenneth Riley's photo always warranted a second look. He was a handsome golden-haired former designer-underwear model who was rumored to have slept his way aboard the council. It was also rumored that his campaign fund, among other things, was well endowed.

Next was Brewster Wilks, who held the lengthiest tenure of any councilman. He'd been a part of the city's government for twelve years and didn't plan on being removed anytime soon. Wilks's reputation for digging up scandalous scuttlebutt on his challengers has sent chills down the spines of most would-be contenders. The pool of rivals with guts enough to oppose him was extremely shallow.

Now, Jonica Wannamaker, she was a real piece of work. After marrying a wealthy oilman forty-five years her senior, she cleverly took over his business, sold it off piece by piece, then divorced him when the money was all hers. It was done so ingeniously that it had to be her plan from the outset. Although she was the sole woman among the group, her fangs were certainly the sharpest and her venom the most lethal.

The remaining collection of city councilmen stiffs was not connected to the scheme so little attention was wasted on them. Nonetheless, each one of them was a part of the investigation.

# Chapter 16

# *Life Left to Live*

Sissy was anchored on Ms. Mary Lee Jackson's front porch, beaming with excitement although her arm was in a brand-new white cast. She brushed at her mauve outfit to remove a speck of lint from the jacket as if she were gearing up for a business interview rather than a casual meeting with a new friend. After taking a deep breath, she knocked solidly on the wood plank next to the door, just as she had the first time she visited. Almost instantly, a voice from the inside shouted with exuberance.

"Okayyy . . . keep your pants on, I'm coming."

Sissy laughed to herself at Ms. Mary Lee's words.

Just as she'd done before, the woman on

the other side of the door had the toughest time getting it open. Sissy nudged it from the outside with her shoulder until together they successfully forced it open.

"Hey, young lady," the woman hailed with a friendly wave.

"Wow, Ms. May'Lee, I didn't think we were going to be able to do it this time."

Glowing like a beauty pageant finalist, Sissy reached out to hug the frail older woman as if she were a bouquet of long-stemmed red roses. "How are you this afternoon, ma'am?"

"Looking at the way you've got all that plaster mounted around your arm, I'm doing a might better than you," was the woman's spicy reply.

Ms. Mary Lee was dressed in her usual long faded pink terry-cloth bathrobe and matching slippers. However, something was different this time. She was all grins. Sissy picked up on it right away.

"What's going on, Ms. May'Lee? I see all of your teeth today."

"Child, come on in and rest yourself."

As they moved into the living room and made themselves comfortable, Sissy's oldest new acquaintance smiled even more brightly than before. She was excited to share some good news. "Well, I had a lot of time to think since you came by here. I thought a lot about your pappy, too, and that beautiful wife of his, Magnolia. Mmm-mmm-mmm, they did so much for me and other peoples who didn't have no way to get around, and your mama made quilts and wonderful-smelling candles, long before you could buy 'em at the supermarket. Since I feel like meeting your folks was a blessing from God, then you just might be one, too, and I don't want to refuse no blessings from Him, so I decided on something."

"Yeah, so?" Sissy squealed, with excitement. She was on the edge of her seat, honestly having been concerned with the dangerous living conditions of a poorly maintained wood-frame house more than sixty years old.

Ms. Mary Lee rocked her head back and forth in a slow methodical motion, as though she had to reassure herself one last time. "Even though I thought I'd never leave this house unless they was coming for me with a pine box, I think maybe it's time to see how much living I can get done outside these here four walls."

Sissy extended her legs straight out and kicked them up and down. "Ohh, I'm so happy you made that decision. I've been just sick worrying about you here. Now, I know you love this house and I don't blame you. I'm sure you've had so many good times in it."

Nodding again with a waning smile, Ms. Mary Lee put it to her in terms she could understand. "This is a good house and it's been good to me. It is old, though, and seen a lot of years, just like I have. Some good and some bad, too, but like a true friend it's always been here and never once let me down." She looked around the small living area, filled with exquisite trinkets and keepsakes, while trying to hold her composure. "Shoot, this old house is just too old to be putting up with the likes of me. I'm always meddling with it, up and down all times of the night. It won't never get no rest as long as I'm here stirring about. Anything that gives all the years of faithful service like this house has given me, deserves to be retired."

Sissy ran her fingertips along the rims of her eyes, wiping away her happiness, which continued to flow despite her efforts to stifle it. "I'm sorry, but I'm just sooo glad for you."

After handing several sheets of tissue to the young woman the matriarch quipped,

"What you cryin' fo'? I'm the one gotta leave my home."

When Sissy peered up and met with Ms. Mary Lee's effervescent grin, she knew that in spite of Ray, by convincing the old lady to move out she had done the right thing.

"Okay, okay. Let me get a hold of myself." Sissy fanned her eyes with a nearby church fan, which displayed a picture of JFK on one side and a funeral home advertisement on the other. "Okay, when do you want to get out and look for your next home? I'm sure that I could come back with my sisters this weekend and we could set up a date to look all day long if you like." Sissy thought she'd keep the birthday celebration a secret until she could return with the rest of the planning committee members.

"I was thinking more like getting out today," the lady of the house answered. Her voice was filled with certainty. "It hasn't been so hot lately and I sho' could use some fresh air."

As soon as Sissy consented to spending the entire afternoon with a woman whom she'd come to respect and admire, the wonderful older woman stood up and drew back the bathrobe, then shrugged it off her shoulders like a Spanish matador tossing his cape aside. Underneath the faded pink shroud was a remarkably fitted black satin pantsuit, much sexier than the one Sissy had on.

Just about speechless, "Ooooh, look at you," was all that Sissy could utter, while watching the tremendous spectacle of life left to live standing in her presence.

"Well, I told you I wanted to get some fresh air and I figured you'd be coming by again sooner or later and I wanted to be ready when you did."

Sissy was still in awe. The smaller woman sauntered into the bedroom before returning with a new pair of black patent leather flats to complement her stylish suit and a shoe box filled with hair-care odds and ends. She calmly handed the shoebox to Sissy as if she'd done it a million times.

"Now, I hope we have time to do something to my hair, 'cause I like to look good when I step out on the town."

For the next half hour or so, Sissy stood behind the woman greasing her scalp while doing the best she could at creating an acceptable hairdo. With long thick strands of hair dangling between her fingers, Sissy couldn't help but travel back in time to her childhood. She remembered how her sisters were responsible for repeating the same act of wrangling with hot combs, curling irons, grease and more grease, although she was always too young then to handle the friendly end of a searing hot pressing comb herself.

After discussions about what made life worth living, Sissy was happy to share some of her own dreams of being a big-time lawyer and owning a business or two of her own, as her sisters did. Ms. Mary Lee assured Sissy that her father would have liked that a lot, then added, "He always talked about black people owning their own businesses, especially women, 'cause then they wouldn't have to bend for no man, no matter what color he was. I'll never forget it. He said that's the only way a black woman can truly be free in this country."

Pride filled Julian Hampton's youngest daughter. Each time Sissy visited with Ms. Mary Lee, she gained a better appreciation for both her parents and the strength of black women in general. Each time she spoke with the elderly woman, growth and self-awareness seemed to follow her home; that part of their relationship she hoped would never change.

Ms. Mary Lee wanted to ride in Sissy's

Mercedes coupé with the windows down so the calm summer winds could brush softly against her face. "Janeese, let these windahs down a bit so's the wind can say hello proper. You know I've been cooped up for a while."

Whatever the woman asked for she received, including an old-fashioned hamburger, a red cream soda, and vanilla ice cream. After that, visiting the best retirement villages in the city was just icing on the cake. The women laughed and enjoyed each other's company. Shady Acres, the most expensive and luxurious retirement complex in the state, was a unanimous selection for both of them. Although the accommodations were superb and reasonable for the money, the total-care assisted-living monthly price tag was nothing to sneer at. Regardless of how much it may have set her back financially, Sissy was willing to do whatever it took to make it happen. As far as she was concerned, their relationship had become priceless. Smiling to herself, she realized that the trap Ray used to snare her had introduced a valued person into her life. If Ms. Jackson did decide to move, her quality of life would assuredly improve substantially, with better living conditions and a myriad of activities to enjoy with other seniors.

While leaving the retirement village, Sissy received the best squeeze around her waist that she could ever remember getting. Ms. Mary Lee looked up at her with twinkling eyes. Somberly, she said, "Thank you, Janeese. Now I'm *sure* you're an angel sent to me from heaven to remind me that even though I might be old as dirt, ain't nobody tossin' none of it over me yet."

Upon returning to the little house that Sissy's newly adopted grandmother had called home for more than six decades, neither woman wanted to say good-bye. Helping Ms. Mary Lee out of the car and up to the front door felt good but Sissy couldn't wait to visit her regularly in a much nicer and safer place like Shady Acres. There she would have full-time attendants and be catered to. At Shady Acres she would be treated like a queen for the rest of her life.

Before they parted ways, Sissy was assured she would receive the signed deed after Ms. Mary Lee's hundredth birthday in two weeks. She couldn't wait to deliver the news to Ray and tell him that she had finished doing his dirty work, once and for all.

# Chapter 17

# *Cheaters in a Liar's Game*

Outside Val's hospital room at Medical City, Dr. Pam Jeffrey explained to Janeen that her friend had ultimately succumbed to an anxiety attack, not a heart attack. After further explanation that Val's weight problem and heavy smoking did increase the chances for heart disease and other related ailments if she didn't get her present condition under control, Janeen felt responsible somehow for her friend's health and welfare.

Janeen sat at Val's bedside from three until seven o'clock, when visiting hours were over. During that time, thinking about Rollin and the words he'd said to her regarding a lifetime of promises and so forth just didn't seem fair. How could she think of herself at a time like this, she thought, dealing with a dear friend who was unconscious and sedated, and Lord knows what had pushed her over the edge.

Janeen meditated before whispering a nearly silent prayer for a woman who had been much more than an executive assistant for seven years and at times had even been closer to her than either of her own sisters.

Once she concluded her sacred thoughts, faint words emanated from Val's still body. Leaning in closer, Janeen asked her to repeat what she'd said, thinking she must have been asking for water or something to eat.

Val raised her head a little. "I said, amen to that, sistah."

When Janeen realized her prayers had been overheard by someone other than the Creator, she cringed. "Oh . . . You shouldn't be trying to talk, and anyway, you weren't supposed to be listening." She began to fuss over Val the same way she looked after Sissy's needs.

Val attempted to sit up. "Well, at least ain't nothing wrong with my ears."

"Uh-uh, lay down, Val," Janeen demanded. "You get your rest, then we can talk about how to make sure this never happens to you again."

The evening nurse checked the room and reminded the visitor that her time was up. Val rudely waved the nurse off as if she were a bothersome fly. "We'll be finished in a minute. G'on now!" The nurse gladly left the room. She'd have all night to get even with her grumpy patient.

"Janeen, press that button on the side there," Val commanded. "Raise this bed up for me, then get my purse."

Janeen did what she was told but felt as if she was the one taking orders for a change. "You sure are pushy for a person who had to be brought down here in a meat wagon," she joked, to lighten the mood.

Passing up on an opportunity to share in the laughter, Val frowned instead. "Janeen, what I need to tell you is serious and it's not pretty."

"All right. I'll be serious but there isn't a purse in the room. Maybe they didn't put any personal items in the ambulance with you."

Val's eyes squinted into thin slits of suspicion. "By the way, who told you what happened to me?"

"Who? Uh, Scarlett Dun'ker, Rollin's assistant told me. Why?"

"Scarlett, huh? I should have guessed it.

I'd like to dunk-her head underwater and see how long she can relax." Val was still angry about what had happened and since her notes seemed to vanish into thin air, she figured that Scarlett had taken them from her while she was fainting. "Scarlett," Val repeated. "I knew I couldn't trust her. What kind of parents name their daughter after a scandalous white chick from Atlanta anyway?"

Janeen agreed. "You know, that's exactly what I thought, too."

While looking seriously at her curious girlfriend, Val started off slowly and filled her in on everything that happened earlier that day. The mayor, seeing the double-dealing tire changer again, all the photos, Rollin's apparent leadership of whatever was going on, and her vanishing notes were all clearly delineated.

Janeen sat quietly the entire time. Although none of it made any sense whatsoever, she continued to listen attentively until Rollin's name came up. From that point going forward, Janeen refused to listen at all. If she had, she would have had to lend credence to the unbelievable accusations. Caught up in the life she envisioned having with him, she couldn't help but retaliate by talking louder than Val. Before she knew what happened, the hospital room exploded with both women shouting at one another like archenemies until Janeen became too upset to continue the conversation, which had spun completely out of control.

Val wanted to help as much as she could, but her boss's reluctance to share or further discuss the news she'd just been saddled with brought the matter to a screeching halt. Janeen didn't know what to make of what sounded to be unsubstantiated rantings of a heavily medicated woman. Before the conflict between trusting Val or believing that *her* Rollin could actually be facilitating some elaborate sting to take her down could get any more out of hand, the evening nurse reappeared, having heard raised voices. She quickly introduced Janeen to the hallway.

"I'm in this damned hospital for trying to look after you!" Val screamed, after Janeen had been ushered out of the room.

Janeen wanted to turn around, go back, and make amends for the fight and try to get some further explanation, perhaps some proof of all the allegations. Val was not known to be a liar, but none of that espionage speculation added up. Janeen considered what Val said about Rollin and all that she'd seen, which suggested Sissy, Ray, Janeen herself, and a whole assortment of wealthy, influential people were in on something that warranted an investigative task force of some kind. That was ridiculous, Janeen decided finally. Plain nonsense.

Long straight lines painted in thick strokes of vibrant primary colors on the sparkling white floor marked differing paths leading to various departments of the hospital. Following the red line led to the cardiology wing. Blue led the way to neurology, and yellow went all the way to the obstetrics ward. Janeen took the path of least resistance and watched the yellow strip in front of her until she was staring through the plexiglass into the faces of an entire room of newborn baby boys and girls. Most of the tiny miracles were resting soundly, no doubt sleeping off the effects of the traumatic experience of being born, while others clamored loudly for attention, warmth, food, and more than likely dry diapers.

Janeen pressed her open hand against the window to say hello to a baby girl who reminded her of Sissy as an infant. "Hi, cutie. You are a special one. Yes, you are;

yes, you are. You'll grow up to be beautiful like your mama, and be as smart as a whip like me. Yes, you will, because you're special. Yes, you are, yes, you are." She continued making faces at the child for several minutes.

Eventually, the child's father appeared at the window to request the baby be taken to the mother's room. Janeen waved good-bye to the baby girl being pushed away in a transparent plastic tub of a crib on wheels.

Further along the window, two pairs of eyes had observed the heartwarming occasion. Bertha and Lila Crowe, Janeen's distant cousins who were also from Newberry, Louisiana, had witnessed Janeen making goo-goo eyes through the glass. Bertha's and Lila's fathers were second cousins and Janeen's father was also related to them somehow. Janeen remembered that it seemed most people from Newberry were related in some way or another.

Looking on from a few yards away, Bertha called out to her, "Hey, Janeen."

Surprised to see her relatives, who were also book club cohorts, Janeen waved her hand as she started out their way.

"Hey, Bert, Lila," she greeted. Her eyes asked the question she didn't dare voice aloud. *Why were a couple of lesbian cousins hanging around a hospital maternity ward?*

Lila, the better looking of the two women, pushed her fingers through her short bleached platinum-colored hair. A closer look revealed that Lila's eyes were dim. It seemed that she'd been crying recently.

"Hi, Janeen. I never expected to see you here. Believe me, I understand," Lila said solemnly, while looking up at Bertha. "You could come here every day and it wouldn't get any easier."

"No," Bertha added, as an exclamation point, "it sure wouldn't."

Simultaneously, both women peered through the window again to catch another glimpse at the new babies being brought into the nursery.

When it was obvious that the couple seemed to openly confront the pain they obviously endured from regular visits to the ward, Janeen had her answer. Bert and Lila wanted a baby of their own to raise together and because it was well-known that Janeen was incapable of conception, the ladies assumed that she suffered from the same distress they did.

Consequently Janeen felt sorry for them. Too sorry to correct their false assumptions and explain that she was there merely to visit a sick friend and was only stopping by the nursery to peek at the little people on her way out.

"Well, I need to be moving on," Janeen said. "Try not to think about it too much, girls."

Bertha's eyes grew dim as well. "Yeah, thanks, cuz'. You neither."

Bertha's role as the protector and the stronger shoulder of the pair kicked in automatically. Janeen had previously shrugged off the rumors associated with her distant cousins for years, but there was no doubting them now as she turned away to follow the thick painted line toward the exit.

"Ohhh . . . Hey, Janeen!" Lila yelled, headed in her direction. "I almost forgot — the novel, *The Women of Newberry*. Have you . . . had a chance to read it yet?"

Janeen had to think for a moment. "Novel?"

Lila's expression was purposely blank.

When Janeen remembered, she felt out of sorts. "That's right. The book club meeting is this Saturday night. So many things have happened in my little corner of the world that it slipped my mind."

Instantly Lila's unbridled concerns were revealed. "My goodness, Janeen . . . you haven't read it, have you?"

"Shoot, I've been so distracted lately, nothing in my life is on schedule anymore." Noting how wide Lila's eyes were then, she became a little concerned herself. "Hey, it's just a book. I'll get to it sooner or later. Kyla will just have to forgive me this time."

Lila took a closer step to her. "You have no idea what the book is about, then? Humph, we need to talk."

In the back room of Luther Griffith's modeling studio, which also doubled for a late-night booty-movie film set, Kenneth Riley and other councilmen listened intently as Jonica Wannamaker made her point so plainly that everyone knew where she stood on the matter at hand.

J. W. Blake continued to peek at his diamond-encrusted Rolex watch, a gift from Ray, every five minutes or so like a dope addict who was behind schedule for his next fix.

Sweat beaded on the forehead of the Honorable Brewster Wilks as Jonica ranted on about being behind schedule and how one property could cost them the whole deal. Councilman Wilks had more at stake than the others, much more. And he was scared.

"Listen closely because I'm only going to say this once!" Jonica exclaimed loudly to gain the undivided attention of the other five city officials present. "We all know how much this deal means to the city and to us. It has taken a lot of time and money to even get a seat at the table, and I don't know about the rest of you but I'm not close to conceding defeat. I not only came to play, I expect to win the damned game."

Each person who sat in that back room knew exactly what she meant. They had all contributed too much time and effort to allow their plans to falter. They were in far too deep to turn back no matter how thick the plot had become. The deal she referred to was a complicated scheme to win the bid for future Olympic Games to take place in Dallas.

About six months previously, a number of councilmen from the city began receiving letters asking if they were serious enough about winning the Olympic bid to stake some of their own money along with funds from investors and be willing to take on a partner with very private interests who could hand them a can't-lose proposal guaranteeing the bid from the Olympic Committee. Some of the council members balked at the proposal because they had the good sense to know that can't-lose proposals often cost everyone involved more than they were willing to pay, financially and otherwise. Another red flag that couldn't be overlooked was the criminal record of the front man responsible for brokering the deal, Ray Gilliam.

Despite becoming a successful construction company owner, Ray was tired of working to make a living, a legit living, anyway. Years of walking the almost straight and narrow had finally gotten the best of him. His past criminal activities included a prostitution ring, drug dealing, petty larceny, and a few fraudulent credit-card capers. But he'd promised Janeen he'd go straight fifteen years ago. Ray had kept his nose clean for the most part. At least he hadn't gotten caught up in anything he could have gone down for, that is, until he came up with this plan.

Through a fact-finding mission and a fifty-thousand-dollar cashier's check drawn on a company that for all intents and purposes didn't actually exist, Ray had discovered what objections the Olympic Committee had to naming Dallas a front runner. He'd learned during a late-night poker game that the city lacked the necessary hotel capacity near the site where most of the summer sporting events were to be held, just north of downtown. To the immediate south of that were the Trinity River; to the west was overdeveloped industrial communities. The east was occupied by an older, largely Hispanic community who wouldn't think of selling out. If hotels were going to be built and space allocated for them, southeast Dallas, widely known as the historical South Dallas District, had to be the place. Ray used that information for a chance at setting himself up for early retirement. If it all worked out as planned, he could say good-bye to small-time hustles and get his turn to play with the big boys. It was too bad that Ray didn't know that sitting at the high-rollers' table had a very high cost associated with it.

Ray's past forced him to stay in the shadows as best he could on this one. Of course, the council members who were involved knew him well, but no one publicized their affiliation. To make sure that none of the politicians backed out on him after all the cards were dealt, Ray began feeding some of their habits. He arranged illegal specialty gifts for them under the table and also helped to facilitate adulterous affairs, and videotaped as many of the rendezvous as possible.

Unbeknownst to Sissy, she orchestrated two of the major aspects of the scheme. Initially she was paid handsomely to convince homeowners in the community to sell their properties, later to be developed for megahotels only minutes from downtown. Her second duty was to supply the councilmen with safe female companionship when they needed a diversion from suburbia. Sissy didn't have an inkling of how dangerous it was associating with powerful people who, when backed into a corner, just might bite back.

Six months of planning, loads of preparation, and ample unrest kept the group of conspirators closely bound together, but the end was near and it all seemed to be going under.

Ray arrived twenty minutes late for the meeting at Luther Griffith's which he'd actually set up. Jonica was livid. Wilks continually bit his nails, thinking about a bastard child who would never get a chance to be born. Bernard Mecheaux, the sole black man on the council, couldn't keep his eyes off Kenny Riley's tight slacks as the pretty boy paced the floor nervously.

"I never signed on to get sent to prison," Riley informed everyone. "You know what kind of hell I would expect to go through if I went to jail?" Of course everyone knew. Blond pretty-boy ex-underwear models would be considered a rare delicacy at an overcrowded Texas penitentiary. "Well, I like my freedom, dammit!" Riley added like a frightened rabbit.

Luther stood up and placed both hands in his trouser pockets. "Let's all just calm down. We knew the job was dangerous when we took it and each of us still agreed to invest, so let's just get on with it."

"Now, that's what I like to hear," Ray said, clapping his hands slowly and puffing on a Cuban cigar. "People, we've come too far to drop the ball now. Only one property stands in the way of all our dreams coming true, just one, and I have someone on it as we speak. I'll have the deed to that property signed by the weekend, I assure you."

Jonica leaned over to place her hands on the thick conference table. "You'd better deliver by this Saturday, Gilliam! A very important plane is due to arrive here on Monday from Germany and if we can't deliver what we said we can, we may as well shoot ourselves in the head for all the good the past six months has cost us."

Feeling the youthful gutter rage he'd tried so hard to shake as an adult, Ray bit his lip and remained silent. He would force himself to do whatever it took to close the last deal or risk looking like an ordinary street punk. It was his brainchild from the outset. He'd put his own money into the kitty and still held the last cards to play. Ray knew what it might take to come away from this with the whole pot, and he wouldn't hesitate to get his own hands dirty if that would cinch it.

# Chapter 18

# Backward and Forward

Sissy couldn't wait to hit Ray with the latest update on the last piece of property. Wanting badly to let go of the life she found herself leading after agreeing to work for him, she felt good about giving it all up and moving forward. The money was nice but she couldn't remember her last night of peaceful sleep.

On her way to Ray's construction company, Sissy felt something tugging at her heartstrings. That something was J. R. Cooper and the fact that she hadn't seen him in a few days. It gave her an excuse to drop by Kelvin's automotive shop. While driving down the interstate, she was troubled about Cooper's and her lengthy separation and why it occurred in the first place.

When she arrived, Kelvin was feverishly twisting at something underneath the hood of a shiny red Lexus 400. Not wanting to bother the busy mechanic, she passed him by and made a quick tour around his place of business. The twins, Orang'jello and Le'monjello, worked just as diligently on their own projects. With all the cars in need of repair stacked deep in the service bay, Sissy had to watch her step and weave in and out between the oil pit and one large obstructive machine after another. Ultimately she had to approach Kelvin for assistance.

"Hey, Kelvin. I didn't want to bother you but I . . . wasn't able to find Cooper around. Is he on break?"

Kelvin could smell her perfume wafting through the dense aroma of oil and sweat but he didn't look up to acknowledge her, nor did he stop wrestling with what had him so frustrated.

"Naw, ain't seen him for a couple of days," he answered eventually. "That's why we have so many cars piled up and my phones ringing off the hook with people wanting to know why their cars ain't ready yet."

*A couple of days, huh,* Sissy thought to herself. That was interesting. One of the last things she heard him say was how much he liked working at the shop and being around people who cared about doing quality work. "He didn't say anything else, just left?"

Kelvin rose from his tiresome task and stretched his back with a long yawn. "Yep, just like that, and I thought he was going to make something of his self too. He was the best mechanic I ever had. He could do twice the work of those two." He pointed at the twins. "Ain't no use in complaining 'bout it, I guess. But if you see him, I'd appreciate it if you told him that he'll always have a job here waiting on him." He paused to get another look at all the cars yet to be diagnosed and serviced. "Uh-huh, we sho' miss those magic hands of his."

Kelvin assumed it was common knowledge that Cooper had served time in prison, although he had neglected to check the yes box next to felony conviction on his job application. After being around enough ex-cons to spot one at first glance, Kelvin was sure of it but didn't press the issue. Most of them wanted to forget the crimes and the time they'd done, and not one of them was in a hurry to discuss either.

"All right, then," she said in a tone devoid of hope. "I'll tell him if I see him first. And I'm asking you to do the same if he comes back here. I miss those magic hands, too."

Dejected, she climbed back into her car and redirected her attention toward the original plan, handling some old business and seeing Ray about quitting the mortgage game.

Before Sissy returned to the interstate, she made a quick stop by the bank to hit her checking account for a thousand-dollar withdrawal. Sitting outside the branch in the busy parking lot, she received a phone call from one of her working girls. Although she had mixed emotions about taking the call, there was no time like the present to begin dissolving troublesome relationships. She found herself despising the situation she'd cherished just a few days before.

"Hey, GiGi. I always know it's you. Caller ID, remember? A girl shouldn't leave home without it."

Sissy slid five one-hundred-dollar bills into a bank envelope and wrote the letters *G. G.* on it before shuddering at the idea of making one last transaction in the flesh trade, then sealed it.

The caller seemed hesitant. "Well, look,

I know I'm supposed to do this thing tonight, but I'm not so sure it's a good idea now."

"I was wanting to talk to you and the rest of the girls about that. After today, I'm getting out of the hustle for good so you'll have to make arrangements on your own after this one. I'll see if I can round everyone else up this evening and discuss outstanding matters." There was a long pause on the other end. "GiGi, you there?"

"Yeah, I'm here."

Woman's intuition warned Sissy that something wasn't quite right with her associate. "Hey, what's wrong?" she asked. "I'll take care of the tab for tonight's date you've already booked. Actually, I've just made your bank and I'll take care of the back end myself, so don't worry about it." Sissy typically paid her call girls up front and collected the money from their dates afterward.

"No, that's not it at all. Doesn't it even bother you that Morgan's missing?"

"Missing!" Sissy shouted into the receiver. "What do you mean? I just talked to her the other night."

"It's been all over the news. The girls on campus are freaking out because her apartment was ransacked and things were smashed but the police said there was no sign of forced entry. That probably means —"

"I know what that means," Sissy interrupted. "I know." No sign of forced entry usually meant that the victim knew her assailant and probably willingly let him in.

"I'm really scared and so is everyone else," GiGi advised. "We all know Mo's situation with the baby."

Sissy thought back to the last conversation she'd had with Morgan about the pregnancy and then remembered the threatening phone call from someone claiming to be the councilman's wife. Suddenly she felt ill. "GiGi, I have to go. Tell the girls to sit tight and I'll contact them later. If anyone comes around asking questions, don't say a word about our business. You got that?"

"Yeah, yeah, don't worry. I won't tell."

Sissy disconnected the call. If only she could have just as easily disconnected the mess she was surely in now, and the onslaught of bad things likely to follow Morgan's disappearance. There was nowhere for Sissy to turn. It was inconceivable to share this jam with Janeen, even though she always knew how to fix things. Sissy didn't want the person she respected most to know what she was involved in. If Joyce found out, she would only condemn Sissy's actions, she would also pray for her lost soul until the cows came home. As far as Sissy was concerned, that was a fate worse than death. J. R. Cooper was missing in action too, although she wasn't quite sure of how he could have helped her deal with this. Regardless, she still hoped he would turn up soon, if not for a strong shoulder to lean on perhaps for a warm body to lie next to and blur reality just long enough to forget about her dismal circumstances for a while.

While still idling outside the bank, Sissy noticed a thin young man approach the ATM from an old rusted Chevrolet Impala. There was something familiar about his movements, although the back view was the only one she had. Without giving it another thought, she grabbed her purse, climbed out of her car and made her way over to the man, who was staring down at his ATM receipt.

"Hey, don't I know you?" she asked, loudly enough to cause the man to flinch.

He stepped back while bracing himself for a would-be attacker. "Naw, you don't know me 'cause I haven't ever seen you before."

She was insistent. "Yes, I'm sure I've seen you some where."

Just then, Sissy heard someone yelling "Dahhh-dee" from the man's relic of an automobile.

After approaching the man's car with caution, Sissy leaned in closer to the back window to get a better look inside. There was the same little girl with the swollen head whom she'd laughed at while smoking pot.

When she recognized the little girl and her father from the park, the shame she'd felt afterward made a guest appearance. Sissy's eyes grew big with surprise. The little girl remembered her, too, and quickly placed both hands over her eyes and screamed hysterically.

"Please don't scream," Sissy whispered. "I'm sorry. I didn't mean to hurt your feelings. Please don't scream. I was just having an awful day and made a terrible mistake. Please, please stop screaming. I'm so sorry."

The thin man pulled Sissy away from the car by her arm. "What in the hell are you doing to her?" he yelled. Neglecting to give Sissy the chance to explain, he opened the back door and began to console the little one. "It's all right, Maggi. It's going to be all right now."

Sissy didn't move an inch, she couldn't move. She stood there mortified, staring at the two of them as the girl whined loudly. The man looked at Sissy with the strangest eyes she'd ever seen but she still didn't move.

The man became more enraged, finding it hard to believe that she was still awkwardly gawking at them. "What are you doing here? Haven't you done enough already?"

Maggi, the little girl, whispered something into his ear. He took a second look at Sissy then at her shiny car. "I'll be damned. It is you." The look he shot her cut like a knife but his next comment almost ripped the heart out of her body. "My daughter has trouble sleeping now, thanks to you. She cried for days after you made her ashamed to be different. I prayed we'd never see your face again."

Finally Sissy attempted to defend herself. "Sir, I'm sorry for what happened at the park that afternoon, and not a day goes by that I don't regret it. I messed up and I'm sorry about that, you have to believe me." Sissy took a deep breath to calm down. "I've prayed over it also and if you don't mind telling little Maggi that, too, I would appreciate it. Please try and help her to understand that sometimes grown-ups make dumb mistakes."

When it seemed that all the appropriate words had been said, she turned to walk away while the angry man listened closely to something else little Maggi wanted him to hear.

"Hey, lady! Wait up!" he shouted in her direction before hurrying over to her car with a fast gait. "Wait a second," he insisted, "Maggi said to tell you how pretty you are and that she forgives you. She made me come over here and say it before you drove off."

The man stood firm with his hand stuck out. Not quite sure what to make of it, Sissy also extended her hand to shake his.

"Hi, I'm Byron Reed. Maggi's my daughter." The little girl was waving enthusiastically, as if nothing had ever happened. Sissy was amazed at how children forgive so easily and always look to see the best in others. If only adults could follow their examples.

"And I'm Janeese Hampton, but my friends call me Sissy," she said happily. "Looks like Maggi's smarter than the both of us."

"Yeah, looks that way." Byron's face softened into a kind expression. "Sorry to yell at you and all, Janeese, but I just got laid off my job and Maggi hadn't been feeling well. It was just bad timing."

Sissy looked at the ATM and remembered that Byron didn't get any money from it. He simply took his card back, then stared hopelessly at the receipt. Suddenly she nodded her head knowingly. "Hey, uh . . . Byron, I really don't want to get in your business, but do you mind if I ask you what kind of work you did before you lost your job?"

"I worked at Sampson Trucking for two years, servicing diesel engines. You know, automotive stuff. Why do you ask? Can you hook a brotha up with a job or something?"

"Actually I think I might be able to do a little sum'm-sum'm." She reached into her purse, pulled out a business card, and scribbled some numbers on the back of it, then handed it over to him. "Here, take this and call Kelvin Clark. He owns the place."

Byron's face lit up like a neon sign. "Are you serious? This is for real?"

"Yes. I just stopped by there and he's swamped. I'm sure he could use someone with experience." She noticed that the light in Byron's face began to fade. "Is there something wrong?" she asked.

Byron was embarrassed and more than reluctant to speak up. "Pssh, it's nothing. I should probably give this card back."

"Why would you want to go and do something like that? I mean, you do need to work, right?"

Taking a long look at her expensive car, Byron shook his head in despair. "You wouldn't understand. With a car like that, I'm sure you have the lifestyle to go along with it. You couldn't know troubles like mine."

She smiled sadly at his comment, knowing that things were rarely what they seemed. "You can never judge a book by its cover. And *we* definitely don't need to be doing that to each other. So out with it."

He flicked the card off his thumb a few times to work up the courage to say it. "It's just that . . . well, it's the reason I was laid off. After two years of not missing a day, the man found out I had some trouble with the law before I was hired and he said he couldn't use me no more."

Knowing what she did about Kelvin's desire to help men with undesirable histories, Sissy insisted he still make the call. "Don't you worry about that, just be honest and I'll take care of the rest."

Byron said thank you and immediately headed back to his car but Sissy knew there was another thing she could help the young man's family with.

"Oh, Byron. I have something else for you. Here, take this, too." She handed him the envelope she had previously prepared for GiGi. "It's five hundred dollars," she informed him. "I know how times can get rough between jobs but I wouldn't want to offend you."

In total awe, Byron held the envelope up to get a good look at it. "Oh, offend me. O-ffend me!" Sissy couldn't help but laugh. "Wait a minute," he said, looking suspiciously at the envelope. "What do I have to do for this? I can't accept no handout."

"It's not a handout," she corrected him, "it's a hand up. Just pay it forward when you get the chance to help someone else."

"I'll do that. Thanks, Sissy."

As Byron and Maggi drove away, Sissy played the scene over and over in her head, backward and forward as many times as she could to impress it on her memory. Like an eight-millimeter film shot in slow motion, the rusting frame of that old Impala coughing up smoke from its tailpipe and Maggi jutting her head out of the back window, smiling and waving so long to her new acquaintance. That scene rolled continually until Sissy was back on the interstate and on to her next destination.

# Chapter 19

# *Casting the First Stone*

As Sissy strutted up to the front door of the Rayjan Construction Company, she held her head high and swore it would be the last time she'd set foot inside that building again.

When she stepped over the threshold, chills ran down her back although the temperature had teetered over a hundred degrees for more than two months. On the inside, administrative assistants answered phone calls, pushed paper, and went on about their day-to-day activities. Sissy spoke casually to the women who did bother to look up, and some of them responded. Her carte blanche around the place didn't sit well with most of the staff, who had to answer for their whereabouts when out of the office. Jealous co-workers used to upset Sissy until she realized it was their problem, not hers. Besides, the fewer people who spoke to her meant the fewer people she had to speak to in return. All in all it was a win-win situation, no wasted words.

Upon approaching Ray's office, imagining him in the arms of the other woman gave her pause before entering again without notice. "Hey, Rosie, is he in?" Sissy asked, addressing Ray's most senior secretary.

"Yep, been in all day with it closed."

Rosie was at least twice Sissy's age but wore more makeup than a teenager with her first Fashion Fair cosmetics starter kit.

"Has anyone been in to see him?" Sissy inquired, staring at his closed office door.

"Uh-uhhhhh, you got the wrong number, sistah. Information is four-one-one, and I ain't never worked at the phone company."

Sissy knew she was pushing it with that last question. Rosie didn't tell anybody's business unless there was something to trade for it, no matter whose sister-in-law Sissy happened to be.

Like clockwork, Sissy pulled her wallet out and pretended to be looking for something when purposely allowing a crisp c-note to fall to the floor on the side of the secretary's desk.

"Oooh, look at that, Rosie. You must have dropped that hundred-dollar bill."

The woman, with well-documented situational ethics, looked at her motivation waiting to be hoisted up off the floor. "Yeah, I thought I had but I wanted to make sure."

"You'd better pick up your money, girl-friend, before someone else claims it." That was Sissy's way of letting Rosie know the offer would be made to another employee if she didn't act fast.

Slowly and methodically the older woman politely lifted her large handbag from its resting place underneath her desk and calmly set it atop the motivator before rudely sucking her teeth. "It ain't going nowhere," she replied with a knowing smirk. "Now, what was it you asked me?"

"I wanted to know if anyone's been in to see him today."

"Oh. Not today," Rosie answered flatly. "Been refusing every call and visitor. Said he won't see nor talk to nobody until he heard from you. Go 'head on in, he's waiting and ain't too happy 'bout it, nei-ther."

Sissy felt like the ultimate chump. One

hundred dollars lighter in the pocket and what did she get for it, probably just another makeup kit for Rosie. Good thing she planned on never again setting eyes on his office crew.

She left Rosie's desk with a bad taste in her mouth and a strong desire to handle her business and get the heck out of there. Before she could reach his double doors, Rosie had already buzzed her boss to inform him of his visitor's arrival.

Once he received the call, Ray stood up from his documents and made his way across his sizable office. He took a labored breath, poised himself, then whipped the door open to invite her in. His stoic expression met her head-on.

Quite surprised, Sissy hesitated before accepting his invitation to enter. "Now, that's service," she joked, to lighten things up. However, Ray was not in a laughing mood. His day had been a long one and a pressing chain of events held him in a snare.

Disappointed in the way his plans had developed, Ray found it difficult to look at her. "Come on in, Sissy, and sit your ass down," was his best greeting.

She took him up on his offer but held reservations, looking at him curiously after he slammed the door hard behind her. She was confused, but too angry now to be scared of him.

"Now, then," he continued, "where in the hell have you been? I been paging you all day."

"Excuse me!" she spat back. By this time, she wasn't in a pleasant mood either. Ray's foul disposition was highly contagious "You'd better check who you're talking to. My name ain't Rosie." Her bad attitude mixed with his aptitude for being bad was a recipe for disaster.

Ray clenched his teeth together to make his point. "You heard me, and I know who I'm talking to. Where in the hell have you been?"

"I've been busy. I just dropped by as a courtesy to tie up some loose ends anyway. I forgot to inform you, I quit yesterday."

Ray's chest heaved with disgust. "Don't play with me, bitch! After all this time, I know you got something for me."

" 'Bitch'?" Sissy repeated while chuckling. "Oh, I see. You must have me confused with Tee-nah."

She couldn't believe he had the audacity to disrespect her as if she was nobody. He'd never before used that tone or language in her presence. Obviously over a barrel himself, he lacked the wherewithal to handle a delicate situation like this one with sufficient diplomacy.

"Look, I don't give a damn about you quittin'. Should have fired your sorry ass a long time ago. Where is the Jackson deed, Sissy?"

She sat in the chair steaming, looking away from him and contemplating her next course of action. "Okayyy, I'm *sorry*, huh?" she asked venomously as she rose from her chair to leave. "Screw this, I'm out!"

As she took her second step toward the door, Ray sprinted to cut her off. Grabbing her by the shoulders, he slammed her against the doors with enough force to rattle both of them. He was enraged. Saliva gathered at the corners of his mouth. "You out cho' mind? You think you're running this and can up and leave when you want to? Don't mess around and get yourself hurt."

He glared down on her, his face a few inches away from hers. His expression was desperate but Sissy didn't waver. The only thing moving was her shaking head pivoting slowly from side to side. She still tried hard to believe what was happening. Her sister's husband must have gone over the edge and snapped. Being the stand-up woman she was raised to be, there was nothing left to do but put up her dukes and fight back. And that's just what she did.

"You must be crazy to think I'm gonna let you manhandle me like this," Sissy contested loudly. "And don't you threaten me, Ray. There's nothing you can do to me that I haven't already done to myself."

Sissy was filled with remorse because of the dirty work she'd agreed to carry out. His threats paled by comparison to what was eating her up inside. It was easy to see that his approach was leading him down the wrong road. And for the first time since she arrived, Ray actually took her feelings into consideration.

Backing away to collect himself, he lowered his head. "Sissy, I didn't mean to come at you like that, but I have some heavy people expecting big thangs from me and I promised I would come through for 'em. Come on, let's go right over there and get the deed executed."

Sissy awkwardly peeled herself away from the doors. She planned on sticking around just long enough to tell him where he could stick that lame apology. "Uh-uh, I wouldn't go across the street with you after what you've pulled on me. But I will say what I came to say." She didn't blink once while Ray waited to hear the details that had him on pins and needles all day. "Ms. Jackson has agreed to sign the deed over after her hundredth birthday, which is next week on the second."

Desperate, he took another daring step in her direction. "Sissy, that's not good enough! I need the papers signed by this weekend or else."

"Or else what, Ray, or else what?" she asked. "You going to send someone after me? Tell 'em to get in line. It's over, Ray, over! I've washed my hands of it. That little wood house might not even stand for another week anyway. I told the woman it wasn't safe but she has her heart set on waiting till her birthday. So, you'll just have to wait."

Ray couldn't afford to wait, he'd have to try another avenue to get what he wanted. Sissy was of no further use to him in the grand scheme of things. He smiled peculiarly as he opened the doors to see her out. Several of his staffers pretended not to have been hanging on every word of the heated conversation they overheard.

Sissy stepped through the doorway as he held it open for her. "Oh, and another thing . . . *negguh*," she exclaimed louder than necessary, in order to be heard clearly by all interested parties. "You ever come at me like that again, it'll be the worst decision you'll ever make. Have a bad day."

Ray thought about chasing her down to do her bodily harm for getting in the last word and embarrassing him in front of his staff but thought the better of it. Let Sissy think she got away with something, he resolved. He was sure that another time would present itself to rectify the situation. Until then, he'd bide his time and simmer from the other side of the doors he'd slammed behind her.

As Sissy regained a reasonable facsimile of the power strut she initially walked into Rayjan Construction with, Rosie stood to salute her. "Humph, it's about time somebody *went there*, honey." She gladly handed back the crisp c-note that she'd received from Sissy earlier. "Here. And I owe you another one. That was worth two hundred if it was worth a dime."

Every woman who previously neglected to greet Sissy gave her respectful nods and said their good-byes on her way out. And come what may, she was done with it.

With bruised shoulders and fresh imprints of the door on her back to show for her opposition, she basked in the thought that at least she wouldn't be going back there. She was willing to die first.

# Chapter 20

# In Plain View

Janeen crossed her legs and leaned back in her high-backed office chair as far as she could. The letter she'd received from the city lay on the edge of her desk with trifold creases still evident although she attempted for several minutes to press them out with her thumbs. It was a notice, a final notice in fact, informing the owner that the home at 2053 Peabody Street was due to be demolished according to the safe-housing mandates of the city of Dallas. Since Janeen kept up the taxes on the house, she was due proper notification of destruction.

She took in the tone of finality of this notice compared to all the others she had received before it. This one had each of the housing code numbers that were in violation, the official dates of notification, and a large red rubber stamp making it all legal. Janeen knew the codes, laws, and measures the city had to take in preparing to level someone's home. She'd had ample time to stop the process if she had wanted to but there was no logical reason to save an old wood-frame house that had become a haven for crack heads and tired prostitutes too weary to go home after a long night of cheap tricks.

It finally dawned on her that this was it. Sometime during the next day, no later than 5:00 p.m., the first house in the city her family had called home would cease to exist. She felt compelled to visit the site where her young life had turned around and thumbed its nose at the past. She had to see it one more time.

"Excuse me, I hope I'm not bothering you," a strong but soothing voice called out from her doorway.

Janeen recognized Rollin's voice before she looked up from her daze. He was immaculately dressed as usual, draped in a charcoal gray four-button suit.

"Hello, stranger," she said back to him.

"Stranger, huh? I'll bet I'm no more stranger than you are."

"Well, you going to stand out there

making jokes or are you coming in?"

On cue, Rollin placed both hands in his trouser pockets before strolling in to take the seat on the opposite side of her desk. His eyes wandered over the notice on the desk where she'd left it.

"Looks serious," he suggested. "The letter, I mean."

"Official, too," she added, exhaling deeply in a prelude to a myriad of questions she needed to get off her chest.

She liked everything she knew about him, but finally realizing just how little she actually did know, a disturbed expression replaced her smile.

He must have read her thoughts. "Something on your mind I could help you with?" Rollin's tone was reassuring.

"Funny you should mention it, there are some things about *you* that seem more mysterious all the time."

Rollin had been expecting this. "Janeen, I know we talked about getting to know each other better and I have been out of pocket. It's after five, what do you say to us getting out of here and grabbing dinner somewhere quiet and easy?"

She gave his proposal serious thought before answering him. "That . . . sounds tempting but I'm afraid I'll have to take a rain check. Too many errands to run tonight, including hopefully saying good-bye to an old friend."

Rollin conceded. "Okay, I get the message. The offer's still on the table, though. Consider it a standing invitation."

When he started to get up from the chair, Janeen decided to ride out his unexpected visit a little more. "Hold on, now, you don't have to rush off just because a girl has other things to do than spend a cozy evening with you." Saying those words as if the two of them had a long-standing physical relationship, Janeen stretched her neck to see if the man was married. It hadn't occurred once to look before then. She'd just assumed he was single after allowing herself to fantasize, as soon as she first laid eyes on him.

Rollin was still concentrating on Janeen's last statement when he noticed her looking at his left hand curiously. "What?" he asked, holding his hand up to help facilitate her search for signs of holy matrimony. "Oh, you're looking for a wedding band. No, I'm not married."

"Ever have been?"

Her second round of questioning suggested an interrogation instead of friendly chatter, and Rollin picked up on it right away.

"Are you sure we couldn't do this over dinner? I'm a big man and missing lunch wasn't one of the smartest things I've done today."

Janeen picked up a small brass clock about the size of a bar of soap from her credenza. "No, I can only spare a few more minutes, then I have to be leaving whether I want to or not. Too many things on my plate and they're all time sensitive. Anyway, I'd better tell you before you hear it from someone else. Monday will be my last day here. I've made a deal with Mr. Bragg and it fell through, so . . ."

"There must be something that can be done," Rollin insisted. "I just feel you're making a big mistake. Let me talk to him, who knows, maybe I'll be the one leaving on Monday." That was a nice gesture to in-sinuate that Mr. Bragg would have chosen Janeen over him if the offer were made to him.

"I wouldn't count on it," she advised him. "Seven years at this company and all I really have to show for it is this five-year-anniversary catalogue clock and too many disappointed hopes to go with it."

"My showing up here didn't help your

situation at all, I'm sure."

"If you honestly want to know the truth of the matter, ever since I knew you existed, my world has treated me like a red-headed stepchild."

Caught by surprise, Rollin leaned back as if he were dodging her words. "I'm sure I deserve *some* of that, although life has been quite kind to me since the first time you crossed my path in New York."

Now Janeen was surprised. When she was formally introduced to him by Val, Rollin didn't show one inkling that he remembered her or knew a thing about her, other than what her résumé and company profile provided.

"New York?" she repeated. Was this the venue for true confessions? "Maybe you had better explain, because you acted as if I didn't exist, all those days at that boring conference."

"Let me . . . let me come clean. You're right, I noticed you during registration, checking into the hotel, and every day of the conference too. But come on, Janeen, you're beautiful, you're smart, and *you're married*. When I arrived here, I just wanted to fit in. A brotha didn't want to make any waves that didn't have to be made. Not one ripple."

"See, that's what I'm having a problem with, you coming here and taking my job, and being perfectly charming, mind you, while doing it. Too perfect, maybe. I want to know who you are, Rollin, I mean really. Where did you come from, how did you get here, and why does my assistant think you're investigating me?"

He knew Janeen had become suspicious but wasn't sure when she'd come right out and ask. Either way, he was forced to skirt the issue as best he could without outright lying to her. Obviously prepared for her line of inquiry, the comfortable sitting position with his muscular legs crossed hadn't changed after hearing the pointed questions.

"I'll try to answer them in the order you asked, if that's all right with you." Janeen nodded that it was, and he continued. "You know my name. I'm one of two children from hardworking parents. I grew up in Baltimore, moved to D.C. and attended Howard University to study accounting among other things, and later, a master's program at Yale. I travel a lot, always have. Born to roam, I guess."

Janeen was drawn in by his frankness. "Roam or run from?"

"I'm not sure I'd say run from, it's more

like run toward. The family used to be close but my folks died young and all I wanted to do was conquer the world after that."

Of course Janeen could relate because her father had been killed in an automobile accident by a drunk driver over two decades ago. The witnesses reported that a clean-cut man in a business suit rammed him at top speed, then stumbled up to the crash site to view the wreckage before making his way back to the car to flee the scene. Janeen's mother lived another ten years after that but breast cancer took her slowly. Oddly enough, Janeen felt even closer to Rollin after learning more about his story.

"So you've been bouncing around from town to town since?"

"Yeah, pretty much. It's been more like bouncing from assignment to assignment. Which brings me to your other question." Rollin paused to collect himself because he didn't like to lie. "I'm not quite sure why your assistant Valorie thinks I'm anything more than I am. Now, I can tell you that the mayor is involved with Mr. Bragg in a huge business venture, but that's all I can say for now." The way he explained it made Val's accusations all seem plausible, and the rest could be chalked up to Val's suspicious nature and far too many hours devoted to TV police dramas. "Any information past that is top secret," he advised her jokingly. "I could tell you more but I'd have to kill you."

Smiling sheepishly, Janeen said the first thing that came to her mind. "Oh yeah? Kill me with what, I wonder."

Rollin's face brightened. Her comment rubbed him the right way. However, he'd have to wait until the dust settled to see where they stood then. "Janeen, I know you need to be heading out but I have one question for you." He licked his lips to moisten them. "On that last day in New York, at the lecture hall, I couldn't stand seeing you without getting a little bit closer so I sat down right next to you but before I could tell you my name and invite you for coffee afterwards, you bolted out of there like you owed me money or something. Why?"

Janeen stood up and casually collected her purse among other items she'd need during the evening. She paused, wanting to watch him while he looked her over until she finally got around to a reply. "Rollin, I may as well just lay it on the line. You were the nicest piece of fantasy I've seen in quite a long time, and I needed that. Style and substance incredibly and profoundly meshed together to create one fine specimen of a natural black man." She eyed him blushing back at her. "It was simply too much for me to handle. Good night, Rollin."

After massaging his ego and saying her piece, she sauntered past him. He was still blushing, speechless, and basking in her beauty. "Don't forget to lock up, now," he heard her say on her way out.

An hour later, Janeen sat on her bed thinking about her recent conversation with Rollin while changing into comfortable jeans and sneakers, which she liked to call traveling clothes. He more than occupied her mind as she drove to the bookstore. Although she was not at all satisfied with the extent of the information she acquired about his personal life, at least she had something to go on. Surely Val didn't imagine the things she saw in his office, and he did admit to the mayor's involvement in some business venture with First World Mortgage. Like the 2000 presidential election, it was still too close to call, so she'd have to wait until all the ballots were in to declare whether this one was a winner or not.

The country's bestselling novel, *The Women of Newberry*, had been all the buzz on TV and radio talk shows across the nation since reaching number one on *Blackboard*, *Mosaic*, *Essence* magazine and *The New York Times* book lists. There was even talk about Oprah's production company, Harpo Films, making preparations to option the award-winning book. Janeen wasn't surprised that it was sold out at the local bookstore. Fortunately, her niece, Kyla, had previously made arrangements to have enough books for her club put aside until after Eric Bynote, the author, made a special visit to their tenth-anniversary meeting.

The store manager checked Janeen's name off the list and returned the remaining books to their hiding place. "Ma'am, novels like this don't come along every year," she commented when ringing up the sale. "And to think, all of those horrible goings-on in one little town in Louisiana. Mmm-mmm-mmm. You'll love it. I read it straight through. Couldn't put it down."

After purchasing the book, Janeen crossed that off her to-do list. Next she headed over to Kelvin's automotive shop. Cars were aligned neatly the way she had seen before at commercial dealerships, making it easier to get through rows of them.

"How's my favorite in-law?" Kelvin yelled from his service area as she stepped into his small, dusty building. He double-checked the recent improvement in service and nodded his fat head while grinning the whole time. Byron Reed had made the call, and his skill and dependable presence were both greatly appreciated in Cooper's absence.

"Good evening, Kelvin. How are Kyla and the kids?"

"Oh, they're doing just fine. Ain't y'all s'posed to be having somebody famous coming to sit in on the book meeting this Saturday? Ky's been running herself ragged trying to get everything ready for it. Say, that book's s'posed to be really something."

Janeen held reservations about reading the novel; she was forewarned that the issues would be more painful to her than to the average woman. "Well, I'm sure it will be talked about for years, if what I've heard about the story is true."

"Uh-uh, I know you didn't pick this particular time to stop by and chew the fat about some book, so what can I do for you?"

"Kelvin, normally I wouldn't ask this kind of favor but I really do need your help."

She asked him what the likelihood was that a roadside tire service would fix a flat without removing the bad tire. Kelvin explained that although tires were not his forte he'd have one of the twins take a look at it but there would be only two reasons to repair a flat tire without changing it. "If a nail was still sticking in it or if it was to patch a slow leak to be fixed later. A roadside tire service wouldn't consider doing it that way, though. Their job mostly consists of changing flat tires using spares."

While Orang'jello attended to her car, Janeen took a seat inside after deciding to make good use of downtime. She called Joyce, who should have been wrapping up her day at the child-care center.

"Joyce's Joy, this is Joyce," her sister announced before screaming, "Constance, please get Hakim off of that table!"

"Joyce, it's Janeen. Catch you at a bad time?" Janeen pressed the phone firmly against her ear, then plugged the other one with her finger to block out any extraneous noise. "I'm sorry, Joyce, but it sounds like a war zone over there."

"Who is this? Hold on. Let me get the door closed." Joyce pointed instructions to her assistant through a glassed-in office and waved at several parents arriving to take their bundles of energy home after a long day's work. "Okay, now go ahead."

"Joyce, this is Janeen. I wanted to ask you if Jonathan Holloway has been by yet to pick up Trip?"

Flipping through the sign-in book, Joyce ran her finger down the page for three-year-olds. She began to read the names. "Hall, Halsworth, Hill, Holloway. Here it is. Nope. He's still here. No one's signed him out yet. Why?"

"Good, I need you to do something for me. I'm on my way over to the old house to say so long because of the demolition tomorrow."

"They should've knocked it down years ago," Joyce remarked, bitterly. "It's a shame how crackheads misuse everything standing still in the old neighborhood. Nothing's safe anymore."

"So I guess that rules out you coming along, and I can't catch up with Sissy. I guess I'll be all right by myself. But please tell Jonathan to call me. Give him my cell number if you don't mind." Suddenly Joyce was quiet. "Joyce, you still there?"

"Yeah, I'm here." The powerful, commanding voice she answered the phone with and used to yell orders around the day-care center had diminished to a low, insecure mumble. " 'Neen? Have you read the book yet?"

Asking what book would have been ridiculous, so Janeen didn't bother. "No, I haven't," she answered rather defensively, "but Lila called herself preparing me for some of the things discussed in it. She said, just in case some of them applied to me. I just picked up the book a minute ago."

"Well, you go on and do what you gotta do. I'll tell Jonathan what you said when he gets here." After another long pause, Joyce pushed harder to reconcile some of the family's old business before it became new business for the entire country. "By the way, Janeen, don't you think we need to sit down with Sissy and discuss some things before . . . Well, just read the book and you'll see what I mean."

Janeen agreed, and put the cell phone back in her purse. Kelvin stood in the work area trying to get her attention by waving his arms. She noticed him eventually and headed his way but all of her thoughts were now on the book and what it might say about how things used to be back in Newberry. Whatever it was, the novel had hundreds of book clubs from coast to coast up in arms.

Kelvin leaned up against Janeen's car as if he had a bit of news of his own to share and regretted it because it might not be received too well. Janeen stood there puzzled, waiting for him to say something. When he wouldn't, she did.

"Uh-oh, Kelvin, you don't look so good. What's going on?"

"We didn't find no holes in your tire but we did find this hooked up underneath the car." Kelvin held an object in his hand about the size of a soda can. It was a mechanical device of some sort with a digital readout and other numbers around its circumference. Janeen was clueless. What was this instrument resembling something straight out of a science-fiction movie, and what did it have to do with her? "Janeen, I know it ain't none of my business, and you know you're my favorite, right?"

"Yeah, so?"

"You in some kind of trouble?"

She didn't like his tone of voice any more than she liked the question. "What kind of trouble do you mean? And what is that thing in your hand?"

Orang'jello stepped from the other side of her car. He was wiping grease from his hands and staring at Janeen as though she was the wrong woman to be caught with if the authorities ever decided to raid the place. Kelvin sucked his teeth and nodded for his mechanic to take over the discussion.

"This here is a cousin to the Lo-Jack," Orang'jello informed her, "one of the best tracking devices you can buy, but you can't get this one on the streets. This is top of the line. I'd say government issue, too."

"Government tracking device?" she asked, helpless and confused. "What are y'all talking about? What are you saying?"

"We're saying that somebody is keeping tabs on you," Kelvin concluded. "Chances are, somebody's been watching you around the clock. Hell, they know where you are right now. That's why we have to put it right back where we found it. 'Cause if we don't, they'll be down here to see us, and I can't allow that. All three of my employees are on papers for something or another and heat could send them back to prison. I'm sorry if it jams you up, but like I said, I can't allow that. At least you know now, that puts you one up on 'em."

Orang'jello looked at Janeen with sorrowful eyes but he was glad that it wasn't his sorrow this time. Before letting out a worried sigh, he took the device from Kelvin to reinstall it.

Janeen couldn't think straight. This was all too outlandish for words. She got the same sinking feeling she had the night Val shocked her with her unsubstantiated suspicions. Even though Janeen didn't want to believe it, these incidents had to be related; her tire conveniently going flat so that she would have to take Rollin's car, the photos, and now this. While Orang'jello worked on the car, she tried to snap out of it. *If I'm dreaming, someone please wake me up when it's over.*

Kelvin approached her driver's side door when she was about to pull out. His uncomfortable demeanor was still just as apparent as before. "Hey, look here, Janeen, if I can help you I will, but I'd appreciate it if you didn't come around here until you get this business straight. Also, don't use the telephone unless it's somebody else's, and always watch your back. I'm sorry."

She looked up at him like a woman who'd been evicted from her home with no place to go. She nodded slowly, confirming that she understood and even tried to smile good-bye but the muscles in her face refused to cooperate. Instead she winked, then reluctantly pushed the car back into the evening traffic.

# Chapter 21

# *Hand-me-down Memories*

Upon arriving in the old neighborhood, Janeen viewed the sidewalks on Peabody Street where she'd learned to roller-skate. They were scarred and fractured with neglect. Wide cracks in some places and violent breaks in others closely paralleled so many shattered lives those very sidewalks were meant to protect from the cruel and unforgiving streets.

After she parked the car in front of the house she used to run home from school to play in, Janeen didn't know what to say to it considering what that house had meant to her. Saying good-bye to an old friend that opened its arms to her, when all else seemed desperate, strange, and too overwhelming for a thirteen-year-old from

Louisiana, had to be done right.

Remembering how her father's shadow stretched way down that sidewalk when they'd take slow late-evening strolls around the block, and the joy she had each time trying to stretch her own shadow out enough to measure up to his, it occurred to her how she was just like most young girls, in love with their fathers. She had loved the familiar sound of his voice, his wide-mouthed laugh, the way he held her mother close just because he could, and all the other reasons daddy's little girls adore them so.

The house was painted white, like nearly every other house on the block. Living there may not have been such a big deal to their neighbors but the Hamptons took a giant step moving to Dallas and bidding farewell to third-hand plantation housing that slaves had built for themselves, fare-well to dirt floors too, and good-bye to a code of honor deep enough to kill for. The small two-bedroom house had been a savior to her then. All those years later, it was a shell of its former self. It now suf-fered severely from a case of dry rot, chipped paint, and foundation problems. Much like the old community surrounding it, that house had served a great purpose but neither was ever fully appreciated by the people who'd passed through them as stopovers en route to better lives.

Walking across a dirt lot that used to be a plush deep green lawn that her mother watered every evening, Janeen pressed her hands flat against the house, which appeared to be sinking into the ground on one side. As she stroked the remaining wood panels like a circus handler soothing a fallen elephant, she knew that leaving without going inside was impossible.

The front door was boarded up by the city and all the windows had been broken beyond repair or taken out altogether by neighbors looking to remodel or recycle their own. She thought of all the unlawful activity the house must have seen since anyone had legally inhabited it, when her mother passed away twelve years before. If there had been a way to get in, she would have been willing to take that chance.

There was not one sign of movement down the length of the street in either direction. Fortunately for Janeen, the evening still held at least another hour of light, granting her the chance to walk those hardwood floors once again.

After breaking a fingernail while attempting to pry a large plywood board off the front door, she had second thoughts. Conceding temporarily, a jaunt to the backyard would have to do, so she headed for the side of the house only to end up looking over the same back chain link fences she used to watch her mother hang hand-me-down clothes on. Janeen was encouraged when the hinges on the swinging gate still worked, allowing her to enter. *Thank you. Don't mind if I do*, she thought.

She found herself at the back door with her hands trembling so hard she almost dropped the flashlight she'd brought along. Nervously looking around from side to side again, she pushed her hands into her front jeans pocket and came out with a set of old keys. Janeen didn't think she would need them but for some peculiar reason, she couldn't bring herself to throw them away in all the years that had passed. Not sure if any of the old keys actually fit the present locks, she figured she'd give it a good old college try anyway.

The first three keys Janeen attempted failed. It appeared to be a lost cause but there was one more she hadn't tried yet. She held her breath, aimed the key at the lock and was immediately deflated when the key wasn't even a close match.

In an effort to at least get a good look inside through the small windowpanes set in the door, Janeen placed her hands against the door and leaned forward. Her slight weight against the outside of the door was sufficient to do the trick. Open sesame. The door creaked loudly as she cautiously pushed on it and entered the one place where there was always more than enough love to go around.

Instantly, the smell of baked pies and fresh home-cooked meals came back to her in sharp distinction, they were that clear. Unfortunately, her vision in the dark house wasn't. Careful not to step on anything that remotely resembled crack pipes, drug needles, or used condoms left behind by trespassers, she moved slowly from room to room.

Like faded photographs, each room she entered held minute traces of long ago and conjured up forgotten memories, bits and pieces of a family that used to be. The laughter, tears, struggles, and triumphs were like fragments of scenes from an on-going urban drama, but this one belonged to her family.

After Janeen moved deeper into the house, she came across scraps of paper and other disposable drugstore items that were littered about in the restroom. One good whiff of somebody's business that still marinated in the toilet which no longer worked was reason enough to hurry Janeen along on her trip down memory lane. The stench was so bad that she placed her hand over her mouth and nose while desperately hunting for a place in the house where the rancid smell hadn't permeated.

Coughing and gagging for uncontaminated air, she was doubled over on her knees and wiping moisture from her eyes. Maybe it was a bad idea to have gone in, she thought. Certainly it was a worse idea to go near the bathroom. Then she noticed something that didn't fit. She happened to be in her parents' bedroom, just feet away from the spot that had once been occupied by a tall iron bed. There was a multicolored four-foot-long oval throw rug, too matted, stained, and frayed at the ends to be worth swiping, even by crackheads. It was lying there like a rug was supposed to but this one had no business in that particular place.

After staring at it for what seemed like forever, Janeen recognized it as the one that had strangely disappeared one afternoon. She assumed it had been tossed out. When she pointed her flashlight at it, its filth suggested it had been in that place for a long time. Had it been in that spot all these years? she wondered. And if so, what use would her mother have had for a throw rug underneath her bed? Especially, after hearing her mother comment more than a dozen times that "People are always covering up thangs that don't need to be covered."

Janeen grew concerned at the thought of finding something beneath it. But that had to be absurd. The notion that anything had been successfully hidden in that house was too far-fetched. Doubts about Val, Rollin, Scarlett, and that device Kelvin found beneath her car had gotten the best of her. Now she had suspicious thoughts that included her parents.

As she took a step to leave the house altogether, Janeen found it difficult to make it to the bedroom doorway without satisfying her curiosity first. She turned slowly. Cautiously, she approached the throw rug, then kicked at it with the tip of her sneaker until it folded over. At first glance, the faded shape of the rug was all there was to see, until a daddy-long-leg spider crawled up through a fingernail-size hole in one of the planks and just about made Janeen pee her pants. "Ahhh! Uh-uh-uh! Get away from me." Bugs didn't normally frighten her but one that seemingly walked right out of the floor was enough to shake her up.

Although still reeling from the scare, she had to know if something more than the spider's family lurked beneath the floorboard. Using the largest key like a craftsman's tool, she dug into the finger-size hole and lifted it while holding the flashlight in an easy-to-swing position, hoping it wouldn't come to that. Her heart raced and eyes blinked rapidly as she pulled up on the plank from the hole in it. She quickly found that the loose plank served as a lever to open a small trapdoor. The whole layout was designed so well that it could easily have gone unnoticed even if the rug had not been placed over it. Hidden planks and trapdoors, why not? she thought. That definitely fit in with the odd week she'd experienced.

Janeen heard a car door slam outside the house but was too absorbed to pay any attention.

More interested than ever, she straddled the hole in the floor and shone her light downward. The light illuminated a dusty box, a large round sky blue box with an inch-wide band fastening down the lid. It was a hatbox, no doubt her mother's, which Janeen wanted to keep for nostalgia's sake. Relieved, she took a deep breath after having held it for most of the suspenseful episode.

She didn't bother to replace the plank where she'd found it, nor did she take steps to conceal the trapdoor with the throw rug, which had evidently done the job for years. Having gotten more than she came for, it was time to go. With the hatbox tucked beneath her arm, Janeen headed out the back door. She turned back to get one last look, then walked to the front lawn where Jonathan Holloway stood beside a cream-colored Toyota Land Cruiser, waiting for her to come out. He was handsome, serious, and his complexion was about the closest a human being could get to UPS-truck brown.

Jonathan was a childhood friend of hers, who might have fallen for Janeen himself if she hadn't been five years older and out of his league when their fathers were members of the Black Panthers in the '70s and also worked together for South Side Cab Service.

After years of being a successful banker, Jonathan saw the need for a private investigation firm to suit the needs of the community, so he founded his own. Local law enforcement often consulted him when they needed the kind of assistance he could provide. Ghetto intelligence is what he called it.

"I thought for a minute I'd have to come in there and drag you out," he joked.

Janeen set the box down on the ground and offered her old friend a long warm hug. "You are a sight for sore eyes, Jonathan Holloway. It's good to see you, but how did you know I would be here?"

"Denise went to pick up Trip from Joyce's. She said you needed me to reach you, and told me of your plans to stop by this old house. I figured you'd be coming here and I was right."

"I wish we didn't take so long to visit with each other, but that's a subject for another day."

Jonathan took a second to notice the hatbox still on the ground. "Okay, tell me what you need. You know you're like family to me."

"I really need you to run a check on a name, Rollin Hanes. The hook is Howard University, then Yale, probably class of 1980 or so."

He wrote it down on a pad. "That'll be easy. Anything else?"

"Yeah, there's a lot to tell you and maybe

it'll make more sense to you than it does to me."

She told him all the things that Val shared and about the tracking device on her car. He assured her that he'd have some information first thing in the morning, unless she needed it right away. Jonathan took additional notes and asked probing questions without getting too personal before leaving her in front of the house to do what she had come for, to say good-bye.

With the hatbox resting on her passenger seat, Janeen closed her eyes and envisioned the house strong and steady as it was the first time she saw it. She said thank you and farewell before pulling away from the curb satisfied, with that vision in her mind.

# Chapter 22

# *Arrested Development*

Late into the evening, Sissy marched a narrow path in the carpet of her loft's living room area. Her emotional motor ran overtime due to all of the turmoil she'd experienced and the thought of going through the impending difficulties alone. A full week had passed but there was still no sign of J. R. Cooper. As far as Sissy was concerned, he was out of sight, so never mind — at least, that's what she kept telling herself. Unlike the first time he'd pulled the disappearing act and stayed away for over three years, she secretly hoped this time that his more recent Houdini routine was merely a bad case of the CJs. Commitment jitters was the term she used whenever she heard stories of yet another black man running away from a real thing staring him in the face. All rhetoric aside, Sissy wanted her new old man back.

Despite not having received a response from Cooper as to his whereabouts during those years of love deferred, she was still hopeful that he would return again, take his rightful place in her life and be the man she always knew he could be.

Now conflicted, she refused to leave her apartment until her woeful feelings subsided. However, she was stopped in her tracks moments later. As she began to tidy up her place, she ran across a hand-written copy of her list of clients. Sissy recognized the handwriting as Cooper's but she had no earthly idea why he'd done it or what he was doing snooping in her private files. Too concerned to be angry, she wanted to see him more than ever then. There were so many questions that begged to be answered. Unfortunately, Sissy had to wait and hope that he would resurface to provide those answers.

Both men stared at the small pieces of sculptured limestone carefully arranged on the elegantly crafted chessboard. One of them thought intently about his next calculated move. His name was Special Agent Matthew Clary. His worthy opponent gazed at the fine pieces for another reason. He wondered how long it would take Special Agent Clary to discover the game had been virtually won with his last skillful maneuver. Clary's king had been captured, game over. Check. The winner of fifteen consecutive chess games in the FBI safe house was none other than J. R. Cooper. He'd been counting the days until he could see Sissy and explain how he wanted to help her but couldn't. He also wanted to share how much he still wanted to make good on their secret pact and begin again, if she allowed him to.

Clary may have been qualified to babysit witnesses for the state but his defensive strategy on the chessboard proved suspect. Cooper grew tired of coming up with innovative ways to make the game last more than five minutes each time Clary begged for yet another rematch. If cold sandwiches, stale chips, and root beer weren't enough to drive Cooper mad, being locked in another cage of sorts just might have.

While devising a plan to break out before going stir crazy, he reflected on his brief taste of freedom and had a chance to view a snapshot of what his life might be like if Rollin kept his part of their bargain, but he was reluctant to count on it. What if the government got what they wanted, then re-manded him back to Virginia to serve out the remainder of his sentence? Life on the run would be better than that, he'd convinced himself.

A few minutes passed. Clary continued studying the board, strategizing to win a match before his partner, Rex Flores, returned with Chinese takeout for the three of them. Time was running out for Cooper so he decided to risk it all on a lark.

"Hey, Clary?" he called out twice before getting his opponent's attention from the other side of the small table.

"Yes, sir, Mr. Cooper," he answered, refusing to look up from the game.

"How 'bout we make our tournament a little more interesting? I mean . . . I do have a few more days before this is all over. So I'm proposing that from now on, the matches you win count ten to one against those that I do but there is a catch. With my next victory, I get to make a phone call. Whaddaya think?"

Clary grunted something about not having the authority to make that decision. However, he did agree to think about pitching the idea to his boss.

Cooper was working it from all angles. He'd been keeping his ear to the wall, listening in on privileged information when the agents from the night shift showed up to relieve Special Agents Clary and Flores. Cooper managed to piece together what Sissy was up against but there was no possible way he could call and warn her while under guard. Regardless of being locked down on house arrest, he felt that he had to do something.

"Clary, I'm going to step in the restroom for a minute," Cooper announced. "Don't hurt yourself while I'm gone, and don't cheat."

Clary thought the comment was amusing. He actually felt better now that no one would be looking down on him while he assessed his chances of winning for once.

As soon as Cooper was inside the bathroom, he locked the door and pushed the small window open on the far wall. He mouthed a couple of highly inflammatory expletives when he realized there would be very low odds on his shimmying through it and climbing down three flights of fire escape stairs to freedom in the street below.

After stepping on the sink for leverage, he angled his broad shoulders diagonally through the windowframe. With a few hearty thrusts of his legs, he made his escape out the window before dusting himself off and immediately heading down the street toward Sissy's side of town.

A few minutes later a friendly knock at the front door of the safe house broke Clary's concentration. He hesitated, still surveying the chessboard intently. The knocks became harder and more insistent. "All right! All right!" Clary shouted at the door before reluctantly leaving the table to answer it.

When he looked out of the peephole, he saw his partner Flores standing impatiently with two armfuls of food in white plastic bags. Clary opened the door to let him in, then quickly darted back to resume the chess game, but Flores stopped him.

"Hey, Matt, look what else I picked up while I was out," Flores said, while stepping aside to reveal an embarrassed and defeated J. R. Cooper, who was handcuffed behind his back.

Somewhat astounded, Clary looked toward the bathroom as if he couldn't believe it. Cooper had gained his trust and used it against him. Oddly enough, Clary wasn't all that shaken up about it; at least he'd gotten his chess partner back.

Afterward Agent Flores explained to the prisoner that he didn't want to try that again or they'd have to shackle him to the bed for his own protection. Otherwise he would be sent back to the county lockup, where they couldn't watch his back. Too many people were involved and news of the investigation was leaking out. In the county jail, someone could get to him. For the right price, he could have been killed.

Cooper understood clearly for the first time just how serious this spy game was. His life was not his own until the last arrest was made; then maybe he'd be a free man again.

After having sat at the small table, Cooper winced and tried to adjust himself comfortably with his hands still cuffed behind him. Cooper's frown of disappointment eventually faded to disbelief when Clary rejoined him there as if he hadn't just tried to escape.

"So you want to finish the game, Mr. Cooper? I think I'm really getting the hang of this," Clary said eagerly.

The prisoner shook his head, then directed his attention to the board for the first time since his unsuccessful escape attempt. Cooper had forgotten that he'd nearly won the game before he sneaked out the bathroom window. "Oh, yeah. Checkmate."

Clary studied the game board thoroughly, then threw his hands up. "Okay, okay. Just one more game." Some people just don't know when it's time to let it go and walk away.

Later that night, Rollin called the safe house to check on matters. Flores didn't mention anything about Cooper's bathroom-window escapade. No news was good news considering there had been murder contracts ordered on other potential witnesses.

"Hold on, Flores," Rollin said, hitting another phone line in a downtown federal building office. "Yeah. You've got him? No, I wasn't aware of that." The information he received was distressing. Rollin motioned with his hand for other agents, who lurked just outside, to enter his office. "Well, get him out of there! Hell, I don't know. Just move him. I'm on my way."

He quickly explained to his team of agents that Councilman Wilks had been arrested by the county sheriff's department the night before for physically assaulting a young female. His wife refused to bail him out after she learned the charges and it didn't take long before the news hit the streets. For the same reason

Flores explained the dangers of being locked up with the kind of information that could silence someone for good, Rollin and three of his top agents sped through downtown toward the detention complex eleven blocks away.

Once inside the county jail, they marched past the metal detectors while flashing their badges along the way. The foursome hit the stairs when it seemed the elevator was delayed on an upper floor. The agents were nearly winded by the time they finally reached the cellblock, which housed the holding tank for arrestees awaiting arraignment.

"Guard!" Rollin yelled to the detention officer who was protected by a room encased with steel meshed wires. "Open this gate!"

The officer didn't choose to follow the normal protocol of asking the suits to check in. He'd seen their types before and dared not ask questions when men dressed like them demanded things.

The barred gate slid open, giving access to the long cellblock with rows of small cells on either side. An overweight senior officer hustled up alongside the men as they went from cell to cell frantically looking for the councilman.

"May I ask who you are, sir?" he inquired in a rather perturbed manner. "Visit'n hours are over. Been lights out for over two hours."

This was the senior detention officer's world, where he reigned supreme. This block was his and he wasn't as quick to serve suits from downtown as his junior co-worker was.

Rollin paused long enough to voice his frustration while the other three agents continued to peer in from outside of each cell. "No, you may not ask my name at this time, but if you detain me and my men and let something happen to Councilman Brewster Wilks, you'll know me so well by the time I'm done with you that your mother will hate the day down to the minute you ever saw my face! Do we understand each other?"

The senior officer shook in his boots. His clipboard trembled in his hands as he shined the flashlight on the prisoner list in order to get a better look at it.

"Hey, I think he's down here!" clamored one of Rollin's men as everyone double-timed it down to the cell in question.

"Uh, yeah, this is it," the senior officer confirmed, trying as fast as he could to get that cell door opened. "Hey, it looks like he's sleepin' in there. See, I knew there was nothing to get all worked up about."

Inside the cell, a man lay in a fetal position with his street clothes on. His back was turned away from them. In an instant, the door slid aside. Rollin was the first one in. He squatted down on one knee and began shaking the man.

"Councilman Wilks? Hey, wake up. Wake up!"

With one hard tug on the man's shirt, the body fell over like a dry sack of wheat. Rollin looked away with his eyes closed tightly. When the others saw that Rollin's hands were covered with blood, they rushed into the cell to find a large kitchen knife sticking out of the councilman's abdomen. There was something chilling about the way the dead man's eyes were wide open and looking up at nothing with his face still holding the same tormented, contorted frown from the pain of having a nine-inch blade pierce his intestines.

Rollin had a brief thought of interrogating the prisoners on the cellblock but he was savvy enough to understand why other inmates wouldn't be so quick to snitch on the one who had committed the murder. They wouldn't want to end up like the victim. Rollin looked into the ranking detention officer's eyes with disgust. Since the councilman's body was already turning cold, that meant the death had occurred before the inmates were locked down for the night. Any one of a hundred men had the opportunity to do it.

Rollin was too overcome for words. The case was coming apart at the seams. This wasn't supposed to happen. Someone must have paid to have Councilman Wilks hit before he could turn state's evidence.

Not a second after the body was found, Councilwoman Jonica Wannamaker dialed a number from her office phone and waited for someone to pick up.

"Yeah," a man's voice responded, over the phone line.

"You're not going to believe who's been arrested — that sniveling coward Wilks. He got pinched last night after kicking the stuffing out of his college sweetie. I've got a scoop from the mayor's office that he plans on selling us out to save his own skin. They'll be down to visit him before long and he'll sing, I know it."

"You have my word that he's done talking, permanently," the same voice assured her.

"All right, then. It's your party now," Councilwoman Wannamaker said. "Blow it and I'll have no choice but to institute a very hostile takeover." Silence filled the airwaves between them until the councilwoman spoke up for the last time. "Are we clear on that?"

"Yeah, we clear . . . oh yeah."

Ray Gilliam placed the phone receiver back on its cradle, then lit up a fat Cuban cigar. "Clear as a bell. Clear as a bell." He smirked to himself. He'd paid to have Councilman Wilks murdered in jail just before the final lockup of the day. A young white man entered the councilman's cell asking for a cigarette. When Wilks explained that he didn't smoke, the assassin replied, "Then what good are you to me?" before ramming the butcher's knife into his victim's stomach again and again until his dirty deed was finished, and so was Wilks.

# Chapter 23

# *Not a Day Goes By*

Janeen hadn't seen Ray for several days. There was no reason to believe he'd be coming back soon for the remainder of his clothes so she claimed the master bedroom for herself. After taking a long candlelit bath, which she always did when her woes became too great, she wrapped a towel around her damp hair as if it were an African turban, which made her feel like royalty. It was a trick her mother had taught her as a child.

Still concerned about the strange turn of events, Janeen set the security alarm, then collected all of the candles from the bathroom to illuminate the area around the headboard of her magnificent sleigh bed. Now comfortably surrounded by several oversized pillows to console her, she picked up the book, the book everyone seemed to be warning her about. Even the woman at the bookstore transmitted bad vibes through an otherwise rave review.

Opening *The Women of Newberry* carefully, as if she was peeling back pages of an ancient priceless manuscript of hieroglyphics, the book appeared harmless enough.

She poured herself a stiff measure of white zinfandel and another full glass of wine for the spirits who might be in attendance and thirsty. Next she fought the strange and powerful urge to flip through the pages of the book and read the novel in random spots, although she had never considered such an erratic reading pattern before. As Janeen held the book firmly, fear ran through her but she had to get into it. How bad could it be? she reasoned. With uneasiness, she began to read the first paragraph.

*I was glad that my father was killed before I grew old enough to know him. After you've finished this novel, perhaps you'll understand why I feel the way I do. But first, allow me to introduce you to the small farming community of Newberry, Louisiana, which has the dubious honor of having enjoyed decades of unrivaled prosperity in the shadows of shameful and unforgivable sins. This is one of many stories . . . The Women of Newberry.*

Reading the author's description of the backwater town she'd spent the first twelve years of her life growing up in made Janeen feel warm inside. Watching the candlelight's reflection against the wall helped her to remember the past as the writer did, in dim hues of unrighteousness and broad strokes of vivid truth, both of them in Technicolor.

The deeper she went into the book, noting the characterizations, who all sounded quite familiar to her, the more engrossed she became in the lives of the people depicted in black and white. Memories of circular hand-cranked washing machines, wooden-planked front porches, entire houses sitting three feet above ground while resting on concrete blocks, metal washboards, and long summer days that went on forever brought smiles to a woman who'd expected horror to abound.

Instead of becoming emotionally rocked as she'd planned, Janeen sipped wine by the glass while gliding through the first section of the book with relative ease. One of the biggest dilemmas the main characters experienced was whether to have watermelon or ice cream for dessert. Times were that simple once, she thought. And, much like her own family, the young couple depicted in the story had two daughters but neither parent had any idea of the troubles and worldly woes coming around the bend with the reckless abandonment of a runaway train.

Janeen closed her mind and locked out her instinctive caution about this seemingly harmless piece of literature. After she let her guard down, the next section of the story ushered her down a path she could not have imagined. She'd later regret reading what she did next.

*Beginning on a warm September Sunday morning, the local Catholic church overflowing with black parishioners followed all the customary traditions facilitated by a white priest, just as it had for as long as Negroes have been free in Broussard County. But that Sunday was different. That Sunday, a young girl's mother hurled accusations of moral impropriety at the priest. The woman fell down on her knees in the middle of a prayer and wailed, crying out strange babblings of hell's fury and unforgivable sins committed against her and hers, all commingled intermittently with speeches in undecipherable tongues.*

Janeen actually remembered that incident from her own childhood. Just as the book noted, it had begun as an ordinary Sunday morning. Other than being on the warm side, church services had gone on without a hitch. Janeen and Joyce sat calmly on the wooden bench, bracketed between their mother and father. The girls wore identical yellow sundresses in a flowered print, which their mother had made by hand.

The priest, a short, thin brown-haired man who was barely thirty years old, was beginning Communion when the back door of the church flew open and slammed loudly against the wall. Several people jumped at the startling sound. Janeen was one of them. Her eyes widened when a dark-skinned mountain of a young woman with a larger than normal frame for a female stomped through the open door like a two-hundred-and-forty-pound rhino storming through the Kalahari.

The thin material of the woman's pale housedress waved back and forth as she began to lengthen her stride. She approached the pulpit with one of her thick fists balled up like a meaty ham, a small girl dressed in faded jeans and a striped pullover begrudgingly in tow. The girl looked to be about ten years old and despite the long pigtails she shared her mother's sturdy build and facial features, although it was hard to tell because she kept her head lowered in a childish, shamed manner the entire time.

The priest couldn't help but stammer back when the woman took her stand only a few feet away from him. Despite her interruption, he attempted to continue with Communion as if nothing had occurred. His hands that held a gold wine chalice were steady as he tried to look past her toward the spellbound congregation.

"The shame you should feel ain't nothin' compared to the devil I'm gonna beat outta you for what you did to my Billie Jean!" the large woman shouted. "Look at her! Take a good look, 'cause where you're goin', ain't nothin' this sweet gonna be round you for miles! You stole my baby from me. You took her innocence like it was nothin' and threw it away. As God is my witness, He saw for Hisself what you did!"

With shaky hands, the priest began to notice that his church members were listening as attentively as they could. "All right, now, Miss Kr-Kremley . . ." he stuttered. "You can't just come up in the Lord's house disrupting service like this. Uh, this — this isn't the place to discuss your concerns. . . . I'll be happy to meet with you later to — to discuss things in my office." He tried to calm her but his words didn't come out in the way that he'd hoped, as she used them against him immediately.

"What you mean, this ain't the place? This is where you took her womanhood! Now the doctor say her womb is spoiled. No babies, not ever!"

The priest's hands rattled noticeably then, to the point that wine began dancing above the chalice rim and ran down his wrist. Despite having red liquid dripping down off the embroidered cuffs of his white robe, he refused to set the goblet down.

As the priest turned as white as a sheet, the woman sank to her knees and forced her daughter to do likewise. "Lawd, send Your angels down on this here earth and smite the devil standin' befo' me right now. He done ruined my child and I say befo' all these people that I will kill him myself if'n You don't. I'm prayin' You release the hounds of hell and *all* of its fury on him this day, Lawd. Strike him down! Strike him down! Ohhh . . . make him bear the weight of his unforgivable sins against me and mine. Hemessa hemessa muertes abomini! Abomini!"

After the woman's cries had panicked the priest into silence and awe, five grown men from the audience gathered her from the floor and wrestled her out the back door. Her daughter, Billie Jean, followed quietly behind them with her head solemnly bowed down, refusing to make eye contact with anyone. Not one teardrop welled up in her eyes, not one. It was a painful display of innocence lost.

Although the incident had happened many years ago, Janeen actually remembered being so frightened by the distraught woman's boisterous display of unbridled emotion that she had hid her face in her small hands when it occurred. Peeking through the spaces between her fingers, she could see the priest's face clearly. He was the most terrified of all those who had witnessed the spectacle. Despite it having been the priest's felonious activities that were the cause of the woman's outbreak, several men from the congregation stepped in to take the hysterical woman away, kicking and screaming to the high heavens about vengeance being the Lord's.

However, various parts were left out of the author's rendition of the story in the novel, purposely, it seemed. There was no mention how the priest disappeared within hours of that unbelievable scene or how, trapped in her misery, the distraught woman was found days later hanged by the neck in her landlord's smokehouse. Her charge, for the record, was disrupting services with unfounded gossip and unholy tales of debauchery.

Hanging on every word, chills danced down Janeen's spine again as she thought back on the priest's expression of fear. She'd never seen a white man that scared of anything before or since that dreadful day. It was as if he came face-to-face with his demons and recognized them for what they were. Back then, Janeen wished she knew what could have possibly put so much terror into the heart of a man like that. Little did she know that in the unhinged woman's hate-filled outcry, it was the priest's own reflection that he saw, turning him sheet white in the pulpit.

Shortly after vividly recalling that scene, Janeen found herself drinking her glass of wine and the other one reserved for the spirits. As she recognized the story all too well, she began to feel the harsh effects of drinking far too much wine on an empty stomach.

Janeen could not resist the urge to read on. Her heart fluttered as the pages turned at a furious pace until she suddenly came to a passage she could have easily written herself. Reading it aloud, word for word, "Sins of my father visited on me," caused more pain and suffering than she thought humanly possible. It came back to her as if it had occurred just yesterday. Some of the most insignificant details about the tragedy that she'd long since tucked away in her subconscious screamed loudly for attention.

Before Janeen's eyes, a writer whom she didn't know had told her own earth-shattering story line by line, and each despicable incident frame by frame. "Awwwwh!" she screamed suddenly before hurling the book across the room. The novel crashed into the wall and fell to the floor, sprawled opened like the pages of her past. She was turned upside down emotionally at coming full circle back to childhood memories that wouldn't die or stay locked away where they belonged, in the dungeon of long-forgotten yesterdays.

Janeen felt like someone who'd been exposed before the world with no warning. What's more, other people near and dear to her now knew her secrets, too. The secrets that she thought were hidden from sight had reemerged somehow and stared her in the face just as the priest's secrets had done to him.

With a suffocating sense of urgency pushing on her, she experienced a desperate need to breathe but she couldn't. Coughing and gagging, she began vomiting up the wine that her stomach vehemently rejected.

She sprang up to a sitting position and her condition abated to painful dry heaves. Janeen was an emotional, physical, and spiritual mess. A woman with so much love to give should never have feared or despised her mistakes to such a painful degree.

Janeen needed to do three things to begin moving forward to conquer her past. First, she had to take a new look at her old self. Second, decide to and then begin to get over it, and third, invest in some new sheets. Once they've been soiled, they could never be the same.

After sleeping through her alarm clock's lengthy summons and ultimately awaking to children riding bicycles and gleefully roller-skating down the streets, she knew right away that she was extremely late for work. Through severely squinted eyes, she attempted to find her way around on the floor, which served as her resting place for most of the night.

While crawling on her knees to the edge of the bed, she discovered that there was no position in which she could hold her head that didn't hurt. It ached even more when she was reminded of the night before.

"It can't be ten-thirty already, and I know I didn't let that damned book get the best of me," she whispered to her reflection in the bathroom mirror. "Don't kid yourself," the reflection answered back. Two and a half hours late for work and she wasn't close to being ready to attack the day head-on. But there was no one to call and report her tardiness to. There were no pressing reports to be completed and no important papers to be signed that couldn't be handled later. Thursday was nearly half gone and with no apparent reason to show up for work on Friday, Janeen decided to take some personal time to get her head together after reading the entire book in a ten-hour span. Dealing with a twenty-seven-year-old crime and a new tell-all book describing the whole episode in detail wouldn't be so easy. Janeen needed some time to absorb it all and figure out a way to get past it.

As she stood in her closet deciding what to wear, Janeen reflected back to a time when she'd relished the opportunity to play dress-up in her mother's clothes. Instantly, the hatbox she'd found under the floor of the old house came to mind. She couldn't wait to see which Sunday headdress her mother was so fond of as to reserve a special hiding place for it.

While unwrapping the dusty sky blue box, she began to sing the soft lullaby her mother sang to her. " 'Busy squirrel with . . . shiny eyes, and bu-shy tail . . . so round. How do you gather all the nuts that . . . fall upon the ground?' "

The top eased off. Simultaneously her singing stopped. There was no hat inside of it, instead she found several old black-

and-white photographs of cousins taken in Newberry, cousins she hadn't seen or thought of for many years. One of the photos pulled laughter from so deep within Janeen it almost hurt her when it came out. She pressed the faded snapshot close to her heart. The black-and-white coloring had become a light rose-brown somewhere through the years but it was still clear enough. It pictured her favorite girl cousin, named Odessa, wearing a floral dress, about fifteen years of age at the time. She was sitting on a dusty wood-planked porch holding a baby on her lap. Janeen flipped the square photo over. The words on the back read: *Odessa and child, Eric — age two.* When it occurred to Janeen what that implied, she was saddened all over again.

Janeen felt a need to look through the other pictures, too. After studying three more, she realized there were stacks of hand-written letters lying beneath them, about forty, most of which were addressed to Mrs. Magnolia Hampton and bound with a thick blue hatband. They were mailed from her father's first cousin Pearl, all the way from Newberry, Louisiana.

There was no way Janeen could have foreseen the magnitude of importance the letters held. Yet upon finding them, her anxiety caused both her hands to tremble. The same peculiar feeling that she was about to have her world rocked again revisited her. Well acquainted with that feeling, she knew this time to heed further warnings, sit down, and hold on tight.

Lieutenant Drennon stood quietly against the window of his office. With his back to Rollin, he looked over the city's fabulous cosmopolitan skyline. The investigation had been going on for five months and passed the deadline authorized by the mayor for his assistance. All they had to show for it was an impressive collection of surveillance photos, a lot more rumors than facts, and one dead councilman, a situation that no one was ready to deal with. Because the rate of progress in the investigation had waned, the powers that be turned to Rollin for answers.

"It's coming undone, you know," Drennon said, still looking the other way. "The mayor came by earlier today and he was not a happy man. He said we should have pulled the plug on this thing months ago." Drennon turned to make eye contact with the investigation's lead agent before continuing. "But I assured him that you could handle things. *Can* you handle things?"

Rollin looked away briefly, then answered reluctantly, "Yes, I can. And I will."

Suddenly Drennon developed a pompous attitude. "The problem is, I've heard that before, Rollin. Frankly, I for one am tired of hearing it. Now, I'm not doubting your commitment or talents in the least but she's doing a number on you. Maybe it's clouding your judgment. So don't . . . insult me by denying that some sparks have kicked up between you and Ray Gilliam's wife."

Since there was no point in arguing whether the woman in question had in fact "done a number on him," Rollin had to let it slide and focus his attention on the myriad of circumstances leading up to this juncture, adding frustration to an already difficult undertaking. What bothered Rollin most was knowing that Drennon was right. The mayor was also right and so far Rollin had been wrong. He was also wrong about timetables, indictments, arrests, parties involved and one nasty conspiracy theory. From the outset, something in Janeen's folder suggested she was not the average businesswoman and Rollin wanted to take his time to dot every single *i* and cross every little *t*. The time had come for him to prove why he'd been selected to put the task force together from a short list of top-rated special agents in the country.

Rollin's neck was on the chopping block for the first time in his career and he felt quite uncomfortable in that position. He cleared his throat. "Janeen Gilliam is an attractive woman, I won't dispute it, but that's not why I'm convinced that she doesn't know anything."

"You just might be right," Drennon agreed. "But we can use what we know about her past to get next to someone who does know something."

After reaching inside the breast pocket of his suit coat, Rollin pulled out a handwritten note. He looked it over, then folded it twice before returning the note to his pocket. It was a message from his assistant, Scarlett, which had "J. M. Bynote" written on it.

Torn between knowing what the right thing was and yet feeling reluctant to do it, Rollin acquiesced. He decided to go along with the program, no matter how bad it made him look or feel. "All right, I'll do it. I'll bring her in after the weekend."

"No, you'll bring her in now!" Drennon

insisted. "We've wasted enough time, waiting for someone to make a mistake. Today, someone did. They killed a man who could have cinched our case for us." He leered at Rollin suspiciously. "There is a leak and I don't like it, but the only way to squash it is to put the whole thing to bed, once and for all. By Monday, I want this to end or your superior officer had better be explaining to me in triplicate why the hell it hasn't yet."

Rollin had received his marching orders from the top. He had to do something and get it done fast.

# Chapter 24

# *Old News*

Joyce fanned her face from the midday heat while standing outside Janeen's front door. She wanted to say a short prayer to help get her through what she figured was about to drop a bomb on her and her sister. Closing her eyes to meditate didn't help. No matter how hard she tried, not one word came to mind. Joyce couldn't remember ever feeling so far from God. Guilt about her avoidance of the Church for more than twenty-six years kept her from saying how sorry she was for it. Having heard once that a person's sins can separate them from the one entity that could restore faith, she finally understood exactly what that felt like. Her soul hadn't rested since she turned her back on the

Church and every custom that went along with it.

"Come on in, Joyce," Janeen said when she opened the door to welcome her older sister in. Janeen's voice and mood were somber.

Joyce took a moment to survey the large sitting area. "Is Ray at home?"

As Janeen shook her head slowly, embarrassment forcing her to look away. "No, I haven't seen him in days." Joyce opened her mouth to speak but Janeen raised her hand to stifle her sister's words. "And Joyce, before you start, I *don't* want you to pray that he comes back. Believe me, it's better this way."

Placing her hands on her hips in a defensive manner, Joyce made her point regardless of the forceful attempt to silence her. "Humph, I was just going to say, good for you. If you ask me, you should have put his tired butt out a long time ago and changed the locks."

They laughed as well as they could, considering the difficult chore still at hand. Janeen invited her into the kitchen where the hatbox sat on the floor next to the table. Four stacks of sealed personal letters sat on it. Only one letter had been opened. Joyce didn't know what to make of the sight. The phone call she received said there had been something found in the old house that couldn't wait to be dealt with and that she needed to take the afternoon off to help sort it out. A whole afternoon meant that it had to be serious.

Without thinking, Joyce sat her purse down on the floor. That was something she'd rarely done because of another old superstition suggesting once a woman's purse touched the floor, the owner's potential to accumulate wealth was greatly diminished. Janeen noticed but didn't bring it up. Although Janeen didn't subscribe to the old wives' tale herself, she knew that Joyce believed in it wholeheartedly. Joyce had given away more purses than she readily admitted, all with the same disclaimer: "You can have it, but I need to tell you that it did touch the floor. But if you want to risk it, then it's yours."

After fixating on the letters, Joyce wandered over to the table with trepidation. The letters were intriguing but they were way too much to process at first glance. "Are these the letters?" she asked, neglecting to look away from them.

Janeen was surprised. "You knew about these? Why hadn't you ever said anything?"

Joyce took a seat at the table. "Because I couldn't prove they still existed," she answered, still refusing to look away from the collection of multicolored envelopes. Janeen selected the seat across from her and placed a box of tissue on the table, then waited for an explanation. Although Joyce agreed that her sister deserved one, it didn't make coming up with one any easier as she adjusted herself in the seat.

"Janeen, do you remember that last week Muh'dear was in the hospital and you were studying for your finals?"

Janeen noted Joyce's uneasiness before she answered. "Yeah, how could I forget?"

"Well, one night she woke up from the coma and asked for you. I never told you because I knew it would have hurt you not to be there and besides there was nothing you could have done. I mean, you couldn't be by her side every second." Janeen's eyes grew dim, thinking back on their mother's last days of battling cancer as Joyce resumed. "I was reading the funny pages to her. Remember how she liked that? Suddenly, Muh'dear opened her eyes like she'd been asleep for only four hours instead of four weeks. I almost peed my pants. We talked for a while before she grew too tired to go on but the last thing she said was to get you the letters so you could get over what happened when we were kids. After she passed on, I tore that house apart trying to find them but I couldn't. I thought maybe they had been thrown out by mistake. Then, so many years had passed that I'd just forgotten about them."

Janeen nodded her agreement with the decision Joyce made years ago to keep silent. "You were right not to tell me about all that. It probably would have killed me to know and not be able to do anything about it. Thank you, Joyce, that was very thoughtful of you."

They sat there, both afraid to touch the letters until Janeen spoke. "I arranged them by dates." She picked up the pile farthest away from her and unfolded the only letter she'd already read. "This is the first one Muh'dear received." She began reading the letter aloud.

*"Magnolia, I'm glad you made it there safely. Is Texas as big as they say? You'll have to write me soon and tell me all about it. Newberry is never going to be the same since y'all left. Sheriff Kileen came by the next morning asking all kinds of questions then kicked in the door to y'all's house*

380

*and spent a lot of time looking for something. The next day, the newspaper said that the state bank was robbed of $200,000 and they had some idea of who done it. Two weeks later, they stopped talking about it as if it never happened. I'm so glad you changed your name, in case they come looking for Hampton, I mean, Julian."*

Joyce's eyes were big when the implications became clear. *Daddy?* was her solitary thought, as it occurred to her that the stolen money from the bank robbery was how their father helped finance their college educations when working hard as a lowly cab driver. No matter how difficult times got, he always found a way to come up with extra money for prom dresses and little knickknacks all young ladies need but poor parents can scarcely afford. She also remembered how many times a day their father made them repeat their new last name, which was his birth name, when they first arrived in Dallas. Their father, Hampton Julian Bynote (pronounced By-noh) became Julian Hampton, and all the girls took the same surname. Each of them kept their middle name of Magnolia after their mother. One of the Black Panther members, who met Hampton at the cab company, made some calls to a friend at the county records office and arranged to have new social security cards printed for the entire family. For twenty dollars apiece new identities were created, although their memories would never die. It took some getting used to and neither of the older daughters fully understood, but they accepted the changes and never looked back.

As Janeen read on, their past was discussed in detail. All the things they had promised never to speak of again were written down in faded ink. Eventually, Joyce read letters aloud too while Janeen made coffee and finger foods to satisfy their hunger while digesting the stories of old. So many terrible events had transpired in the little town of Newberry that both sisters were in awe of how it survived without imploding from all the drama written about in those letters.

Included in the letters were newspaper clippings of numerous trials, homicides, and reports of scandals involving members of the Catholic clergy including the alleged rapes of several young girls. And every minute detail was explained in Pearl's letters for their consumption. One letter caused Joyce to hyperventilate. Their mother's name was mentioned in the same line with the man who'd caused most of the conflicts back home, a young priest named Ellis O'Leary. It seemed that he'd left many towns in Louisiana with deflowered children throughout his infamous religious missions. If the incidents hadn't taken place in their own hometown, neither of the sisters would have been able to imagine that such atrocities were true. But they were true, each story, each line, and each tragedy.

Hours later, after reading the remainder of the letters on the table and finding that many mysteries were revealed in them regarding their own family, Janeen's eyes were red from lack of sleep. Joyce was speechless. Their dark family history had clawed its way back from an uncovered grave, alive and breathing on Janeen's kitchen table beckoning to be dealt with.

"You know we have to show all this to Sissy right away," Joyce insisted.

Janeen knew this time would come but had not prepared herself for the inevitable. However, Sissy was after all as much a part of it as either of them was. "I know, Joycee," Janeen agreed. "Soon. I just need to make peace with it first. Soon."

An unexpected doorbell chime caused Janeen to jump as if someone had trespassed into her secret world. "I guess I'd better get that."

She stood up from the table and attended to the door. It was Sissy, excited and about to burst with exuberance. "Is Joyce here? I saw her car out front."

Janeen looked right through her. "Uh, yeah. She's here."

"Good, I've been calling her all day and no one answered at your office so I figured I'd try here next." Sissy noticed something strange about the way her sister just stood there blocking the doorway. "Is something wrong?" she asked. "Why are y'all both playing hooky from work today?"

"Just girl talk," Janeen answered, and not too convincingly.

"Girl talk, huh? Good, I could use some of that myself, so step aside."

Janeen eventually moved out of the way to allow Sissy to enter. Halfway across the room, she remembered the hatbox and all the letters piled up on the table but it was too late to do anything about it. She didn't want Sissy to find out like that.

When Sissy made her way into the kitchen, Joyce stood up from the table and welcomed her with open arms. She squeezed Sissy so tightly that it almost hurt.

"Hey, not so hard!" Sissy pleaded. "I'm still kinda sore."

Much to Janeen's delight, there wasn't an inkling of what caused the room, only moments before, to be filled with grief, self-reflection, and animosity. The hatbox and all traces of its contents had vanished. Janeen shot Joyce a wide-eyed surprised look, which was returned with a quaint I-handled-things smile.

"So, what are we talking about? Girl talk, I mean," Sissy questioned.

Joyce let a few moments float by without offering an answer, once again allowing Janeen an opportunity to come out with it, all of it. When nothing happened, she took over the strained situation. "Oh, Sissy, we were just talking about this and that. I met a new man and I'd love to introduce y'all to him but I'm not quite ready yet, you understand."

Janeen's heavy sigh of relief was over-shadowed by Sissy's surprise. "Dayyy-um, Joycee, a man?" Sissy squealed. "So when are you gonna let us check him out? You let him dust the cobwebs off it yet?"

"Ooh, I know you didn't, with your fast tail. It ain't none of your business," Joyce responded, playfully. "Besides, a lady never tells."

"What lady?" Sissy said, laughing.

Joyce quipped back, "Well, it would take one to know one."

The pensive mood was irrevocably broken as all three ladies laughed together with the youngest of them leading the pack. "Oh yeah, speaking of ladies, I hope y'all remembered promising me to go see Ms. Mary Lee Jackson to discuss her birthday celebration," Sissy said to jog their memories of the planned appointment, though the other two ladies seemed baffled. "You know, old Peach Cobbler."

"Ohhh," Janeen said, finally remembering also. "Was that this evening? I guess it did slip my mind."

"She's expecting us and said she was fixing something special. I can't wait to head over there. If we hurry, we can make it just before dark."

Joyce hid her discontentment regarding Janeen's continued refusal to spill the family beans. She didn't think it was fair to withhold the information from Sissy but she understood that the timing had to be right.

Janeen went upstairs to get dressed in

casual attire while the others waited. Immediately Sissy began pumping Joyce for information about her new love interest. Joyce filled her in until Janeen returned. Not one word was said about the hatbox or sharing it with Sissy on their way to the other side of town.

Not three seconds after Janeen exited the expressway onto Metropolitan Avenue, Sissy stretched her neck to look into the distance. "Something must be going on. The traffic shouldn't be backed up this late in the day. Maybe you should take this side street and go the back way."

Janeen did as she was advised but there was no relief. They inched forward as far as they could until a fireman with a heavy yellow suit and hat waved them on to a detouring road. Suddenly Sissy jumped out of the backseat and sprinted toward the epicenter of the commotion, where all the fire trucks gathered to battle a blazing house. Janeen slammed on the brakes and followed after Sissy, frantically calling her name. Joyce feared the worst while stepping out of the passenger-side door.

"Sissy, wait!" Janeen screamed, among the multitude of people gathered around watching the fireworks. "Sissssy!"

As observers pointed toward the woman knocking over barricades to get closer to the tiny wooden house burning out of control, Janeen heard someone yelling, "Stop her! She'll be killed!"

Panic overcame Janeen when she recognized that the panicked woman was Sissy, who like a lunatic made an attempt to enter the blazing house. Despite the overwhelming heat and flames reaching skyward, Sissy fought three firefighters decked out in full protective gear to get in.

After they tackled her on the lawn and struggled to contain her, Janeen figured out what Joyce surmised from the outset. The woman they were to meet and plan a birthday celebration for was spending the last minutes of her life engulfed in flames inside an inferno she called home. It just wasn't right for anyone to die like that, Janeen thought, standing at a safe distance behind the firemen's barricades.

Sissy fought senselessly to break free, crying "Nnnnnno!" and screaming out the woman's name.

Several yards away, Rollin watched the incident in its entirety from the backseat of a shiny black Chevy Tahoe. He'd received an anonymous tip that an old woman living at that address was in danger but he arrived too late. After he'd seen enough, he ordered the driver to move on. And just when he thought his investigation couldn't have gotten any more upside down, it did.

# Chapter 25

# *Crossroads*

Hours after the smoke cleared and Ms. Mary Lee's body had been taken away to the morgue, Sissy cried herself to sleep at last when all emotion was spent. In Janeen's favorite upstairs guestroom, Joyce watched over the youngest of the three for as long as she could, then headed for home shortly after ten o'clock in the morning. While Janeen prepared to make Sissy breakfast in bed, Jonathan Holloway stopped by and dropped off a file folder with the requested information. He said that it looked as if the facts she'd given him checked out. In return, she explained Sissy's traumatic experience and a few other concerns, then thanked him for making a special trip to her home.

When Sissy awoke, still disheveled and

utterly debilitated, Janeen had to coax her to eat something and begin getting over what she'd witnessed. But each time Sissy tried to talk about it, tears clouded up her fragile world again. Janeen knew then that she couldn't hit her brokenhearted houseguest with more drama, especially something devastating enough to shred the remaining threads holding her life together, so she decided against sharing the hatbox letters.

After several attempts at consoling her younger sister, whom she always felt responsible for, Janeen adjourned downstairs to clean up the kitchen from breakfast. The file folder Jonathan dropped off was pleading to be examined. Janeen stepped away from the sink to do just that.

There was a notice from the Howard University yearbook organization, exclaiming that any information found in their archives could not be utilized for financial gain without consulting them first. She casually flipped through other such disclaimers until she ran across something that looked inviting.

As Janeen collected coffee cups and china plates from the table to be added to the rising soapy water in the sink behind her, she paused to read the bio twice under the name Rollin Hanes Jr.

" '*Senior Debate Club President. Barons of Intervention President. Glee Club.*' Humph, I wonder if he can still carry a tune," she said aloud while looking over the remaining documents. Thinking that the yearbook picture looked nothing like her Rollin, she was glad some men got finer with age. She smirked and dismissed the folder's remaining contents until one page jutted out in a read-me fashion before she could throw the papers away and trash all of her suspicions as well.

The information from Yale provided more background than the previous document had. True enough, Rollin was a regular fixture on the Dean's List, Phi Beta Kappa key recipient, and star Debate Club honoree. But she was hit with an uneasy feeling when she looked over his graduate school photo, which looked even less like him than the other one did.

She picked up the sheet of paper with one hand and transferred dishes to the sink with the other. While viewing additional information listed under his name, she neglected to notice the water level nearing the sink's rim. She plopped the china down into it, not taking her eyes off the page that appeared peculiar.

When she returned to the table to retrieve the last of the morning dishes, Janeen skipped through all the other documents and grabbed at the last page. A Where Are They Now? addendum to the yearbook archives for Yale University revealed that Rollin Hanes Jr. had met his untimely demise while hang gliding off the coast of Barbados in 1987. *Untimely demise? 1987?* Janeen continued repeating it to herself until the words printed on that page sank in. She let go of the expensive serving dish. It shattered into several pieces when it slammed hard against the tile floor. Janeen disregarded it as she felt the undeniable need to sit down before she fell over. A puddle of hot water pooled around her feet but she couldn't stop looking at those words that put her in a trance, words that proved beyond a shadow of a doubt that Rollin Hanes was an imposter. Wondering who this man was that she'd fallen in love with, yearned to be with, and confided in, made her sick to her stomach. The same questions she'd dismissed returned. Why was he in her life? Why now? Suddenly Val's unfounded accusations didn't sound so far-fetched after all. Even though she didn't have the answers, the questions mounting inside of her fueled intense anger. If hell hath no fury like a woman scorned, a woman who'd been lied to, tricked, and made a fool of was sure to snap.

Sissy entered the kitchen rubbing her eyes like a small child who'd lost too much sleep warring with bad dreams throughout the night. "Janeen!" she yelled when her tired eyes discovered the broken dish and a flowing stream of water pouring over the sink onto the floor.

Janeen didn't move or acknowledge that someone had come into the room. Her eyes were glazed over and her teeth were gnashed tightly together. She looked as if she could spit nails and much worse.

"Janeen!" Sissy yelled again, tiptoeing through the rising pool to shut off the water. "What in the world is wrong with you? You're gonna ruin this Aztec tile you spent all that time looking for."

Janeen rose from the table. Her expression was blank. She took a brief assessment of the damage, then apologized for making the mess, as if it were someone else's house. Without another word, she lifted her pant legs above the standing water, collected the papers, tucked them

394

into the folder, and sloshed out of the kitchen, muttering "I'll be back" over her shoulder.

Not sure where to begin looking for Rollin Hanes or whoever this man really was, Janeen rushed to First World Mortgage. She decided to look in the company directory for a home number. When she pulled into the parking garage, Rollin's car was there. "Good," she huffed. Now she could get to the bottom of this. The elevator couldn't have moved fast enough for her.

The minute she stepped off on the seventeenth floor, Janeen bolted for the long corridor leading to both his offices. Scarlett was busy at her desk, filling storage boxes with mounds of brown hanging folders. She was surprised to look up and see Janeen storming by, giving her very little opportunity to detain the woman on a mission. "Wait! Hold up!" Scarlett protested.

Janeen gave her a stiff forearm to move her aside. Scarlett returned the aggressive move. Her initial thought was to go off but it was too late. Janeen was already standing over Rollin, who was completing an important phone call at his desk.

"Yes, today. She just walked in. Okay, I'll let you know."

He placed the receiver down and stood slowly to meet her face to face. The way Janeen breathed smoke was a good indicator that this would not be a friendly visit. Scarlett stood behind her, waiting for the go-ahead nod to get even. Instead, Rollin asked her to step outside and close the door behind her. Reluctantly and tight jawed, Scarlett did as she was instructed but that didn't stop her from listening to their conversation from the other side of the door.

Once he and Janeen were alone, Rollin looked down at the papers clutched tightly in her hands and poised himself for the onslaught destined to ensue. Although he had no idea what information those papers contained, he was certain that the jig was up.

Feeling a bit relieved, he said, "Hello, Janeen, I knew you'd be coming here sooner or later. We may as well talk about it."

She stood back, further assuming a put-up-your-dukes posture. "Yeah, that's a great idea. Let's do that, uh . . . I can't call you by your name because I don't know *who the hell* you are!"

Beyond frustrated, she flung the papers in his face. As if he'd received a swift backhand he knew he deserved, Rollin didn't attempt to dodge the flying documents. On the contrary, he took a moment to glance over a particular page that happened to land on his desk. After reading it completely, he wanted to apologize.

"I probably earned that and more, but please let me explain. If —"

"Tell me how you're going to explain walking into my life and tearing it apart piece by piece. I hate that I trusted you. I confided in a man, who I thought felt the same way about me but all it was . . . All you are is one big lie. How could I have been so stupid?"

Rollin took a step in Janeen's direction. She reacted with a defensive step backward. He understood that she didn't want him near her and he easily understood why. His successful career hinged on how at ease he made people feel while he was undercover. What he hadn't planned for, which was in direct conflict with government policy, was falling in love with a prime suspect. Unfortunately, she didn't trust him anymore and the ugliest part of his job had yet to make an appearance.

With hopes of calming her somehow, he

threw his hands up. "Janeen, please. Let me begin at the beginning. It would make this whole thing easier if you took a seat."

"Easier?" she shouted. "Nothing has been easy for me since you came along. Tell me why I should make this easier for you?"

Rollin opened his top drawer, reached his hand in it, and came out with a slip of paper with the name J. M. Bynote on it. It was a photocopy of the original he'd kept with him every day since they had been formally introduced.

He slid the paper across the desk so she could see it for herself. "I didn't just mean easier for me, Janeen Magnolia Bynote." This Rollin knew had to happen before the investigation could proceed further. He regretted having to go there but it was inevitable.

Lying just below her on the edge of his desk was a copy of her birth certificate. Janeen Magnolia Bynote born to Hampton Julian Bynote, Father, and Magnolia Odessa Bynote, Mother. Broussard County Hospital, Louisiana.

Janeen's knees got weak when those words cut right through her and when she began to look faint, Rollin rushed over to her aid. Pulling out the chair for her to sit, he noticed she was too shaken up to resist his help. Actually, he was glad that she didn't have the will to fight with him any longer.

It had been twenty-six years since Janeen had heard somebody call her by that name and seeing it firsthand on a legal document made it even worse. She couldn't lie about the information just revealed if she'd wanted to. Rollin had the goods on her, indicating that the government or whoever he represented had the goods on her, as well. For all those years, she'd walked along two roads that were bound to cross. She knew they would, sooner or later they had to. It was then she decided to go along with Rollin, or whoever he was, and move forward with her life.

"What else do you know about me?" she asked softly, with her head slightly bowed.

Hearing the pain in Janeen's gentle words, Scarlett tiptoed away from her place against the door feeling guilty for listening in on a conversation that no longer had anything to do with her, although she already knew it all.

Rollin almost winced when Janeen's expression displayed just how deep her wound really was. "I'm sorry. Please believe that I am," he said, almost remorseful for taking the assignment in the first place.

All was silent until Rollin took a seat across from her and searched for an appropriate place to start. "Wheww, Janeen, I know that a man named Hampton Bynote moved his wife and two young daughters out of a troubled town in Louisiana in the middle of the night some years ago. And on that night a bank was robbed but neither the money nor the bank robbers were ever found. I could guess who robbed that bank but that's water under a very old bridge. Besides, nobody cares about that anymore. I also know what kinds of things happened in that town around the time your family left it. I know that a priest was shot to death on the same day that the robbery took place. I don't know the particulars, nor do I care to. I've also learned that a man with three daughters showed up in Dallas seven months later from Houston; before that, whereabouts unknown. That third daughter is probably what threw the law off his trail because your family no longer fit the profile and in those days one bank robbery wasn't worth pursuing past a couple of months."

Janeen stared at him curiously in an attempt to discern whether that was all he knew. His relaxed expression confirmed that it was and she was glad. He might have drawn his own conclusions but without knowing the complete truth, she felt safe. There was still an ounce of hope that when it all came out, it would be on her terms.

Lifting her head a bit then, Janeen sought to get what she came for. His story. "Okay, I know when I'm licked. That's black history on me, what about you? Who are you and why are you here to spy on me?"

Rollin stood up to open the large doors of the bulletin board behind his desk. He paused, allowing his suspect time to prepare herself for what she was about to see. "You know, I wanted to take this down but thought better of it. This is something you would need to see anyway, to believe how serious this is."

When the doors of the locked bulletin board cabinet opened, Janeen gasped, holding her shaking hands over her mouth to muffle the sound of her inner being crying out. Just as Val had warned, picture upon picture stared back at her, one stuck on top of the other to form a snapshot of her life over the past few months. She recognized photos from events that happened before she met Rollin. That was the most exasperating part of all. She felt violated, stalked, and wronged.

"Just how long *have* you been watching me, Rollin?"

"For just over five months, Janeen, and by the way, my name is Hunter . . . Hunter Green. You may as well know that I'm a special investigator for the FBI."

She shook her head when a thought came to mind followed by another one to quickly chase it away. "You still haven't told me why you had pictures of me, my husband, and sister Sissy taken, and what they are doing up on that board."

He stepped aside to collect his thoughts before getting any deeper into the discussion. "Some time ago, I was approached to head a task force to look into some matters concerning members of the city council and an attempt to defraud the city. It was suspected that your husband, Ray, was linked to them, and he was later determined to be the ringleader of a vast high-level conspiracy involving foreign investors, mortgage fraud, and the Olympic Committee. That investigation led me to you, and after some digging into your past, well . . ."

Stunned didn't come close to describing the dissonance she felt then. "Ray isn't connected enough to be the lead in a high-level anything," she protested. "He owns a small construction company and that's it."

"You've underestimated him. See here," he said, pointing to a police mug shot of a much younger Raymond Gilliam. "He was arrested for murder once. We're positive that he slit his girlfriend's throat after he caught her with another man, but the local police botched the case and he was released on a technicality. Did you know that?" Her disbelieving eyes told him that she didn't, but she knew he was into a lot of criminal activity when they met. "What about these?" he continued, while pulling down several photos of Ray meeting with businessmen at restaurants, car washes, and several other out-of-the-way places. After lining up the pictures on his desk, he asked Janeen if she personally knew any of the people in them.

She nudged herself forward in the chair to take a quick glance at each photo. "No, no, I don't personally. Some of them I do recognize from stories on the news."

The agent smiled. "I knew you didn't, but I wasn't sure of that when I took this case. Nor did I know that your name is listed as the principal for your husband's company, Rayjan Construction, where he has been laundering money for years. But we can't prove it without the other set of books that we're sure he has hidden someplace. Before we began watching him, it appeared that you were the brains of the outfit."

Too confused about the murder accusation involving Ray to be concerned with his business, Janeen was still far from possessing a complete understanding of Rollin's role so she pressed for more information. "Rollin, uh, Mr. Green, how did you end up with a job in this company, in this office? What does Mr. Bragg have to do with this?"

"He doesn't have anything to do with it really. We approached him and laid out what we thought about you and wanted to see if you were double dealing here as well because people doing wrong usually do it wherever they go. Fortunately, Mr. Bragg believed in you so much that he offered us this space to operate from and gave me a manufactured temporary position to thoroughly inspect your life, inside and out. He was sure you had nothing to do with whatever Ray was up to."

Janeen felt good that the old man trusted her and stood by her side even though she was totally oblivious to the speculations about her. Now she understood what he meant when he said something about things happening that were out of his control. He'd gone out of his way to help her and she was proud to know him because of it. "I'll have to thank him for that, won't I?"

"I would," Mr. Green agreed.

Janeen shook her head to the slow beat of her own befuddlement. *"Mr. Green?"* She pronounced his name with emphasis, still attempting to get used to saying it. "When did you know for sure that I wasn't involved in any of this city council stuff?"

He leaned back in his chair and interlocked his fingers just below his chin. "The day we had lunch at the Rib Hut."

"When I caught Ray with that young girl in the parking lot?"

"No, when you wiped the barbecue sauce from the corner of my mouth. I knew that a woman who'd take care of a man like that couldn't be all bad."

That was almost enough of a compliment to make Janeen blush. Both of them shared a much-needed exchange of pleasant glances. But it was short-lived. Agent Green went into his drawer again. This time he pulled out a photo of Sissy with Cooper outside the automotive shop.

He handed it to Janeen, who accepted it, then hunched her shoulders.

"What, a picture of my sister and her friend J. R. Somebody? Is he a special agent, too?"

"No, he's J. R. Cooper. I can't share with you what he brings to the table but I will tell you that he's not only her friend, he's also her husband."

"Husband? Sissy's never been married." *This couldn't be right.*

"I assure you she has, at least once," he said, while nodding his assurance.

Back into the drawer he went looking. Janeen was filled with anxiety now and demanded more proof. Out he came with a marriage license naming Janeese Magnolia Hampton as the wife of Jeremiah Reynoldston Cooper III. "They were wed in Shreveport, Louisiana, four years ago."

"Well, I'll be," Janeen replied, somewhat in shock. "I'll kill that heffa."

"Before you do that, we need something from her and I'm not sure you want to hear what I have to say, but it could save her life."

Janeen sat up straight in her chair. "Go on, then."

The agent took a more formal posture as well. "Sissy, as you call her, became involved in the Olympic conspiracy too, unknowingly, I hope. She took a job securing property by convincing homeowners in south Dallas to sell out. Although Ray's company purchased the homes at a sizable profit to the landowners, it was still an unconscionable act. The property would be worth three times as much if the city of Dallas wins the bid to host the Summer Olympic Games. That's not a federal offense but there are some ethical issues involved worth doing state time for."

She didn't follow his logic. "I don't condone her actions or choices, especially since I was responsible for helping a lot of those families get homes in that community, but if she didn't break any federal laws . . . why would the FBI be concerned?"

"Her husband and other witnesses have connected her to the city council through her small but profitable prostitution ring."

"Sissy's a prostitute? No way. Uh-uh! I didn't — we didn't raise her like that."

Mr. Green raised his hands up to bridle her emotions. "Heyyy, slow down. I never said that she was prostituting, I only meant that she operates the escort service that supplies college girls to politicians from time to time. I'm betting that Ray set it up and then used that information as black-mail to keep his foot in the door."

Janeen was as still as standing water, thinking back on all the things she'd been told. Numb and worn out mentally, she looked up with helpless eyes. "Now what, Mr. Green?"

"Hmmm, now that we've got all that out of the way, I need you to talk to Sissy about turning state's evidence against Ray and all the councilmen she's providing services to. Mr. Cooper can't help us because they're married and he's got to keep a low profile for his own sake."

"I'll talk to her," Janeen assured him. "She'll do what she needs to. I'll see to that."

Mr. Green was as relieved as she was to get it all out in the open. "If you can locate Ray's other books, that'll put this thing to bed, and Sissy can walk away from this virtually unscathed. Oh yeah, one more thing. We've been watching your house. Have you heard from Ray lately?"

The fact that people have invaded her personal space didn't matter anymore. She just wanted to get through it. "No," she answered quietly. "I haven't."

"Well, if you do, page me nine-one-one. He's a wanted man and might not act rationally if he's cornered. I'll have someone keep watch on your house until we find him."

Desperately trying to figure out what she must have done to bring all those woes on herself, Janeen struggled to kill the pain inside or subdue it somehow. Time and prayer would prove the only remedies to bring about the changes she needed to take place. Time and prayer, heavy doses of both.

On her way out of the office, Janeen turned back to look at the man who she thought would save her, the man she wanted to love and have that love reciprocated by. She was hurt by his actions but realized he had merely done his job, what he was trained to do and was good at it.

"Hunter Green, huh?" she said, to remind herself of the man she didn't know and the one she'd lost. "You should have chosen something more original. I see why you adopted a dead man's identity."

"Oddly enough, Mrs. Gilliam, Hunter Green is my real name. My mother was an interior decorator with a sense of humor."

She tossed him a faint smile when there was only one thing left to say. "So long, Mr. Green."

Janeen left the building with all the wind

taken out of her sails. She was spent, with barely enough energy to drive home. Nothing seemed real anymore. And as for Sissy's trifling business undertakings, they would have to be addressed as soon as she could clear her own head. Walls were closing in on Janeen fast. She had to do something to sort out the details and make a plan for resolving them, much as she'd done whenever troubling business concerns cropped up. Unfortunately for her, this wasn't business at all. It was life.

# Chapter 26

# *Revelations*

After Ray circled the block several times in a rented white Ford Taurus, he concluded that his hunch was right. Someone parked across the street in a faded blue plumbing van was watching his house. Speaking into a cell phone, he told someone on the other end that a limousine would be waiting at the airport for a special arrival on Monday to seal the deal, then he disappeared down the block.

When Janeen made it home, she eyed the van, too. She may not have been bubbling with joy about the surveillance but she did feel secure that the van was anchored there and that she had allies if she needed them.

At Joyce's home, her daughter, Kyla, was percolating with excitement as the time drew near to meet the author of the Newberry book and gain insight into the story. Book club members arrived bearing gifts and food dishes to begin the feast of southern cooking and literary discussion. Joyce had helped to decorate the house with streamers and confetti although she was uncharacteristically quiet the entire day and hadn't once threatened to pray for anyone.

Bertha and Lila were rather quiet as well. Normally they would have been the life of the party. Kyla noticed the change in their behavior. "Y'all sure are being good tonight. I know we said we'd watch our P's and Q's for the author but you two are taking it a bit too far. Loosen up. Haven't you met a writer before?"

As the book club members milled about, visiting with one another and catching up on trivial aspects of each other's lives since they last met, someone shouted, "Oh, look and see if that's him," when they heard a car door close outside.

"No, it's only Janeen," someone else answered. "I hope he hurries because it looks like we'll finally get all that rain they've been promising. I'd sure hate for him to get caught in the storm."

Kyla greeted her aunt at the door and

welcomed her in. "Hey, you. Glad you could make it. Mama's been looking out for you. She said to tell her when you got here."

"Thanks, Kyla, I'll find her myself. Is she in her bedroom?"

Kyla shrugged and bounced away. Janeen looked over all the friends and family present. It seemed more like a coming-out party than a book club meeting.

After peeking her head into Joyce's room, she called out her older sister's name. "Joycee? Joyce, are you in here?"

"I'm over here," a familiar voice called back.

Janeen made her way around to the vanity area on the far side of the room where Joyce clipped on a sparkling set of earrings to complete her ensemble. "You look great," Janeen nervously complimented the woman of the house.

Joyce manufactured the best smile she could. "Don't I, though."

They embraced, feeling closer than ever. Janeen closed the bedroom door and filled Joyce in on all she had learned while in the secret agent's office. She spoke of Sissy's wrong-doings, what had been discovered about the family's exodus to Dallas, and what the authorities knew about the details leading up to that point. She also shared news of Sissy's secret marriage, prostitution business, and the whole kit and caboodle regarding Ray's past and present enterprises.

Understandably, Joyce was stunned. She felt so sorry for Janeen. It was hardly comprehensible. What's more, she felt as responsible for the messed-up state of affairs as Janeen did. What happened before they left Newberry could have ended differently had Joyce taken the steps Janeen was afraid to. Although Joyce was nothing but a child herself when all the drama began, the self-imposed guilt she'd been carrying around like an albatross around her neck wouldn't allow her to find forgiveness from the one from whom she needed it most, herself.

"Hey! How are you?" they heard people say loudly through a closed door, followed by a string of "He's here!" and applause.

The moment both sisters dreaded was finally upon them. They embraced firmly again, then took a second to check their makeup in the vanity mirror.

"Looks like it's show time," Joyce joked, with a hint of reluctance.

"Yeah, I think so. How should we play it?"

"Straight down the middle for once," Joyce answered. "Straight down the middle."

"And so it begins," Janeen concluded, "finally."

Joyce left the bedroom first. She immediately introduced herself to the celebrity guest, as did the other women who were worked up into a mild frenzy. Eric Bynote gladly made new acquaintances before he could even set his shoulder bag down.

He was a handsome man in his late twenties. Brown curly hair covered his head and tan-colored skin covered the rest of him. He appeared to be of Cajun descent or Creole and could easily have been mulatto.

After the author began sipping from a glass of wine offered to him by Kyla, everyone chose places to sit. While the members settled in for the discussion, Janeen appeared from the hallway leading to the front of the house. As soon as their eyes met, Eric quickly rose from his seat and extended his arms.

"You must be Janeen," he said, as if he knew her well from long ago. "Thanks for the e-mail letter you sent me yesterday. It really patched up a lot of holes that I've been wondering about for years."

"Hello, Eric," answered Janeen in a kind tone as she accepted his warm embrace. "You have your mother's eyes."

Just about everyone else in the room was spellbound. Joyce, being the eldest, was the only one who knew the whole score. She fought back tears when they held on to each other like a mother and son separated from birth. One look at him and Joyce knew who his father was. The resemblance was uncanny. He and Sissy could have easily passed for siblings, probably because they were just that, brother and sister.

Janeen finally let go of the guest and turned to face all the puzzled women gawking at her and the talented writer they'd been waiting eagerly to meet. "Let me introduce y'all to someone," she announced. "This man is my second cousin on my father's side."

A great amount of confusion filled the room. Joyce was sufficiently prepared for what was to follow, or so she thought. After so many years, it was time to explore and openly admit the sorrow that had plagued their family for what seemed like forever.

Kyla was the most perplexed. "Why didn't somebody tell me? I *am* the one who wrote the essay explaining why Eric should visit our group opposed to anybody else's."

"And I'm so glad you did, too," Eric thanked her, "or I might have never found y'all."

Still confused, Kyla just didn't have the wherewithall to understand. "Found us?"

"Yes, growing up and hearing about family that vanished in the dark was difficult. It wasn't until my grandmother Pearl died a few years ago that I found out the stories weren't merely folktales. When I received your contest entry, stating that your family roots went back to Newberry, I knew then where I had to come. That was the main idea behind the book club contest and the real reason I asked for the names of your members. I wanted to find y'all, especially Joyce and Janeen. When their names were included on your membership list, the coincidence was too great to deny."

The other members felt special. Blood relatives or not, they were honored to be a part of the reunion. Soon enough they'd share in the family's ghosts as well.

"Have a seat, Eric," Joyce insisted. "Make yourself at home. You're among friends and family."

Kyla assumed temporary control of the meeting again. "Let's see. I don't know where to begin. Now that I know we're fam-lee, I'm too geeked to think straight."

"I'll start," Tomeka, one of the youngest members, proclaimed heartily. "Uh, while reading this story, I was blown away at the detail you poured into the events. You put me there when the wagon collapsed, when the church exploded, and I had to close my eyes every time the priests got together and plotted to snare their next victims."

Others voiced their agreement and praise for a story well told. Kyla asked how a man could write a story that affected as many women as it did. Eric waited for Janeen's okay before answering it. She told him to go ahead and share everything he knew, and that she would fill in the rest.

"I've been asked that same question by thousands of readers since this book hit the stores." His voice was shaky and unsettled. "And my pat answer is that I've tried to put myself in their shoes although I'm a man and was a child when all of this was going on."

"Eric, are you saying this was a true story?" someone asked, from the group.

"Yes. It was based on a true story, one that needed to be told."

Mouths flew open around the room as members looked to one another in utter surprise as well as for support. The unnerving story line was hard to believe. Knowing that countless women and little girls were often raped, molested, and co-erced into sexual affairs with ordained men of God, merely for the sport of waging bets to see which priest could rack up the most conquests, was sickening.

He continued, "The character of Roxanne was based on my mother, Odessa. As a young girl, she was told by my father, who was a traveling priest, that she was chosen by God to be cleansed of all of her sins. He also told her that —"

"That she was special and it was the only way her parents' sins could be cleansed too," Janeen interceded. Her knowledge of the lies commonly told to unsuspecting girls admitted her involvement in the injustice.

In the split second it took for the others to catch on, Bertha was the first to break down. She tried to leave the room with her head in her hands but Lila held her tightly by the arm until the urge to flee subsided.

"Uh-uh, Bertha," Lila demanded, while welling up herself. "We've been running from this for most of our lives, and dammit, I'm tired of running. We ain't running no more."

Their confessions hit Janeen about the

same time it tugged on Joyce, who immediately felt sorry for all the gay and lesbian jokes she'd made over the years at her cousins' expense. She reasoned that maybe their encounters as girls with grown men whom they trusted may have turned them against a man's natural love and into the arms and comfort of other women.

What Janeen had been dealing with all that time didn't seem to amount to much then. She felt ridiculous for keeping it hidden and holding on to it. Letting it go was the answer. Letting go and facing it, as Lila said.

Makeup-stained tissue began to mount up, and sobs filled the room and caught up every woman except Janeen and Joyce. They attempted to comfort the others who had the same kinds of sins committed against them by late-night sneaky uncles, unscrupulous stepfathers, or men their single mothers had carelessly brought home and allowed too much access to their young daughters.

Watching the women attend to each others' woes was the reason Eric felt it necessary to put his mother's story down on paper. He'd seen it ruin her life by turning her to the bottle, then later to the needle. He wanted to help other women of

Newberry get on with their lives and over their experiences, which wrongly imprisoned them through no fault of their own.

Joyce pulled Janeen aside and hugged her close. "Neen," she said, sniffling and choking back the tears, "I've never told you this but I'm so sorry that I didn't report it when I saw what that man did to you, but I was just glad that he'd stopped doing it to me." Overwhelmed with guilt, Joyce let out a loud cry. "Oh, God!"

That was the first time Janeen could remember seeing her shed tears since the incident, and they'd promised on the way home not to ever tell a soul. Practically holding her older sister up, Janeen buried her face in Joyce's thick hair. Although Joyce had just enunciated the words plainly enough, Janeen still felt compelled to ask. "You too, Joycee? Joycee, you too? How come you never told me, how come?"

" 'Cause . . . I was supposed to be there for you," she replied in a tidal wave of emotion. "I'm the big sister and I was supposed to be there for you. I came back after getting candy from the store earlier than I was supposed to when I realized he might try to hurt you, Neen. I . . . ran . . . all . . . the way back but it was too . . . late. I saw him on top of you and it was too late.

I stood on the other side of that door and watched him hurt youuuu. I'm so sorry. I'm so sorry. Please forgive me, Neen, pleeeeease forgive meeeee."

Everyone in the room heard Joyce's outpouring of confessions, the cries of a repentant woman and of a sorrowful child. She was stricken with grief. Stricken with the realization that she, too, needed to let some things go, Joyce dropped down on her knees as the others looked on.

Janeen took her place beside her weary sister and motioned for the others to follow suit. Instantly, as if it were customary to do so, they all knelt down together. While holding Joyce's hands tightly, Janeen knew what her sister wanted to do but couldn't, so she stepped up and did the honors herself.

"Lord God. Please hear our cries, O Lord. We're hurting, Father, trapped in a world of pain and suffering. We've tried to conquer this thing ourselves but it has us in a bad way and won't let go. We come to You collectively and individually, on one accord, asking You to find forgiveness for those who harmed us and stole a piece of our innocence from us while we knew not our rights nor wrongs, and Father, please help us to find that same forgiveness for ourselves. The guilt that we might have done something to cause this kind of sin against us gets heavy. We're asking You to take this burden from us so that we can go forward and leave it behind us for good. We know that through You all things are possible. Please hear our cries, O Lord. We're hurting, Father. It is in Jesus' name that we pray and deliver it up to You. Amen."

The exact moment Janeen completed her prayer and the last amen was mouthed, a booming thundrous roar was felt throughout the room. Lightning flashed brightly outside, followed by another chorus of bloodcurdling thunderbolts banging against the sky.

Despite the force of nature kicking up outside, a quiet calm befell the members in attendance. Eric felt that telling his story was at last vindicated. "I think He heard you, Janeen," Eric whispered. "And I know He'll answer. I know He will."

After the group picked at dinner, not really eating much, the writer said that he had to catch a plane home. He thanked the Good Book Club for their hospitality and love.

As Eric Bynote prepared to go, he presented Janeen with a package. It contained all the letters her mother, Magnolia, had sent to his grandmother, Pearl. She thanked him for them, then handed over the ones he knew must have existed somewhere too. They exchanged personal contact information and made plans to stay in touch.

His parting words were enlightening. "Janeen, my mama missed you every day of her life. She died apologizing for not warning other girls, and you especially, about what she'd been put through."

Just as he had appeared out of the night, he dissolved into it like an apparition from another lifetime while Janeen watched him from the window through rain falling down in sheets. Eric Bynote had changed Janeen's life that evening, then departed from her in the midst of a flash flood, leaving behind him a forecast of clearer days and restful nights.

Later, Joyce handed Janeen a mug of coffee. "What now?" she asked, still somewhat subdued.

"From now on, we'll play everything straight down the middle. Straight down the middle."

Janeen found herself pulling alongside the curb in front of her house. Unfortunately the garage door opener refused to function when she sought refuge from the nasty weather. Steady rain was still coming down so heavily that she had trouble seeing the walkway to the front door. Months of dry days were forgotten during two hours of constant rain falling sideways but she couldn't avoid seeing the plumbing van still parked across the street.

Filled with ambivalence about the van's presence, Janeen decided to address its occupants on the following day. Paramount now, though, was getting out of the terrible storm.

When she pushed the car door open, cool rain attacked her before she could manage to get the umbrella to open. Halfway down the drenched pathway, a strong gust whipped the umbrella inside out. She was so glad to finally reach the porch and shelter from the rain that she failed to notice Sissy's car parked on the side street next to her house.

Janeen feverishly shed her long gray raincoat at the door, then she tossed the broken umbrella back on the porch before stepping inside and closing the door behind her. After stripping the wet clothing from her tired body, she sat down on her bed and thought about getting in touch with Sissy to share all that had transpired at the book club meeting. Janeen actually looked forward to explaining every hideous detail that Sissy should have known about years ago, no matter how much they were certain to cause a great deal of trauma. It was a discussion that was long overdue.

She leaned over the sink in her bathroom and looked intently at the new Janeen who was on her way to recovery. She liked this new Janeen who wouldn't let anything or anyone stand in her way. She *was* going to heal.

While drying her hair with a bath towel, she thought she heard a strange noise but disregarded it. But there it was again. Janeen put on her housecoat and slippers to investigate. It sounded like something or someone was knocking but there was no one at the front door when she checked. Again she heard the faint bumping sound. Maybe the wind had blown a shutter loose upstairs, she thought.

After flipping the upstairs light on, she climbed the last step of the winding staircase and approached the guest bedroom that Sissy had slept in the night before, when suddenly the bumping became urgent. Upon opening the door to darkness, she reached for the light switch. Someone shouted as the room lit up.

Something slammed hard against Janeen's face, knocking her against the wall, where she fell. She tried to focus and gain her bearings before struggling to her feet. Through somewhat foggy vision, Janeen saw Sissy, who was black and blue from being severely beaten and gagged with a headscarf. She was lying on the floor with only a bra and panties to cover her.

Meanwhile, someone in the van across the street turned on the dome light inside the oversized vehicle. "That upstairs light just came on. Someone is up there," Scarlett said. "I don't like this. With the rain coming down so hard, someone could easily have slipped in through the back door or a window and we couldn't have even seen them."

Her male counterpart went back to reading the sports page in the comfort of his dry working environment. "It's probably nothing. We're supposed to sit here and watch the house. That's it," he argued, "nothing more."

"Nah, I'm going in. I'll stay inside until our relief comes. I'd feel better about it if I did."

Scarlett's sixth sense adamantly beckoned her. Deciding to give in to it, she pulled a clear rain poncho over her head and darted across the street. She hid from the rain on the porch, quickly shook the water from her clothes, then rang the bell.

Upstairs, Janeen grimaced when someone grabbed her by the nape of her neck and pulled her from her squatting position. She clawed wildly at the man's face while he yanked her to and fro like a rag doll.

"Come on, baby, and join the party," the angry man's voice dictated, as he threw her onto the bed. "I heard your sistah likes it rough."

"Ouch! What in the hell is going on, Ray? What have you done to her?" Janeen screamed. Too much was happening all at once. This was the man she'd loved and opened her heart to. She was horrified to see him carrying on like a maniac.

When she gathered herself to make an attempt to untie Sissy, Ray wouldn't allow it. He kicked Janeen in the stomach for good measure and began to taunt her.

"Uh-huh, baby, you like that? Huh? You never told me you like it rough, too." Ray punched her, this time in the head. As she lay groveling on the floor, near senseless, he stared at her wildly, long enough to be sure that she wouldn't be getting up soon from the last blow. "That's for drinking my orange juice. Told you you'd be sorry for pulling that shit! Bet you're real sorry now."

Soon Ray began placing items from a closet safe into his gym bag. He held up the signed deed for Ms. Mary Lee Jackson's property to make certain it was the document he needed. After he had everything he came for, Ray walked toward Sissy and knelt over her. Janeen watched him as he began to practice his strange brand of torture, deliberately dripping hot wax from a lit candle on Sissy's back and bare legs.

In the midst of Sissy hollering out, wincing in torment and squirming on the floor, Janeen imagined that she heard the doorbell ring. She held her face with one hand and made another failed attempt at fighting him off Sissy, the whole time wondering what had gotten into Ray and if she could stop him. She'd never seen him like this and had found it hard to believe when Agent Green had informed her that Ray did in fact murder a girlfriend of his some time ago. She wished that it was Ray who'd been killed instead. But he was very much alive and reeking of liquor while acting worse than a crazed animal.

Ray spat in Sissy's face and proceeded to laugh again. "You almost cost me millions and I'm going to take it out of your hide. When I mess up that pretty face of yours, nobody'll want you then."

Planning to make good on his threat, he took out a black-handled switchblade knife from his jeans pocket. The doorbell rang once more. For the first time Ray heard it, too. He turned toward Janeen. "You expecting comp-nee, huh? Maybe it's your boyfriend, that pretty neggah from the Rib Hut? Why'ont you go see who it is and tell 'em to come back, because we're tied up in family business." His joke made him chuckle uncontrollably.

In an attempt to save Sissy's face from the knife, Janeen dove off the bed onto Ray's back. He struggled frantically to get her off him, then backhanded her across the mouth with enough force to send her flying across the room. She screamed as she sought to break her fall, to no avail. When she hit the floor, excruciating pain ripped through her face. It felt as if it were falling off. She was dazed and seeing double. Placing her hand on her face to soothe it didn't help but seeing her own blood from a split lip gave her the strength she needed to continue the fight.

"See! See what you made me do?" Ray yelled at Sissy. "You made me hurt my woman! Because of you, my whole life might not be worth a damn no more. Oh yeah, you're gonna pay for it every time you look at your face in the mirror and see the tic-tac-toe I'm gonna carve in it."

Janeen scanned the room for something to hit him over the head with. During the search, feeling came back to her face. She almost gagged from the blood collecting in her mouth and dripping from her chin. While using the bottom of her housecoat to wipe it away, she noticed that the material seemed heavy, then remembered that the gun was still in the pocket from the last time she heard noises late in the night.

With no time to spare, Janeen wrestled the pistol out and quickly pointed it at Ray's head. A crazed scowl covered her face like a dime-store Halloween mask's. "Get away from her, Ray!" she demanded. "Get away from her *now!*"

In an overt act of defiance, Ray grabbed a handful of Sissy's hair, his back to her. "Or what, Janeen? Or what?"

Sissy had been physically and mentally abused to the point of giving up. Her spirit was on the verge of being broken altogether until she observed Janeen standing there with a cannon of a gun in her hands. Sissy's surprised expression caused an alarmed Ray to turn around.

"Or else, Ray," Janeen answered calmly. "Or else."

Once he saw the shiny automatic weapon she held, Ray quickly placed his arm around Sissy's neck and began to squeeze. "I'll kill her. I swear. I'll snap her neck. Why'on't you toss me the gun?"

Sissy began to struggle as Ray increased the pressure on the choke hold around her neck. "Ray, for the last time, let her go," Janeen insisted. "Let her go, Ray, or my mother won't be the only woman in this family to blow a man's head clean off for putting his hand on her daughter."

Ray's unsure expression mirrored Sissy's. Neither of them could fully comprehend what she meant initially even though they both heard her loud and clear. Janeen often feared Sissy's finding out about her real parentage in a way that might prove to be irrevocably damaging, but now it was beyond her control, so they'd just have to deal with it.

"Yo' daughter? Well, I'll be damned," Ray said, laughing hysterically.

"That's right, Ray, you may very well be

damned if you don't let her go! Sissy's my daughter and I won't let you harm her anymore. I know about the prostitution, the city council scam, and everything else. I even know about the girl you killed." She took the safety off the gun and steadied her hands as she took aim.

Ray continued to laugh while popping open the switchblade. "You ain't gon' use that, *Mrs. Gilliam*. You still love me. Besides, I made you. When I found your pitiful ass, you were scared of your own shadow. You think you can shoot me before I slit her throat, huh?" He placed the blade against Sissy's neck and threatened to press down.

"She might not be able to, but I am," Scarlett exclaimed with certainty from behind Janeen. "Step aside, sistah, I get paid to do this."

Ray shook his head as if he'd been drugged and was hallucinating. "Ain't this a bitch! What the hell y'all thank this is? Y'all s'posed to be Charlie's Angels or somebody?"

Scarlett moved next to Janeen and began convincing her to lower her arms. "Janeen, he's not worth it. Don't do it," she reasoned with a woman who wanted that man dead so badly she could taste it. "Please

433

don't, he'll get his. I promise he will."

When Janeen agreed to lower her gun, Scarlett immediately resumed the game of nerves as if it were second nature to do so. "Come on, Mr. Gilliam, let's end this charade. You don't want to cut her and I don't want to kill you, but I'll do what I have to if it'll save her life. It's like I said, I get paid to do this and I'm still on the clock."

Sweat poured off Ray's brow and Sissy was turning blue. His hand, holding the knife, began to shake. The standoff was nearing an end but if something hadn't happened fast, Sissy might have died in the midst of it.

Adding to the tension, a large black man stepped through the door, out of breath, with his gun drawn. He pensively surveyed the room while assessing the situation, then he twisted his thick lips when he realized that it was much more grave than he imagined from his van across the street. He was the cook from the Rib Hut.

"Brisket?" Janeen mouthed, just above a whisper.

"No, ma'am. That's the name on my daytime job," he corrected her as he inched toward Ray with his gun pointed at her husband. "On my nighttime job, they call me Special Agent Harvey Hall. See,

Brisket . . . now, he smokes meat, uh-huh, but Special Agent Harvey Hall, he smokes bad guys like a pack of Newports."

By this time, the long-barreled tip of Brisket's gun was pressed against Ray's nose. Brisket was grinning like the Cheshire Cat and Ray was scared because the agent seemed to have a loose screw. "Nowww, that's nice and cozy, ain't it, Mr. Gilliam? Ah-ah-ahhh. Don't think about it too long. You know you don't want me to start smoking again, now, do you?" He pressed the gun a bit harder to deter Ray. "I'm still not too happy about having to climb all those stairs over there. Why the hell don't stuff like this ever go down on the first floor?"

Giving it one last thought, Ray moved the knife downward and away from Sissy's neck. Brisket knocked it from his hand and rolled him onto his chest before sticking his knee in the middle of Ray's back. Brisket purposely allowed all of his 260 pounds to rest on the suspect's spine while he took his time cuffing the prisoner. Ray wanted to protest but he couldn't expand his lungs enough to breathe, much less complain.

As soon as she could, Janeen made it to Sissy's side with efforts to revive her.

"Sissy, come on, every thing's going to be just fine. Come on." Eventually, Sissy coughed and sputtered. Her color was returning slowly. "That's it, baby. That's it," Janeen whispered softly, brushing her daughter's hair with the palm of her hand. "That's my girl."

Brisket sat Ray on the downstairs couch until local black-and-white squad cars pulled up and waited outside in the ensuing storm. "Come on, Sugarfoot," he said, pulling on Ray's collar to lead him out.

Ray responded with a wisecrack. "Hey, Special Agent Brisket, you know they won't be able to pin nothing but assault on me. I'll be out in six months, then I'll be a rich Sugarfoot. Hey, hey . . . then you can come and cook for me. I could use a good house niggah."

Upstairs, Sissy came to her senses while Scarlett dumped the contents of Ray's bag onto the bed. Out came his second set of financial books, three designer neckties, an assortment of diamond watches and rings, and a crystal ballerina that she took a special interest in. Scarlett observed it thoroughly and looked under its base. "Hmmm, I collect fine crystal but I've never seen such an exquisite music box," the agent mentioned to no one in particular as she wound it up.

As music emanated from the crystal box, the ballerina initiated her rhythmic circular dance. Sissy heard the tune and instantly perked up from a slight daze. Her mind replayed the last time she'd seen the box with the dancing ballerina. "That's it! Ray killed Ms. May Lee!" she screamed before snatching Janeen's gun off the dresser and bolting down the staircase with Scarlett after her in hot pursuit.

Brisket, Ray, and four police officers proceeded out of the house and up the walkway. Brisket was the only one covered by an umbrella. Through the pounding rain, Ray's smile was visible despite getting drenched on the way to the squad car.

Sissy hit the front door with the gun hanging by her side. Scarlett trailed her. She couldn't allow a prisoner in handcuffs to be gunned down in cold blood on her watch.

Sissy shouted, "Rayyy!"

Instantly Ray turned around, still smiling. A gunshot sounded. The bullet hit Ray in the chest and jerked his body back against a squad car. The police officers dove out of the way and took cover from the shooter when they saw blood pouring from his body. Scarlett stopped chasing Sissy when she saw Ray's body drop to the ground.

Across the alley on the next street, a lone gunman hastily climbed off the roof dragging a high-powered rifle behind him. Having witnessed the dramatic event play out in front of him, Brisket began humming a carefree tune as Ray lay face down in a puddle of water and blood. Janeen couldn't move from the entrance of the doorway. Like a stone monument, she was numb to the world around her. She couldn't hear Scarlett offering her condolences and regrets that it had to end the way it did.

Finally every lie had been exposed and Janeen's old troubles came to rest. A lifetime of troublesome woes was reconciled. Time and prayer heals all wounds, they say . . . heavy doses of both.

# Chapter 27

# *After the Storm*

Monday morning came too fast for everyone except the mayor of Dallas, whose press conference rolled on the heels of highly publicized police arrests of five city councilmen. Their charges ranged from soliciting prostitutes to conspiracy to defraud the city government, all the way up to and including murder and conspiring to commit murder. One local news station was tipped off as to when and where each arrest would take place. Some of the accused hid their faces as they were cuffed like common criminals and paraded for the media when placed into custody. The mayor went to great lengths to prove that his administration gave no favoritism to rogue politicians. By 10:30 a.m. Monday, all the stations covered the story in detail and interviewed other members of the council who claimed to have known nothing about the alleged crimes of their contemporaries.

As Shuna Jamison reported the activities leading up to the arrests, except for Sissy's part in it thanks to the anchorwoman's relationship with Janeen, flight number 191 on American Airlines deplaned at Dallas/Fort Worth airport. A group of distinguished, well-dressed German investors headed up the skywalk toward the baggage-claim area. They, along with many other passengers who'd just arrived in Big D, watched the startling news reports on the airport televisions. When the newscast concluded, they quickly collected their luggage and immediately headed back to the ticket counter to purchase one-way fares to Houston. There they could do business without the scrutiny of camera crews and FBI agents watching their every move.

Around noon, Janeen showed up at First World Mortgage. As she walked gingerly through the rows of cubicles that led to her office, employees popped their heads over cubicle walls to get a look at the woman whose husband was killed over the weekend and publicly linked to other murders as well as wide-spread city corruption.

At the same time, Val placed the last of her personal items in a moving box and left a note on the top of her boss's desk, where it was sure to be seen as soon as Janeen arrived. Before Val could leave the office, Janeen entered it, too, and closed the door.

"And where do you think you're going?" Janeen asked. Her spirits were surprisingly high.

Startled, Val jumped before answering. "Oh, my God!" Janeen's face was swollen in several places.

"Don't go getting alarmed, I'll be just fine. It looks a lot worse than it is," Janeen offered, to calm her friend's concerns. "Besides, you still haven't answered my question. Where are you going with that box?"

"I, uh, figured since we had words and after hearing the news all morning, that you'd be leaving here, well . . . Anyway, I figured that without you there is no me at this old company, so I decided to call it quits, too."

"That's nonsense," Janeen interjected. "I owe you a debt of gratitude that I could never repay. You've been a good friend and an excellent executive assistant. You've taken care of my affairs for seven years and I *know* I can be a witch at times."

"You? Nahhhh," Val joked.

"Well, I have a proposition for you. You remember the fun we had at Magnolia's, that fancy wellness spa?"

"Of course I do. I have an appointment for tomorrow at three."

Janeen sat down on the corner of her desk and softly rubbed her jaw to soothe it from a spike of pain jutting through it. "I wasn't going to tell you this until your birthday but I'd better do it now 'cause I'm going to be out of reach for a while."

Val's eyes lit up with anticipation. "Well, what is it that can't wait until my birthday?"

"Magnolia's, I own it. And I also own the new one being built on the south side."

"You're kidding? That's just great, Janeen, but can't this wait until . . . you've been through so much."

"I've told you not to worry about me, and no, I'm not kidding, and I have two more of them slated to go up next year and who knows after that. Here's where you come in. I pay my managers ten thousand more than they allowed me to pay you here, but managers have to be formally educated from a four-year uni-versity. I offer paid vacation, medical, dental, child-care assistance, and tuition reimbursement."

"Dayyyy-um, Janeen, that's wonderful."

"That's what I think, too. I want my employees to value their jobs, benefits, and their customers. It should be a pleasure when clients pay their hard-earned money to get some down home pampering, and I know you can feel me on that. So what do you think? I'll continue to compensate you at your current wage and also pay you to finish college. Then, I'll double your salary."

Holding in her tears, Val reached out and hugged Janeen. "You have always been so good to me, well . . . except for that one time in the hospital, but I ain't gonna bring it up."

"Tem-po-rary insanity, girrrl, you know a woman losing her head over a man ain't in her right mind," Janeen remarked, to add levity to her own complicated situation.

"Then you were *sho'nuff* cuckoo," Val asserted.

Janeen laughed hard for the first time in a long time. "Okay, so do we have a deal?"

"Well, it sounds like a winner, but I once heard of a wise man who told his daughters that a woman, a black woman in this country especially, ought to own something 'cause that's the only way she'd truly be free and not have to bend for no man *nor woman*."

Proud as she could be, Janeen patted her protégé on the back. "I see that I've taught you well," she said, with a chuckle. "Tell you what, since negotiation is the better part of labor, I'll sell you the shop at cost after you've graduated from college and have shown a steady profit margin for two full years. I'll invest in you if you'll invest in you."

Nodding and beaming with joy, Val shook on the deal, then ran out and typed up the agreement to be signed before Janeen changed her mind and made the offer to someone else.

Eventually Mr. Bragg made his way down to Janeen's office when he heard that she was in the building. Once he'd gotten over the shock of her appearance, he apologized profusely about all that had transpired over the past month before setting up a meeting with her for the following week to discuss his retirement and the opportunity she had always dreamed about and deserved, the chief executive officer position at First World. During their subsequent discussion, she asked that the offer be tabled and that her colleague Daniel Koster take the interim position in her stead. She remarked that he was capable, smart, and honest, all the necessary traits of a great corporate leader.

While he didn't like her answer, Mr. Bragg agreed to give her the time she needed to sort things out. Janeen also suggested that the elderly head janitor, Mr. Salley, be given an exemplary retirement package and an elaborate send off party, then she handed over a floppy disk from her purse with "Insurance" written on it. "Here, take this. It'll save the company at least three hundred thousand a year in deadweight. See, I'm earning my keep already." Of course, she was referring to the money being embezzled by Edward Greathouse III and Rick Wells, two common crooks who thought they'd never get pinched.

Janeen shoved some personal items into her purse but left her office pretty much as it was. She wasn't sure if she'd ever return to the mortgage company to accept the company's top job but it felt good knowing that it had been offered to her.

After the old man saluted Janeen with a warm embrace, Mr. Bragg handed her a sealed envelope with specific instructions inside. The note read:

*Because of what I do for a living*

*you'll have to pretend that I was never there, but I hope that you won't forget me nonetheless. Please check the closet in my office and take the briefcase to your new son-in-law. Tell him I said the governor of Virginia is up for reelection and insisted on doing the right thing.*

*Signed,*
*Rollin*

Janeen smiled as she read the name Special Agent Green had signed to the note, then she did what the letter asked her to do. When she stopped by Sissy's downtown apartment, Janeen had her first heart-to-heart mother-daughter talk — one that was long overdue.

Sissy answered the door wearing a sorrowful expression of a wayward sinner seeking forgiveness. "Hey, Janeen, or should I call you Mom?"

"Hey, yourself, and Mom suits me fine," Janeen answered, beaming with the pride of a new mother. "Actually, I like the sound of that."

"I still can't get used to saying it, but I always felt there was something special between you and me. Something that exceeded sisterly love."

After sighing deeply, Janeen anguished over what to say next. "Listen, Sissy — Janeese. I'm sorry for keeping our little secret from you but it never seemed like the right time to discuss it, and, well, when so many years passed, I felt guilty for not being woman enough to."

"Uh-uh, you'd better stop or I'll never get off my chest some things I've been meaning to say to you for far too long." Sissy paused to bridle her emotions. "Mom . . . I know you must be ashamed of me for getting caught up in those things I had no business even thinking about. You and Muh'dear raised me better than that. But I'm so glad that you found out and I hope we never have to keep secrets from each other again. No matter what trouble I got myself in, I should've told you about Ray's child and how evil he'd become. And when I think about keeping my marriage from you, I just want to run away and hide."

Janeen leaned over and hugged her daughter as tightly as she could. "What's past is past, young lady, and we all have done a thing or two to be ashamed of, but now we have to move forward and leave it behind. I must admit that it did hurt me when I learned that Ray involved you in undoing the work I loved, helping our people get their own homes, but all is forgiven. Speaking of your marriage, though, if you ever run off and cheat me out of planning such a special event again, I just might have to evoke my motherly privilege and whip that tail."

Sissy actually laughed at the thought of it. "I could probably use a good whippin' right about now."

Janeen informed Sissy that she had a surprise to spring on her. The directions that Rollin included steered her to the safe house where J. R. Cooper had been hidden away. Since Sissy had been asked to keep quiet and await her surprise, she didn't ask who lived in the out-of-the-way apartment building they approached. "You ready?" Janeen asked, somewhat subdued.

"I guess so," Sissy responded with trepidations.

Janeen knocked on the door. Agent Clary answered the door. "Yes, ma'am?"

"We're here to relieve you of your guest," Janeen answered. "Agent Green said he'd call ahead to inform you that the prisoner be released into our custody."

Sissy was more confused than before now. What was this all about? she wondered. Agent Clary nodded, then disappeared for a brief moment. When he returned, Agent Flores was with him. They held their personal toiletry bags in their hands. "Great, please take care of him. He's had a rough go of it." That was Clary talking. "By the way, he's one heck of a chess player." Without giving it another thought, the two men were on their way down the staircase and out of Cooper's life forever.

Before Sissy could make heads or tails of it, Cooper appeared in the doorway wearing faded jeans and a white FBI T-shirt with WE DO IT UNDERCOVER written on it, which he'd won from Clary over the weekend. He was tired and looked as if he needed a long rest and a good shave. Having thought that FBI replacements were at the door, he was overwhelmed when he saw his wife's face instead.

"Oh, baby, come here and let me hold you. I can't believe that it's all over." Now elated, Cooper's eyes flooded with emotion that he'd held in for years.

Sissy lunged into his arms, rocking him back on his heels. She didn't seem to notice the pizza stains or the roughness of his appearance. She was just glad to be with him. "Is it really all over, J.R.? Can I keep you? Please tell me that you'll never leave me again. There's so much I want to tell you."

Like a fifth wheel, Janeen felt out of place. "Uh, excuse me, y'all. It seems that I'm in the way so I'll just go. Do you think y'all can get a ride from here?" When she realized that the two of them were involved in a passionate long-awaited kiss and had not heard a single word, she placed the briefcase at Cooper's feet and slowly backed away.

After the estranged lovebirds completed their deferred salutations, Cooper noticed what Janeen had left and took it inside with Sissy following closely behind him. When he popped it open, he nearly fainted. Taped to the inside of the case was a note, resting on stacks of neatly bound hundred-dollar bills. The card advised Cooper to do right by his bride and plan wisely for their future. And, although nothing could adequately repay him for the time he'd lost while having been wrongly imprisoned, $750,000 was a darn good start at getting on with his life.

"Ohhh, oh my goodness. Oh my goodness!" was Cooper's first reaction. His grasp of reality wasn't sharp enough to take in all the loot that the briefcase held. He was afraid to touch it. Too many things had gone wrong since the sordid incident that stole more than three years of his life.

"J.R., what is this all about?" Sissy asked, while gawking at stacks of hundred-dollar bills. "I don't get it. There is a lot of money here."

"The reason I couldn't reach you, or anyone else, for that matter," he began to explain, suggesting she take a seat. "The whole time I was away, I was in prison for attempted murder. The night I celebrated my graduation at a pool hall near campus, the governor's son and a few of his personal cronies had too much to drink and decided to pick a fight with the only black man in the entire joint." Sissy was shaking her head in disbelief as he continued. "I had to defend myself so I used the pool cue to ward them off. Unfortunately, I smacked the governor's spoiled brat over the head one too many times. They rushed him to the hospital and me off to jail. Every day they violated my constitutional rights by keeping me in solitary confinement, they said for my own protection. I wasn't allowed to use the telephone, and my court-appointed lawyer, if you can call him that, was taking his orders from the governor's office. Not one witness remembered the story the way it actually went down and the others conveniently developed a bad case of amnesia after they were paid off, too. Can you believe that? I didn't know the entire trial had been fixed until it was over and I saw the district attorney hand my first-year court-appointed jughead a fat envelope for his troubles. It was quite a trick to throw a case and not make it look like he was taking a dive. The FBI must have found out about it somehow because they snatched me out of that hellhole and offered me freedom if I went along with a scheme to dig up dirt on Janeen and Ray but I knew deep down inside that everything would work out fine. It had to. I'd given up too much, lost too much already to go back to prison. And, when things got too hot, they stuck me here to ride it out until it was all over. I guess that *He* heard my prayers after all," Cooper added, thinking back to his first conversation with Special Agent Green.

"Thank God. You must have been going crazy in that place! Oh, baby, forgive me for all the terrible things I thought about you for walking out of my life without a trace." She started to cry at the thought of his 1,335 days and nights of loneliness behind bars in a powerful man's sick idea of personal retribution. "And I thought that I had the market cornered on cruel and un-usual punishment."

Cooper held her close with his strong arms. "Please don't waste the tears. And don't ever waste your time thinking about me being locked up again. Hoping that you'd still want me if I ever made it out alive kept me going. To think that I had to lie and deceive you to keep my freedom was unbearable. I'm the one who needs to be forgiven. Mrs. Janeese Cooper, all I want to do is love you each millisecond of each day for as long as you'll have me."

"Mr. Cooper, that's forever," Sissy whispered, wiping the tears away. She could have cared less about the money. She had her man back, the only one she loved, and all she could think about was a whole houseful of babies who looked just like him.

As for all of those evil plans made by the "Scandalous Six," as the indicted coun-cilmen involved in the Olympic scam were often called, they went for naught. Jonica Wannamaker received the harshest penalty. Her most serious felonious act was murder for hire. She'd paid to have a contract put out on Ray. J. W. Blake sang like a bird in order to stay in the free world. He continued to feed his heroin addiction by managing a local hard-rock band. Oddly enough, the charges didn't stick to Luther Griffith but he was ousted from city politics and later built a multimillion-dollar enterprise called Tons o' Fun Gags, an X-rated erotic Internet gift store for overweight consumers. Bernard Mecheaux pooled his resources and called in some old favors of his own, and hired Johnny Cochran, who successfully played the race card. Mecheaux later bought a Minor League baseball team. He now takes in the sights and sips fruity umbrella drinks all summer long in Florida. Kenny Riley left politics for good after serving eighteen months in a minimum-security federal facility. His nerves were frayed so badly after his trial that he ballooned a hundred pounds and went to work as a Tons o' Fun catalogue model for his old pal Luther.

# Chapter 28

# *Kismet*

Janeen tried hard to forget about Jonica Wannamaker and every other name that brought her grief in this lifetime. After laying Ms. Mary Lee Jackson's remains to rest, Janeen said good-bye to Ray as well. She stood at his burial site, not quite sure how to feel. In an odd sort of way, he had rescued her from her fears as a molested child, and provided her with the experience of how a woman should be loved by a man, despite what he had become. Janeen walked away harboring no regrets, knowing that everything in life comes with a price. At last, she felt redeemed when it was all said and done, certain that her sorrows were paid in full.

The following Sunday morning at ten

o'clock sharp, the Friendship West Baptist Church adult choir snapped to attention. Their crimson robes trimmed with creme satin added a majestic touch to the scene as Marcella Sims moved from among the ranks to the front of the group to lead a stirring rendition of "Precious Lord, Take My Hand." Sissy and Cooper sat arm in arm in the third pew. Janeen was perched closely on Sissy's other side. She'd always had a fondness for that particular hymn because it was her mother's favorite gospel number. Likewise, her sister Joyce loved it, too.

The singer, Marcella, who had a knack for knocking the walls down with her powerful voice, began to work the congregation into an emotional cyclone. When Janeen realized how much Joyce would have appreciated a blessed voice crooning her favorite spiritual, she grasped Sissy's hand and began to slowly rock back and forth to the hypnotic organ melody. How wonderful it would be if Joyce could somehow be there, she thought. After all that had transpired, Janeen hoped that maybe her older sister would find a way to forgive herself enough to return to the Church some day.

As Cooper began to say a silent prayer of

thanks for allowing him to be in the Lord's house as a free man, Sissy tugged on his arm. When he didn't respond immediately, she tugged again, harder the second time. He raised his head and leaned closer to Sissy, who had already moved in for an intimate moment. She planted a subtle kiss on his cheek, then motioned with her eyes for him to turn and look over his left shoulder. After he quickly obliged, a grand smile reappeared on his face.

When Cooper instinctively stood up from his seat on the end of the pew and stepped into the isle, Sissy nudged Janeen to get her attention. Before Sissy could apprise her mother of the wonderful news, Janeen witnessed the miracle for herself.

Joyce was taking patient, deliberate steps down the center aisle. She wore a bright yellow knee-length dress accessorized by a white wide-brimmed hat with a small yellow magnolia flower on the left side of it, just as her mother had hundreds of times. Somehow, some way, she had made peace with God, her past, and her soul. It may have taken over twenty-six years to break through the chains that kept her away, but she did it. She'd finally broken free.

Janeen was so amazed by Joyce's presence that she found it difficult to get to her feet. On shaky legs, she nervously took a small step toward Joyce, who was making her way between the rows to take a seat.

"Heyyy, Joycee," Janeen whispered, as they held each other tightly. "It's so good to see you . . . here."

Joyce nodded uncomfortably as she sat down. She responded with a deep sigh and a long look around the large sanctuary. Of course Janeen understood that was the best her dear sister could do under the circumstances. Within a matter of seconds, Joyce instinctively began to rock back and forth with the music just as Janeen had done before she arrived.

While the singer's words penetrated Joyce's heart, the world seemed to stop for a half beat to allow her the opportunity to catch up. At the same time, Janeen lowered her head to say a thank-you prayer of her own. When Janeen concluded with an amen, Joyce added barely audibly, "I hope you prayed this church don't fall down. I had to knock to get in. Guess He didn't really believe I was coming."

The joke that Joyce made about having to knock at the church door, suggesting that God didn't recognize her, made Janeen giggle and that was a good thing.

After church service was over, Cooper excused himself to allow the ladies the opportunity to share in the joyous occasion. They had the best time over their first Sunday brunch together, the three of them — Janeen, Joyce and Sissy, family.

As for Joyce, maybe finding her way back home had something to do with her new man, the handsome deacon with custody of two nieces and no idea how to raise them to be proper young ladies. The congregational chat favored Joyce as the front runner in the Deacon Derby.

Eric Bynote's novel was still in the number-one spot on the *New York Times* bestseller's list. His publisher anxiously awaited a sequel but he informed them that someone else would tell it much better than he ever could. Subsequently Janeen brokered a lucrative book deal for herself, then disappeared from the country for a six-month vacation on the French Riviera.

Somewhere in the south of France, Janeen plugged in her laptop on the sun deck as the breeze gently kissed her tanned skin. Walking the beach every morning proved therapeutic but it wasn't close to what she really needed. She'd begun writing her memoirs, titled *Secrets: Life after Newberry.* As she reflected on the years gone by and worked at getting out the kinks in her dramatically disjointed life, she couldn't help but think of one man, the man who ultimately did save her, just as she thought he would. He also saved her daughter as well as her son-in-law.

After she had been in her hideaway for nearly a month, a strange thing happened. On one cool spring evening, Janeen answered the doorbell in her secluded condo overlooking the Mediterranean. She reasoned that someone must have been lost because she was not used to seeing anyone around her hideaway after the servants retired for the day.

"Who's there?" she called out cautiously.

"Ma'am, you have a special delivery," a strong voice replied. "It's a special delivery of some sort from Texas."

"Texas? Okay . . ." Janeen fumbled inside her handbag until she found what she was searching for. The same gun she'd pointed at Ray was held firmly in her right hand because no one should have been delivering anything at that time of night. She cautiously opened the door with her left hand and hid the shiny gun behind her back with the other one. "I'm sorry, you said Tex—"

Suddenly Janeen melted when she laid eyes on him again. He was decked out in a casual eggshell-colored linen outfit and caramel-tinted leather sandals and a sight for sore eyes standing there posing with a large Rib Hut takeout bag and a bottle of fine Champagne to go with it.

Before Janeen invited him in to stay awhile, she had some questions that needed answers. "Mr. Green, it seems that you came halfway around the world to bring me dinner," she stated with a sly wink. "Might I ask what dish is so scrumptiously delicious that it had to be personally couriered all this way?"

"It's your favorite, a rib plate," he answered. Oddly enough, that was the correct response.

Straightfaced, Janeen was poised to ask her second question. "One more thing . . ."

"Yes, ma'am. Anything. Just ask."

Janeen moistened her lips when a sensual thought came to mind as naturally as the sun shining at daybreak. "Mr. Green, did you happen to bring any . . . *bobby-q sauce* along? . . . Good, there're a few things I've been wanting to show you."

# Reading Group Questions

1. Why do you think Janeen stayed in her bad marriage for so long? Was it wrong for her to fantasize about another man? Do you think she should have handled Rollin any differently?

2. Rollin was in a tough position, having to ignore his emotions in favor of his work. Did you empathize with him, or were you angry at him for not protecting Janeen better?

3. Sissy is an impulsive and not always thoughtful person. Did you like her? Did your feelings toward her changeover time? Was she either right or smart to keep Ray's secrets and help him in his schemes? Does she bear any responsibility for Mrs. May Lee's death?

4. Why did Sissy work so hard to act

cool around Cooper, even when she
was startled by his sudden reappear-
ance? What did you think of her decision to resume her relationship with
him?

5.  Janeen has started two successful busi-
    nesses of her own — the real-estate
    company and Magnolia's. Why, then,
    do you think her job and the respect of
    the Old Man are so important to her?
    Do you think she has her priorities
    straight?

6.  Janeen offers Val a subsidized educa-
    tion and a business to manage at the
    end of it. In what ways will her gener-
    osity pay off?

7.  The book club is an important gath-
    ering place for the women in this
    novel, and discussing *The Women of
    Newberry* was a life-changing event for
    some of them. In what ways can iden-
    tifying with characters be helpful or
    hurtful? What does discussing a book
    with friends add to the experience of
    reading it?

8.  Joyce's feelings of shame kept her from

church, and kept her from having a completely open relationship with her sisters. How else did keeping secrets come between relationships in this novel? Were any of them better never discovered?

9. At the heart of this novel are the relationships between sisters. How do you think Joyce, Janeen, and Sissy will treat each other now that all the secrets are out in the open? Will their relationships change or will they stay essentially the same?

10. Who would you cast in a movie of this novel to play the major characters?

# About The Author

**Victor McGlothin** nearly forfeited an athletic scholarship to college due to poor reading skills. His desire to overcome that obstacle has evolved into a joy in sharing the written word through passionate tales of suspense and drama. Victor is a former bank vice president and lives in the Dallas area with his wife and two sons.